"And we most certainly did not spend the night together. I slept in my carriage."

~~ ∞ ~~

"Your carriage?" Her full laugh filled the room. "You actually worried about my reputation."

"Reputation may seem a matter of ridicule to one such as you, but I can assure you I take it most seriously. And it was not your reputation I was concerned about."

Her laughter died at his words. "One such as I? I don't wish to know what you've heard of me." He heard her slide off the bed. "It doesn't matter in any event. If you'll tell me where I might find my shoes and my other stocking, I'll be gone and trouble you no more. You can forget you ever met me."

If only he could . . .

Romances by **Lavinia Kent**

BOUND BY TEMPTATION
A TALENT FOR SIN

Lavinia Kent

Bound by Temptation

AVON

An Imprint of HarperCollinsPublishers

AVON BOOKS
An Imprint of HarperCollins*Publishers*
10 East 53rd Street
New York, New York 10022-5299

Copyright © 2010 by Lavinia Klein
ISBN 978-0-06-173409-0
www.avonromance.com

First Avon Books paperback printing: February 2010

Avon Trademark Reg. U.S. Pat. Off. and in Other Countries, Marca Registrada, Hecho en U.S.A.
HarperCollins® is a registered trademark of HarperCollins Publishers.

Printed in the U.S.A.

10 9 8 7 6 5 4 3 2 1

For the Lifesavers—Mary, Marsha, and Elaine.
I couldn't do it without you.

Bound by Temptation

Chapter 1

Norfolk, March 1819

It was not the first time Lady Westington had awakened tied to a bed.

It was not even the second.

Clara gave her arm a firm pull, yanking hard at the tie. The room was frigid and she wished to bring her arm into the warm cocoon of covers.

Drat.

Her wrist was very firmly bound, the fabric soft but with little give. She tugged her other arm. It was caught also—the fabric was silkier, more elastic. She tried to twist her wrist, slipping it sideways. The tie moved with it.

Double drat.

Clara did not want to open her eyes. The thick down of the pillow curled against her cheek, and she rubbed her face into it, hiding from the cold. The rough nub of the fabric abraded her skin. This was no China silk or soft linen. She shoved her face deeper.

Triple drat.

It was not her pillow.

She closed her eyes tighter. Dawn was not yet welcome. Waking up felt more painful than usual, her eyes positively blurred with sleep, her mouth dry, her brains still fogged with dreams and possibility—that magical world of possibility that surrounded her just before waking. The bed was cozy. The covers, thick and heavy, were wrapped tightly about her legs. The first rays of sunlight weres beaming across the pillow. Clara could feel their heat and glow beating down upon her hair. Turning away, she refused to welcome the morning radiance.

Strange pillows, bound arms, and all that they meant, could be suppressed for another few moments. Clara had thought these times were far in her past. It had been years since she'd indulged in such game playing, and then it had been only briefly.

At least there was no heavy, warm weight curled against her.

Hopefully, her judgment had not led her too far astray. Her lovers had always been men whom she liked and respected, and she could only pray that this had not changed, that her lapse had not been too great.

She sighed, fighting reality for one last breath.

There was bacon cooking. The smoky, salty smell nipped at the edge of her consciousness. Bacon was almost reason enough to start the day—even a day such as this promised to be. Her nose twitched. She moved to scratch it.

Or, at least, would have moved, if her hand had been free. Unwillingly, she opened one eye.

A white linen neck cloth bound her left wrist tightly to the rough wooden headboard. The frame of the bed rose heavy and dark, not at all like her own delicate mahogany furnishings.

She opened the other eye. The blue wool sleeve of her gown met her eye. She followed the fabric from the fitted shoulder to the small froth of lace at her bound wrist. She wiggled her legs, feeling the warm weight of her skirts wrap around them beneath the covers. The toes of one foot wiggled free, while the toes of her other foot remained snug inside her thin silk stocking.

The villain had tied her with her own stocking! She forced her eyes to focus as she stared about the unfamiliar room.

Bloody hell. Understanding began to descend.

It was not the first time Lady Westington had awakened tied to a bed. It was, however, the first time she had awakened fully dressed, without recollection of how she had gotten there.

An edge of fear fought to hold her, but she pushed it back. There was no time for that now. Lying back, she closed her eyes and took slow, measured breaths. This was not good.

At thirty, she was no foolish girl. There had to be an explanation—she'd been prepared to waken tied to an unknown man's bed, worn from a night of pleasure. She had not looked forward to it, but she'd been prepared to face that consequence.

Why should this be worse? Another slow breath, and it seemed almost possible that this would not be as bad as she feared. Maybe they'd merely fallen asleep before anything had a chance to happen.

Opening her eyes again, Clara considered. Where was she? She tried to sit, but the ties held her tight, limiting her view. The ceiling had once been white plaster, but was now marked with the brownish stain of water and the soft gray markings of candle smoke and soot.

There was a window to her right. An unfinished wooden frame surrounded unwashed glass. The sun shone through it, unblocked by shutter or drape. But constrained as she was, she could see no other furniture or ornamentation. There was the impression of a door beyond the foot of the bed, but she could not be sure.

A horse whinnied. Another knocked its hooves against cobblestones. A boy's high, unchanged voice called out. He'd need another moment to fetch the mash. A maid whistled as a door slammed shut.

If Clara screamed, she'd be heard. She took reassurance in that small fact. Whoever had done this to her had not bothered with a gag.

She drew in a deep breath. She needed to pause and think, to be reasonable. If she screamed, she would be rescued. One layer of worry vanished. Her imminent danger was not of a physical nature. She could be found whenever she wished.

But did she want to be found, lying here, bound

to the bed? The scenes that filled her imagination were not pleasant. The promises she had made to Robert and to herself preoccupied her. Her stepson was engaged to the daughter of the greatest prig in the county, and any hint of impropriety on her part would ruin everything.

Given her history, she could not think of a single explanation that would excuse her circumstances. Countesses, particularly soon-to-be dowager ones, were not supposed to be tied to beds, much less discovered in such circumstances.

Screaming could only be a last resort.

Damnation. Powerlessness was an unaccustomed position for her. She let her head fall back against the pillow and closed her eyes against the bright light of the window.

What had happened last night? Worry worked at her again, and this time it was harder to suppress. Trouble was not unfamiliar, but this blur of memory and thought allowed an edge of panic to creep in.

She'd had Mr. Green to the Abbey for dinner. Upon that point, she was clear. Robert had been out. There'd been roast duck. Cook had surpassed herself, the skin so crisp it crackled like parchment.

And Mr. Green. She shut her eyes tight at the thought. He'd been so young, so hopeful, so completely inappropriate. If she ever chose another lover, it would not be one whom she needed to train.

Clara yanked hard at her bindings again. She

did not think Mr. Green could ever have conceived of strapping a woman to a bed. She doubted he'd even heard of such a thing.

She had let him down gently—she hoped. How he'd ever gotten the idea that she might welcome him to her bed she didn't know, but she'd done her best to let him know it wasn't going to happen. And certainly not in Norfolk. She had never indulged herself here. She had too much respect for Robert.

Robert mustn't find her like this, or even hear of it. Lord Darnell would force Jennie to cry off the moment even a whisper of scandal graced her name again. She had to get free before that happened. She pulled hard again. Leaving your partner trapped had never been part of her play. Equal control was essential in all games.

She pushed with her feet against the mattress, trying to inch her way up the bed. If she couldn't pull free, maybe she could work enough give into the bindings to loosen them. The fine knit of the stocking moved with her, but the cravat might be gaping some.

She worked toward it. Maybe she could get it with her teeth. A good tug and she'd be free.

Damn, she couldn't reach. The other arm held her fast. She twisted and turned, straining hard—

And collapsed backward on the pillows. Whoever had tied her knew what he was doing. She assumed it was a he. This didn't seem like a woman's work.

Stay calm. She repeated it over and over again. At worst this would be a prank—not a kind one, but surely one without real evil intent.

Think logically. Do not give in to desperation.

So what had happened? How did a fine duck dinner and a man who still had fuzz on his chin translate into her current situation?

Mr. Johnson had come by to visit with Robert after Mr. Green left. She had the sudden image of his craggy, old face lit by the dying embers of her fire. Robert hadn't been home. Had she suggested cards? She rather thought they'd played a few hands.

An image of a lively game and the sound of a whistle playing in the background flitted through her mind. It wasn't her home. She could feel the smoothness of cards in her hands and taste the bitter bite of ale on her lips.

The Dog and Ferret.

She'd persuaded Mr. Johnson to take her to The Dog and Ferret. The whys escaped her. She lifted her head and let it fall back into the pillow with a thud. She'd never done such a thing before. Why had she last night?

It wasn't impossible to imagine. It wasn't even out of character. She'd stopped at The Dog for refreshment on many a hot afternoon; why shouldn't she have stopped by for an evening of cards with the local lads?

Well, she knew the whys very well, but it still didn't mean she wouldn't have done it. She'd been Clara Bartom, squire's daughter and local hoyden, long before she'd been the Countess of Westington.

Respectability could only be taken so far.

She lifted her head and pounded it back into the pillows again. She had to get free before she was caught. It took everything she had not to press a futile struggle against her bonds. It was not strength that would free her, but her mind.

She began to recite curses under her breath. A fish caught on the line—that's what she was.

Now if only she knew whose line.

She tried to distract herself by thinking on her life. Her wants were simple: to stay in Aylsham until Robert was wed, and then to return to London and her life—her new life. It was time to begin pursuing the quiet, graceful life she desired, a life with love and a family, a life far different from the one of the past years. It was time.

Only, bloody hell, it was hard to think of a peaceful life when she was flat on her back tied to a bed. There was no distraction from that reality.

Who the hell had done this to her?

As if in answer, she heard the click of a key in a lock, and the door creaked open.

He'd been gone longer than he planned. Jonathan Masters balanced the tray carefully as he turned the key and maneuvered the door open. Luckily, the woman was surely still asleep. He was not much experienced with drunks, but he understood enough to know that it would take hours to waken from a stupor such as hers, and probably longer before she'd admit to being alive. He'd only overindulged on one occasion himself, but that had been enough to know that she was not in for an easy time of it.

She'd probably wish she'd been dead before he even entered the picture.

He pushed at the door with one hip, the tea on the breakfast tray sloshing in the pot. He should have let the maid bring it. The services of a butler were not in his repertoire.

But then, that was the least of his should-haves. He was not a man prone to regret his actions, but last evening there had been plenty to rue. He should not have stopped at this badly managed inn. It wasn't even a proper inn; it was more of a tavern.

He should not have spent six months trapped in a bloody carriage, chasing his youngest sister from one corner of the kingdom to the other and back again. He had responsibilities of his own, and trying to find Isabella interfered with all of them. No sane man would have attempted it. He should let his hired agent act in his stead. And he certainly shouldn't have attempted it over the winter. Even these bloody muds of early spring weren't an improvement.

He should never have allowed his valet to stay behind in Ipswich. Who cared that the man sounded like a frog and was running a fever high enough to heat the carriage to a toasty warmth? It was his valet's place to stay with him, no matter what. He should not have insisted the poor man stay to be coddled by that overly familiar innkeeper's wife.

And he certainly should never have partaken of his evening repast in the public taproom. As they didn't have a private parlor, he should have taken his meal in his room.

And to top his list, he should never have looked at the bloody woman—he allowed himself to curse a second time, a rare indulgence—it didn't matter that she might be the most exquisite thing he had ever seen. She'd been like a porcelain doll on a shelf of—that was much too feminine a metaphor. He should be thinking of toy soldiers or alabaster marbles, but the thought of comparing her creamy skin and dark locks to anything less than feminine was inconceivable.

He should have resisted temptation.

And he certainly shouldn't have been persuaded to pull up a chair in the tavern and play a hand. He had great reason to avoid gambling. It was true that on occasion he might make up a fourth when needed, but he did so only to fulfill social obligation. He knew too well the price of such a vice.

Procrastination was only delaying the inevitable. He had to face her. Tension tightened his shoulders, drawing them up. He stopped, the door halfway open, and considered. He could still call the authorities.

Last night, he'd decided that giving her a good fright was a more fitting punishment than actual imprisonment. It went against his basic beliefs to imprison a barely conscious woman for unsuccessful petty theft. He'd once been given another chance, and had promised to try and do the same.

He was the most sensible of men. How had he ended up with a woman tied to his bed? It was a most undesirable situation.

He should yell for the landlord and be done with it.

He desperately needed to be on the road again, needed to find his sister. The rains might begin again at any time, making his way impassable. He'd heard his sister had found employment in North Walsham near Norwich and he didn't want to miss her again. Too much of the last year had been spent tracking Isabella. He'd only returned to his estates for the final harvesting last fall, and he refused to let this year follow a similar path. He was already missing some of the early planting.

He pushed the thought away.

Instead, he shoved the door fully open and stepped in. He would deal with one problem at a time. Piece by piece was the way to build a tower or solve a puzzle.

He would finish with the woman, and then he would find Isabella. He would not fail her again. Nudging the door closed with his hip, he set the tray on the table and then locked the door with care.

He turned.

The woman was awake.

He couldn't see her face clearly, as she lay sprawled across the bed, but the poker stiffness of her body left no doubt that she was awake. Awake, and not calm.

Why hadn't she screamed? He would have expected her to raise a bloody ruckus. He'd meant to gag her, but had delayed it, given her deep slumber. It had seemed wrong to shove a stocking between her delicate lips while she slept.

He set the tray down on a corner table and strode toward her. Questioning her would take but a moment. He would frighten her with the possible consequences of her actions, and when she was properly chastised he would let her go, sure that she would never resort to such measures again.

He would not let her go the way of his mother. If only somebody had put a stop to her wild ways. This time, he would take control.

Stepping into the woman's view, he met an angry pair of flashing eyes. He had not realized they were golden. He'd sat with her, lifted a pint with her, and he'd not noticed her remarkable eyes.

He would have expected fear, but all he saw was fury.

He glared back at her. He would not be distracted. He had one purpose, to confront the little thief, get her to confess, and scare her into mending her ways.

He waited for her to speak. Silence was power.

She continued to glare at him, her lips pulling into a tight scowl.

He waited.

She pursed them tighter.

He waited—and sure enough it came.

"Who the bloody hell are you and what the bloody hell am I doing tied to your bed and where the bloody hell am I? What on the bloody earth did you do to me last night?"

"That's not very original. Surely you've a more potent curse than 'bloody.'" He ignored his own multiple use of the word in his thoughts mere moments before. He glared down at her. "And I am the one to ask the questions."

She had the lightest sprinkling of freckles across her nose. He shouldn't have noticed.

As if catching his regard she wrinkled her nose. "If you don't release me and answer my questions I'll scream."

He stayed calm. "Why haven't you already done so?"

He watched her swallow, caught the tinge of fear in the movement. She was not as cool as she would like to appear.

She swallowed again and answered with some poise. "I only waited to be sure it wasn't a prank or a mistake. It wouldn't have done to throw a fit before I knew the situation. I can assume that as I don't know you, sir, that it was not a hoax." She held her voice calm, but he could see the pulse racing at her throat, see her thoughts race within those remarkable eyes.

"Please, if you're going to scream, go ahead and get it over with. It can only help resolve the situation faster," he said, letting her know that he was the one in control. Hysterics were the last thing he wanted, but he thought she was too intelligent to bring about her own demise with more speed than necessary. He knew how this game worked. She'd soon start to flirt with him, use her womanly powers to change his mind. Unfortunately for her, he'd long been immune to such forms of persuasion.

His mother had been a master at the art, and he would never follow in his father's footsteps in this manner.

She opened her mouth, and for a moment he thought she was going to surprise him and scream. One loud cry, he was sure, and there'd be a man at the door within seconds. It might not be a well-kept inn, but it was a busy one.

Her mouth shut with a pop, and he could see consideration in the way she pursed her lips. The longer she kept the constables away, the longer she'd have to persuade him to let her go.

"What did you do to me last night? How did I end up here?" she asked.

"You know the answer to that as well as I." He was not going to be dragged into meaningless conversation.

She did not like his answer. Her eyes flashed with anger again, and he could see her consider her best move.

"Untie me." She spoke with the accent and command of the highest born lady, and for a moment he almost doubted himself, but no true lady would be found downing ale and winning at cards. And no true lady would have laughed as she did, the absolute joy of the sound filling the room with sunshine. He hadn't known that sunshine had a sound before last evening. No, ladies did not laugh like that.

"Untie me, or I will scream. You should have gagged me." She definitely knew how to sound like she was used to wielding authority.

But so was he. "You're not going to scream."

"I will scream and summon the authorities and—"

He did nothing but continue to stare down at her, unwilling to let her see his exasperation.

"Untie me." Again the words were spoken with that tone of almost royal prerogative.

"No, I want to be sure you're available for your visit to the magistrate." He needed to frighten her, needed to be sure she would never be so foolish again.

"The magistrate?" A definite edge of concern entered her voice.

"What else would you expect?" God, he wished he'd just called for help last night. He tried to do a single good deed by not sending an unconscious woman into custody, and this was his reward. He had made her his responsibility, and he took responsibility very seriously.

"I certainly don't expect the man who abducts me and ties me to his bed to be the one threatening to call in the authorities." She sounded calmer, more in control. She twisted her head toward him. "I must use the chamber pot. Untie me."

It was probably a trick. Still, he was a gentleman. He walked to the window. It was a good drop down with nothing to grab. She would not be leaving that way.

He turned back to the room.

There was nothing she could use as a weapon. Not a single brass candlestick or fireside poker. She might be able to swing the single chair, but he doubted she could get much force behind it.

He walked to the small table and poured a cup of rapidly cooling tea. It was not of the quality to which he was accustomed.

Cup in hand, he walked over and considered her. She was glaring at him again, those golden eyes shining like a cat's. She made no further argument, but let her eyes do her speaking.

He sighed. There was no help for it. His cravat loosened easily and she brought her arm down to her side quickly, rotating the wrist to loosen the muscles. Her expression did not speak of gratitude.

The other tie was not as easy to undo. The fine knit of her stocking slipped through his fingers as if it were alive. He grabbed her slender wrist in one hand and tried to work at the knot. Her skin was warm in the cold of the room, her pulse rapid beneath his fingers. Focusing on the knot was impossible.

"Get out of the way. I'll do it," she ordered.

His grip stayed firm. He didn't speak, just continued to work the knot. She smelled of cinnamon. How did she manage that? It was almost as if she had biscuits stashed in her bodice. There was a temptation to search.

The knot. Pay attention to the knot.

"Hurry up, or I'll piss on your boots."

"Keep your temper and hold your bladder. Rushing me won't help. You'd have been better off with less fine stockings—your legs must freeze in these. I can't imagine that they don't just slide down under the garter."

She rolled her eyes at him. It was enough to make his fingers stop midtask. The soft silk of the stocking caught on his nail at the sudden jerk. Nobody, save his sister Violet, had ever bestowed such an expression upon him.

"Don't stop. I am not joking about my needs. There was a great deal of ale involved last night." She squirmed, and her breast brushed the back of his hand. Its warm weight tempted him to turn his hand, to cup her with his fingers, to—

No, this was undoubtedly her plan. He would not be tempted.

He kept working on the knot, giving not the slightest indication of his attraction. Perhaps it was his renewed determination that had it slide apart almost instantly.

The stocking dropped to the floor as he stepped back.

"Take care of your needs and then we'll talk." His voice was deliberately harsh and unforgiving.

·

He stepped back to the window and stared down at the cobblestones of the stable yard below.

"Aren't you going to give me privacy?"

"No."

He heard the soft hop of a bare foot against the boards of the floor. The floor must be icy beneath her feet. He could picture her standing, her back straight, and an unforgiving glare marking those fine features. Giving in would not come easily to her.

A smile raised the corner of his lips as he imagined her ire. This was a battle he could not lose.

She stomped across the room and he knew he had won.

He waited and gave her an extra moment before turning. He could afford to be gracious.

The smile on his face grew as he further imagined her expression at his victory. He turned and—

She was eating his bacon. Perched on the edge of the table, the plate on her lap, she held the thick rasher and devoured it avidly. She licked her fingers and smiled up at him. The smile remained as she picked up his cup of cold tea and sipped that also. Her eyes peered at him over the rim of the mug. They were laughing.

She had gone from fear and anger to laughter in less than a minute. His mind filled again with the sunshine of her laughter the night before.

It must be her own private lure, her own scheme to manipulate him into letting her go without calling the authorities.

It was that laughter that had enticed him over

to the card table, that had begun this whole fiasco. His heart hardened against it. He was not a fool.

With firm determination, he walked toward the woman and, reaching out, plucked the cup from her fingers. She did not resist. He grabbed the pot and refilled the cup. Then, with deliberate precision, he drank from the exact spot she had.

He too could play intimate games.

Her eyes narrowed and then relaxed, their focus glued firmly to the spot where his mouth caressed the stoneware.

He could taste the bacon. Her lips had left behind its savory essence. His tongue slipped out to fully taste the remainder.

Her eyes followed the movement, her pupils growing large. She brought the slice of bacon she still held up to her mouth and bit it slowly, the soft crunch causing him to salivate.

He was intensely aware that her lips had been on the cup only seconds before. He had meant his action as a gesture of disregard, but now it was something more.

Her tongue darted out, mimicking his gesture, as she caught a crumble from her lip. He swallowed and felt his nether regions harden. Her eyes stayed locked on his, and he could almost feel the heat of each deep breath that filled her chest.

She took another careful bite, licking her fingers delicately. With deliberate care she ran the tip of her tongue over her shiny lips. Her chin tilted down, but those huge golden eyes still held him. She knew exactly what she was doing. Her glance never left his face, but he could sense her awareness.

She slipped off the edge of the table, her hips swaying in a timeless female rhythm as she approached. A foot before him, she stopped. The hint of a smile marked her mouth, but it was so subtle as to be almost undetectable. "I've stolen your breakfast. Wouldn't you like a bite?"

Her arm rose, and she rubbed the edge of the bacon against his lip. Again his mouth was filled with the rich, savory flavor, but this time he was staring at her mouth, still slick and shiny, the lips slightly parted, the pink of her tongue visible between the small white teeth.

He shifted from foot to foot, uncomfortable. This would not do. He leaned forward and took a bite of the bacon, crunching through it with speed and a touch of cruelty.

She pulled back at the force of his bite, her hand shaking. Then she gathered herself together and let her shoulders fall back, her breasts rising with the movement. Even beneath the warm wool of her gown, their full curves enticed.

Her game was clear.

He stepped back, not in retreat but to gather his forces. His back brushed the cold stone mantel of the fireplace. How had he imagined that there were no weapons for her in this room?

He turned on his heel and walked to the side. He would not be trapped, not by any woman.

"Are you done with my breakfast?" Again, the

words were harsh, but why should he pretend kindness? It was time to be sure she was properly chastised, and then send her on her way. He would not waste any more time.

"I'd actually like more tea." She spoke quietly, forcing him to focus on her mouth. "I find I have quite a thirst after last night. Do you mind?" Her gaze moved to the teacup he still held cradled in his hand.

He bloody well did mind. Damn, he was using that word again. Why did everything seem so damn bloody this morning? "Here, take it." He held out the cup, making sure their fingers did not touch.

She accepted it with a crooked grin. She understood his care and it amused her. She walked toward the table, her skirts swirling about her rounded hips.

He was tempted to stare out the window again, but that would be cowardly. He would give her but one moment, and then be done with this whole affair.

He let his gaze roam over her again, taking every measure of her charms. Then, with cold calculation, he turned back to the fire and rested his head against the high mantel, staring down into the dark ashes. He waited as he heard the slosh of the pouring tea and slight gurgle of her swallow. He kept his gaze firmly on the hearth.

He had intended direct confrontation this morning, but given her seductive games, a less aggressive approach might be called for—might get him out of here sooner, back on the road faster. He would not change his words, but he forced himself to moderate his tone.

"Tell me. Why did you steal my watch? Surely it would have been easier to slip a few notes and some coin from the table? Or did you steal that as well?"

Chapter 2

Clara hoped her mouth was not gaping. Was that what he thought had happened? Steal his watch—the idea was preposterous, even on a dare she'd never committed theft. Well, there were those love poems that her cousin had received, but she'd been only twelve at the time and the poetry had been so truly dreadful as to demand to be read aloud rhythmically.

Steal his watch. She didn't even remember seeing his watch. Granted, given the fact that she didn't even remember him it would have been unlikely that she'd remember his watch. *Don't think about that. Not now.*

Whatever had happened last night to make her forget, she sensed that he had no part of it. She wasn't quite sure why, but she did trust that he believed this situation was as simple as her stealing his watch.

She longed to close her eyes and rub her temples, to wait until this whole mess made sense. Instead, she snagged the last strip of bacon and caught the tip between her teeth, staring at him from the corner of her eye. There was something familiar about him.

It was hard to place. He stood just over six foot, well above most men of her acquaintance. That alone should have made him memorable. When she added in dark hair with just a hint of fire at the ends and eyes so dark a blue they were nearly black, he really didn't seem a man she would forget.

But she had.

She felt a shiver rise, and suppressed it.

Staying calm was most important. She forced all other thoughts back.

"Are we previously acquainted?" She ignored his question about the watch, trying to take control of the situation.

"Do you include last night? I can assure you we were well acquainted then." He glanced toward the bed.

She wanted to roll her eyes again. That had clearly not happened. The very idea was preposterous. The thought helped to steady her. "You're not an accomplished actor. Don't even attempt to fool me. I think this is a moment for honesty."

"I don't see why you should think so. I hardly call stealing my watch honest."

"I did not steal your watch." She had not wanted to confront this so directly. Men rarely did well with a direct approach.

"Only because I stopped you."

She spoke each word slowly. "I do not steal."

He let his gaze rove over her. She knew what he saw, the slightly worn dress over a figure too full and too short to be fashionable, hair that was no doubt standing straight out, skin that no longer awoke each morning as rapidly as the rest of her—she probably had pillow lines still running across her cheek, and eyes shadowed by fatigue and knowledge. She was well aware of her own charms—and her lack thereof. She drew herself taller and forced herself to pretend that appearances did not matter. She waited until his gaze returned to her face and then repeated, "I do not steal."

"Hah."

"Did you just say hah? I am not sure if that makes you sound six years old or sixty."

He didn't like that. His chest stuck out another inch and his chin tilted up. The man was just too tall. It was hard to be commanding when staring at the top buttons of a shirt. He'd left the collar undone.

There was the faintest sprinkling of dark curling hairs peeking above the edge of white linen. She'd always enjoyed the way a few hairs abraded— Where had that thought come from? One moment she was thinking he sounded sixty and the next— This would not do.

"I am sorry, sir, but I can assure you I did not steal your watch. Indeed, the only possible reason I would have done so would have been as a tease and, as you deny any acquaintance previous to last evening, that is impossible."

He pulled out the chair and sat, resting his elbows on the table and cradling his head in his hands. "You are giving me a megrim. This should be a simple matter. I only decided to speak with you as a courtesy. No matter how heart-wrenching your story, I have every intention of having you taken before the magistrate." He sounded so distant, so cold. "It was only misguided gallantry that prevented me from calling him last evening. I didn't fancy sending you into custody barely conscious."

She was glad he was not watching. Her composure was definitely slipping. What had happened last evening? It was true she'd tipped more than one tankard of ale, but she couldn't believe she'd downed enough to place her in the state he described and certainly not enough to leave her with no recollection.

She shivered as she considered all that could have happened. Waking up tied to a bed was mild compared to some of the pictures her imagination could paint. If she wasn't careful she would be sick. Robert would not be pleased at all—nor would Lord Darnell.

"You can't call the authorities." She said it calmly, but firmly. There were some who moved up in the world unexpectedly who never learned how to behave. From the moment she'd become the Countess of Westington, she'd made it a point to learn her position. The quiet voice of command was invaluable.

"Of course I can. In fact, I don't see that I have a choice." He sounded surprisingly weary.

It was her turn to move to the window and stare

out at the cobbled yard. She was still at The Dog and Ferret. He must have just bundled her up the stairs last night. Her fingers dug into her palms as she considered who might have seen her.

"No, really. You can't." Her chest felt tight with the effort of staying upright.

"I can and I must. You are clearly a danger that cannot be left loose." He did not sound pleased by his answer.

She turned back from the window and walked to the bed. It looked so warm and cozy compared to the deep chill of the room. The pillows might not be as fine as her own, but they were still inviting. Just curling up in the bed for the rest of the day and ignoring all this seemed wonderful.

She wondered if he'd curl up with her and let his weariness fade. Where had that idea come from? It was preposterous.

Still . . .

The idea did present possibilities.

She sat on the edge of the bed, allowing her skirts to rise up, revealing her feet and ankles. The bed creaked under her weight. His head lifted toward her. She cocked a hip provocatively. "Really, you can't." She let her voice deepen. It was surprisingly easy to do as she met his cool blue gaze. "I realize it's a mistake to try and tell a man what to do. There's something innate that makes you all object to orders. I think even my footmen sometimes grimace at my commands. They don't think I see, of course, but men are also not good at hiding their emotions.

"You for instance are trying to decide if I really have footmen. You're examining my dress again and comparing it to my speech." She ran a hand along her waistline, letting her fingers play gently with the fabric. His eyes followed. "Accents can be affected and clothing, of course, can be borrowed or bought from shops specializing in the previously worn. I believe my maid makes a fortune taking my castoffs to such a place. But that's only my in-town clothes. Here in the country I much prefer the used and comfortable.

"I can see you are still not persuaded. The cloth is good, heavy and tightly woven, but the elbows are worn, the seams frayed, and there is a singular lack of ornament save for the edging of lace, and even that is slim." Her fingers moved up her body to the rounded neckline of the dress, pausing to press at the thin lace.

It was not her words that held him. It was the low, inviting tone of her voice and the subtle gestures highlighting the curve of her body as she discussed the dress.

Really, men were all the same—give them a peek at a bit of flesh and they were slaves. It had been both humorous and powerful with her husband. Recently, it had been closer to tedious.

Still, there was something in his rigid posture that captured her interest. He might not be able to avoid his baser thoughts, but he was not pleased by them.

"I do not know what the quality of your dress had to do with whether I should call for the authorities. You are a thief; it matters not how fine your dress." He spoke slowly and with precision.

She held his gaze. It was clear he wanted to look away, to avoid temptation, but he did not.

She ran her tongue across her lower lip, watching his gaze move. "We both know exactly what I mean and that it does matter. I fancy you would not like to live in a world in which it did not. I am sure you are very comfortable with your station. The leather of your boots and the cut of your shirt say it for you, as surely as my dress."

"I do not care who you are."

That brought a smile to her face. "Oh, you care a great deal. I have strayed from my point, however. I should not have ordered you. I should have persuaded. Men do so much better with persuasion."

He started to speak, but she brought her finger up to her lips, silencing him. "All that really matters is who I am. I had sought to avoid this, but before this proceeds I should simply introduce myself."

"I am Clara Bembridge, the Countess of Westington."

His face changed at her words, but perhaps not in the way she was expecting. She leaned forward trying to get a better understanding of what she saw in his dark eyes, but they reflected back at her as endless as a puddle at midnight.

"You're Lady Westington?" he could not keep the disdain and shock from his voice. He had heard all about the adventurous Lady Westington and none of it had been good. It explained so much about her behavior. A lady she might be, but in name only—he wasn't even sure how many lovers she'd had. She was a close acquaintance of his sister Violet, and that explained more than enough. No wonder she'd been comfortable in the tavern drinking with such a rough crew.

It was probably a tame evening for her. If even half the things he'd heard were true, then— It truly did not bear thought.

"Yes, I am." She sat up straight on the bed. Her jaw tilted up and it was clear she was ready for a fight. She could see what he was thinking and did not like it.

Raising a hand he massaged the back of his neck. With every word she spoke the muscles were tightening, tension and pain creeping up the back of his skull to his temples.

How had this suddenly become so complicated?

He should have been done with her last night. This was his reward for trying to show mercy. No good would come of this. "Is there not somebody responsible for you? Some man who can come and take you off my hands?"

"Some man?" Her voice was low and he heard the warning in it. A red flush spread across her cheeks. Yes, she would get along well with Violet. He lacked understanding of these women who didn't comprehend their place in creation. It was not such a complex thought. And, ironically, it was always the women who seemed to have a brain in their heads who were given to such fancy.

"Yes, some man, father, brother, son—it matters not."

"Son?" Her eyes flashed as she said the word. "Just how young do you think I was delivered? Or how old do you think I am?"

He was too smart to answer that. Last night, he'd thought her his age or older. This morning, asleep, she'd looked years younger, hardly more than first out. Now he couldn't tell. "A brother or a father then?"

"I am an only child, and my father rests in the churchyard up the hill. I notice you don't mention a husband?"

"You are known to me, if by reputation only, and I am well aware that you are a widow—if of the merriest kind."

She shifted so her skirts dropped, covering her bare toes. It wasn't until they disappeared from view that he realized how taken he'd been by their casual innocence. He'd never noticed a woman's feet before, but those sweetly curled pink toes had distracted him.

He dropped his head back into his hands. If he didn't look at her, his thoughts would be safe.

She didn't speak for a moment, and he sat staring at the scarred tabletop and listening to the jostle of horses below.

"We must determine how I can get out of here without being seen." She spoke finally. "I don't fancy the village knowing I spent the night with you. Assuming, of course, we were not seen last night."

"I don't believe we were. I hustled you up the stairs once I had decided on a course of action. And we most certainly did not spend the night together. I slept in my carriage."

"Your carriage?" Her full laugh filled the room. "You actually worried for my reputation."

"Reputation may seem a matter of ridicule to one such as you, but I can assure you I take it most seriously. And it was not your reputation I was concerned about."

Her laughter died at his words. "One such as I? I don't wish to know what you've heard of me." He heard her slide off the bed. "It doesn't matter in any event. If you'll tell me where I might find my shoes and my other stocking, I'll be gone and trouble you no more. You can forget you ever met me."

If only he could. He couldn't even pretend that he'd soon forget the way her hair had spread across his pillow as she slept, or the glisten of her lips as she licked the last crumb of bacon from her fingers, or that delicious laugh. He rather imagined that last would float around the edge of his dreams for a lifetime.

"There's still the matter of my watch. Lady or not, I will not countenance thievery."

"I can only say again that I did not steal anything. Unless, of course, you added it to the pot and I took the hand."

"You know that is not what happened. It fell from your cloak when you prepared to leave."

She was silent again. He looked up, trying to

determine her mood. He was not used to a woman who could maintain a silence. His sisters had never been quiet women. Violet was always too busy trying to take control of a situation she had no business being involved in. And Isabella . . . well, Isabella simply could not stop talking.

He pushed aside the thought of Isabella. He dreaded the circumstances he might find her in. His own guilt rarely let him rest easy. He curled his fingers into a tight fist. He would finish with this nonsense and be away.

Lady Westington was resting her head against the mantel in a pose reminiscent of his earlier one. She lifted her head and stared at him through weary eyes. "I am not a thief. How many times must I repeat that to make you listen? I certainly have no need of your watch or any proceeds it would bring. I could buy a hundred, I daresay a thousand watches should I need another."

"I have not found that theft is always based on need."

"That is true, but nonetheless it was not me."

"I saw you take it. What other explanation do you offer?"

She rubbed her temple. Perhaps his headache had spread to her. No, more likely it was merely the remainder of her indulgence of the previous night. "I do not feel the need to offer any explanation to you."

"Then perhaps I should have the local magistrate summoned. Even in a backwater such as this I am sure he is up to the task of demanding an answer."

At his words he saw a flash of concern.

She massaged the tight lines of her forehead. "Robert would not take kindly to hearing he lived in a backwater. And it really would complicate everything."

"Robert?"

"My stepson—the current Earl of Westington— and the local magistrate."

"Ah." That explained so much.

"Yes, ah. Normally I would not object to his being summoned. He would vouch for my honesty and none here would gainsay him. The situation is, however, complex. I would rather he not be involved at present."

"I can well understand that. But in truth, my interests are not in what pleases you. I am rather more concerned with justice. And I have only your word that he would speak for you, and I am not inclined to accept that at present." Again he saw that flash of worry.

"You doubt me, but of course you do." She lifted her head and stared at him. Her eyes spoke of knowledge beyond her years. She smoothed a hand across her temple once more and then straightened. He could almost see her muster her forces. "If you are going to summon him, then do so. It will be of inconvenience to me and embarrassment to him, but you have already said that my pleasure does not matter."

There was something in her tone that made him think of other pleasures. She did not speak seductively or with flirtation, but somehow he was left wondering if she doubted him as a lover. He actually opened his mouth to reply to this baseless accusation. He slammed it shut. This was why he hated dealing with women. They confused the issue even when they did not mean to—although it was hard to tell exactly what she meant.

"Well, are you going to summon him?" She sounded suddenly tired. He found he preferred her full of fight and ire. He did not wish to win so easily.

"Jake, the landlord's son is normally about," she continued, rubbing her temple again. "He'd know where to find Robert." Then she changed. Her eyes came up and met his. The fight was not over. She took a step toward him. Daring him on. "Would you like me to call down? Or perhaps I should scream? It isn't acceptable to abduct a lady, you know. I wonder which Robert would find more persuasive—that you claim I took your watch, or that I was found in your rooms after being tied to your bed?"

"Are you sure he'd find it unusual to find you tied to a bed in a strange man's room?"

Oh, she didn't like that one. She spun on her heels away from him. He could hear her pull in each angry breath.

"Then do it. If you do not, I am leaving. And if you try to restrain me I will scream. Based on your words, I no longer have much to lose." She waited a moment and then marched to the door.

Without even trying the handle, she held out her hand to him. "Key."

The command was back in her voice, and it was enough to make him hesitate. He did not want to give in to her.

His mind sped. He could see no point in continuing. He was not going to call the authorities; in truth he had never been going to. Doing so would only delay his journey and complicate matters. Explaining the true situation to her stepson would not be easy.

"Key," she demanded again. "I am weary of this game."

It was only as she spoke the words that he realized how much he had enjoyed the battle. He resented it. He fought against it, but he could not deny that he relished it.

He reached into his trouser pocket and drew out the key. He held it out to her, not moving toward her.

Another of those heavy breaths passed her lips. She measured the distance between them with her eyes and then moved toward him warily. Her wrist shook as she reached out for the key, and he wondered if she thought he'd grab her. Surely, she must know that if he'd been willing to resort to physical force the game would have been long over.

With extreme care she lifted the key so that only the tips of her fingers brushed his palm. Even so, a shiver of awareness ran through him.

He held his palm flat even after she had lifted the key. He watched her walk to the door. When her hand was on the handle he found himself floundering for something to say. It didn't seem fitting that their encounter should end on such a note.

But nothing came.

He watched as she opened the door and stepped through. There was a moment when he thought she'd turn back, but with a decisive click the door shut.

He didn't even hear the tread of her feet as she walked away.

He should be glad that she was gone. That he would be back on the road later this day. He only hoped the rains were delayed.

He stared at the door longer than he should have.

Clara barely resisted the urge to speak. She didn't know what there was to say, but it seemed there should be something. Her honor had still not been defended. He clearly did not believe that she had not taken his watch. Then there was the matter of her shoes, stocking, and cloak.

Her skirts were long enough that unless she kicked up her heels like a young girl nobody would remark on her feet, and the morning sun was still shining bright, giving hope that she would not look too much a fool walking the mile home without a cloak. Her feet might be sore and she'd probably catch a chill, but she would survive.

Creeping down the stairs step by step, she listened for the sounds of anybody passing by. Fortunately, it was late enough that the first rush of morning was past, and early enough that late sleepers were still slumbering away.

She reached the inn door and eased it open with care. She saw Jake's shirttails as he disappeared into the stable, but that was all.

A quick dart and she was free. If she was seen walking along the lane it would be considered odd, but not unduly so. There were some advantages to having an unusual reputation.

Now she could only hope that her luck continued as she walked farther and farther from The Dog and toward the Abbey. Perhaps Robert had been out late himself the previous evening and would not even notice that she had been gone. She crossed her fingers tight.

"Lady Westington." Her name sounded from behind. She turned and looked over her shoulder. Coming toward her, perched high on a massive horse, was the prettiest blond pixie of a girl the world had ever seen.

"Oh, I am so pleased to see you. Robert said you never rose before noon or I would have asked you to ride with me. Or do you prefer to walk? A morning stroll can be quite a wonder. Have you seen any deer or rabbits?" Jennie smiled down at her. Her stepson's fiancée was full of joy, as always.

Clara forced herself to stop, ignoring the icy rocks beneath her feet. It was imperative she appear normal. Jennie, and therefore Jennie's father, Lord Darnell, must never know that the Countess of Westington had slipped again.

"Don't you have a groom with you? I thought

your father didn't like you to ride alone?" she asked. Offense was the best defense.

Jennie blushed like a beet. "You won't tell him, will you? I know that I shouldn't be unaccompanied, but none of the grooms was free and I didn't want to wait."

Clara smiled back. "Don't worry. We can keep this whole meeting a secret and pretend that it never happened. Or if you prefer, we can say that we were together the whole morning."

"Oh thank you, Lady Westington. That would be most delightful."

Chapter 3

~~~~⟨⟩⟨⟩~~~~

The fire danced and jumped, sending a blanket of warmth across the parlor. Morning sun had given way to gray, and the occasional splatter of rain blew against the latticed panes of the windows. Clara curled her toes in the heavy wool socks Molly had found for her. She was lucky she had not been drenched as well as chilled.

That was far away now. She lifted the heavy mug of tea and took a welcome gulp, ignoring her still cold fingers that caused the tea to tremble. Most often she drank from the delicate porcelain cups the house seemed full of, but there were moments that only a mug would do. The heat of the stoneware warmed her lips even before she tilted the cup. An image of other lips placed carefully on the edge of a mug, drinking where hers had been, came to her, but she pushed it back.

Hers were the only lips that would drink from this cup.

Glancing about the room, she tried to decide if there were any items she wished to take back to London upon her return. The house would be Jennie's home soon, and it was an adjustment that Clara needed to consider with care.

Turning her attention to the task proved difficult. Her thoughts kept turning to the blank spots in the events of the previous evening. Her chest ached with the pain of missing parts of her life. What had happened?

"I hear you had quite an adventure." Robert's voice echoed from the doorway as he entered her study, his lanky form disproportionate in this most feminine of rooms.

"Whatever do you mean?" Her fingers gripped the mug more tightly. Had someone at the tavern seen her? Had her mystery man not been discreet? Had he come looking for his watch? Perhaps Robert had just heard of her card game the previous evening? That would be scandal enough. She waited for Robert's answer.

"Jennie said you'd gone out with her early this morning. I am glad you're making an effort to get to know her. I realize my engagement has not made things easy for you."

Clara put down the mug, her ready smile both from Robert's clear infatuation with the girl and her own relief that last night's debacle had not yet come home to roost. "I don't know why you sound surprised. You know I adore Jennie."

Robert took a seat across from her, stretching his long legs toward the fire. "I know you like her, but *adore* seems a bit strong. To be frank, you've always seemed to like her the way a young girl likes kittens—they're cute and warm and don't often scratch."

"That's fair," she said. Robert had always known her too well. He'd been an undeveloped boy of thirteen to her own lofty eighteen when she'd first come here. Michael had been all of thirty-three, not much older than she was now. It had seemed a vast age difference between Robert and her at the time, but even then he'd seemed to understand all her secrets. Twelve years later, she sometimes forgot that he'd ever seemed a child. "I must admit she's always just been about, happy and smiling. But ever since you've shown a preference for her, I've made an effort to better our acquaintance. She has a keen intelligence underneath that gentle countenance."

"You must know I wouldn't have proposed if she'd been all fluff." Robert leaned forward and plucked her mug off the table. He smiled mischievously before taking a deep drink. "You like bergamot too much. I thought I'd brought you around to smokier blends."

Clara could only stare at the mug in his hands. He frequently stole her tea and her biscuits. The intimacy of it had been so familiar that she'd never realized it until this moment. It was a gesture of comfort and family.

She'd appreciated the sensuality and control of the man's move that morning, but not the level of closeness it placed between them.

She swallowed hard and attempted an answer. "I know you're partial to blends that smell and taste like a peat fire, but please spare me. I am after all a lady."

"You are that, Clara. Despite your best attempts to prove otherwise." Robert put the tea back down. "I am pleased by your behavior these last months. I know you don't see it as my place to govern you, but I have worried in the years since my father's death. You haven't always seemed to care about the repercussions of your actions."

Little did Robert know. Her actions had always been formed with a strong understanding of their repercussions. Still, there were some things one couldn't tell one's stepson even if he often seemed more of a friend and she longed for someone to confide in. "We both know I wasn't quite a lady when he found me. I've never felt as if I belonged since he's been gone. But you know I rarely talk about him and those years following his death, and it has no reflection on my current good behavior. I'd be dancing on tables in Mayfair if it weren't for Lord Darnell and his requirements in a son-in-law."

"You've never danced on tables in your life, but I do appreciate your help with Lord Darnell. He was very clear what would be expected of me, and of you, if I was to claim Jennie."

Little did Robert know if he thought she'd never danced on tables. She'd danced on one in this very room, if memory served. Her husband had loved a good laugh and all it could lead to. Clara wondered what Robert would think if he knew that most of the behaviors that society had so objected to had begun in the warm confines of her marriage, knew that it was her fear that she had never lived up to Michael's expectations that had led to so much of her outrageous behavior.

She turned to Robert with a forced smile. Thinking of the past and the mistakes she had made would lead only to melancholy. "You know Lord Darnell has no objections to you. It's me he fears will corrupt his sweet Jennie and ruin his family name. For the second son of a duke, he has a greater sense of importance than several princes I have met."

"I think he still holds out hope that Jennie will land a duke. You are just his excuse—not that I think he would hesitate to force her to cry off the engagement should he so desire." Robert tapped his fingers against the rim of the cup. He shook himself slightly before looking back up at her. "And when have you met princes?"

"Certainly not in Norfolk. I am afraid princes fall into those questions you don't really want me to answer." The smile was easier now.

"Mother, certainly not Prinny—I hope." Robert only called her mother when he wanted either to exasperate her or to make her smile. She reckoned it was both at the moment.

"No, not Prinny—although I have been introduced. And if you had seen him in my youth . . ." Clara said. She wiggled her toes in the heavy socks. Blood slowly returned to them. "I stuck to princes of the foreign variety—Italian, Russian, even an African, I believe."

"You don't mean—" There was both horror and curiosity in Robert's voice.

She picked up the cold tea and took a sip, glancing over the rim at him. He just stared. Finally, she gave in. "Oh, don't be silly. I thought you knew me better than that, and besides, I already told you that you didn't want to know."

"But—"

"But nothing. It's my business and not my fault if I've only confused you more. You did ask." Smiling to herself, she plopped the mug back on the table and stood. "Now I've a pile of correspondence to complete."

She turned to the door, her mind filling with the details of the letters she needed to write.

"No, don't go." Robert's words stopped her.

She turned back, her brows lifted in question.

He hesitated a moment and then started slowly. "I've let you change the subject, but I really do want to know. Why did you get so wild after Father's death? I do remember you before, and you were very different than in those years after."

It was her turn to hesitate. "I wasn't aware that my wildness was the subject."

Meeting her gaze straight on, he answered, "Perhaps it wasn't exactly the subject—but don't you think it's time to tell me? I'll be married soon and I really would like to understand."

Previous misgivings of being unable to share her secrets came back to her, as did the question of sharing such things with her stepson. Still, he was right. He was soon to face his own marriage, and although the history of her own might not help, it probably would not hurt to tell him at least part of the truth. She sank back into her chair. "It's hard to explain. I've never been quite sure I understood my reasons myself, but they always felt right. Do you remember how much your father liked to have fun?"

Robert's eyes clouded for a moment, and then he smiled, a smile that filled his entire face. "It would be hard to forget. I think he started more trouble than I did."

It was her turn to smile. "Yes, I have no doubt that he did. He loved having a son to play with. He wasn't always as sure about his wife."

"He loved you." Robert spoke with absolute conviction.

"Yes, he did. And I, him. But I never pursued joy with the same vigor. He always regarded me as a bit of a stick-in-the-mud. He could never understand why I didn't want to spend my days thinking of nothing but enjoyment. And then he died."

They were both silent for a moment.

Clara drew in a deep breath and then continued. "After his death, I wondered if I'd failed him. If things would have been different if I'd lived more the way he wanted me to."

Robert looked at her solemnly. "I can only say again that he loved you."

She smiled at him again, only slightly sadly. "Yes, but after his death I wished I had tried more to see the world the way he did—and so I decided to try. It made me feel closer to him, and I have to admit that I did rather enjoy myself."

"Well, I should hope so," Robert replied, his lips held tight.

"Oh, don't look at me like that. I am well aware I may have gone a little too far—but your father never did have any limits. And besides, I've decided to change my ways. I've come to understand how much joy there is in life without causing outrage."

Doubt spread across Robert's face.

She wrinkled her nose at him and stood again. "You'll just have to wait and see—and now I really do have to get to my correspondence. Which you also don't want to know about—if only because it is so dull. The only interesting one in the bunch is from Lady Smythe-Burke, and I still must get through three pages about the proper colors for new drapes before she'll get to the gossip."

Robert started to say something—she could see he was not so ready to let the subject of past behavior drop—but after a moment he nodded and answered only, "No letters from Lady Carrington, or the new Mrs. Struthers? I thought your dear friends never let a day go by without putting pen to paper."

She walked to the door and turned back to him. "You must think we have nothing to do in our lives. Violet Carrington has only just returned to London after searching for her sister and is beginning to think about planning her wedding. I swear if she puts the date off one more time I'll have to have a new dress made. And Anna—I'll never think of her as Mrs. Struthers—has her own worries and little time to share them. Even I am only taking up my pen because of this blasted weather. I rather like the country when the sun is out, but cold rain puts a damper on almost anything I desire to do here."

"I don't even want to hear about what you could be doing in Town." He stood also, brushing biscuit crumbs off his pants. "I am sure that is one of those questions I don't want answered—no matter what you claim about your future behavior. And I did not mean to imply that you and your friends have nothing to do. I am well aware that you spend more time running my estates than I do. Women are the backbone of England and I never forget it."

"For all that, you started the conversation implying that you'd like to govern me."

"Don't tease me." Robert joined her in the doorway. "That isn't quite what I said, and I know I'd have as much success governing you as the barn cat's new kittens."

"And yet those kittens will learn to catch rats just fine without you."

Robert walked by her. "I think I'll go hide in my study and stare at the account books. I haven't forgotten that we began the conversation also comparing Jennie to a kitten, and I don't want to imagine her catching rats or learning anything else without me."

He looked like a little boy who had finally beat his father at chess. Clara reached out a hand and patted his cheek before turning and heading up the stairs. His footsteps echoed down the hall below, and she heard the creak of his study door.

She doubted he'd get much work done this morning. His head was too full of Jennie for that. She hoped Lord Darnell would relent and let them marry soon. Jennie was almost the age Clara had been when she married Michael. Her mother had still thought her young, but she was grateful for every moment she'd had with him. Her hand shook as she grasped the stair rail. She closed her eyes for a moment to gather strength.

It still hurt to think about him. She could go for days now without thinking about their time together—and how it had ended. It was why she had fled to London after his death and stayed there for as long as she could—if only she could have been as carefree as Michael had wanted during his life instead of waiting until after. Being in London had made forgetting so much easier.

It did feel good to have talked about it, though. She had told Robert far from everything, but her soul felt lighter for the words.

Being back here was teaching her just how ready she was for change. And it was not as painful as she'd expected. Not even sleeping in the bed that she'd shared with Michael for those precious years had left her bereft. Granted, she'd had the room redecorated, but the bed was still the same, narrow mahogany posters rising to the high canopy. She'd been frightened of the dreams that bed would bring, but she'd slept far better here than she ever had in Town. She really was ready to move on, to start anew. Strength and commitment filled her.

She paused halfway up the stairs and considered as a new thought filled her. Why had she decided to tell Robert so much now? Why did thoughts of Michael surround her?

It was that blasted man from The Dog. She didn't know why or how, but it was his presence that had revived Michael's ghost. There was something in the way he made her feel that made her relationship with Michael come back to her.

A glance across a church fete.

The first innocent kiss.

A second not so innocent kiss.

Refusing him.

Giving in.

Disbelief that he wanted to marry her.

Marriage.

Perfect days.

Angry days. Fighting. Making up.

Fighting, again.

Never feeling she was quite enough.

She opened her eyes and stared at the heavy paned window over the front door. It was amazing how living a life determined not to have any regrets, any missed opportunities, could lead to so many doubts. She would not think further. If she let her mind follow this track, it would lead to that final tragedy, and that could not be borne.

With firm determination, she turned up the stairs. She would read Lady Smythe-Burke's letter again. Plum versus apricot as the prime choice for curtains might not be one of the more important questions in life, but it could certainly be mind-numbing.

"Drat." It was a mild curse and Clara said it without force. She'd been trying to write this letter since this time yesterday and still had made no progress. The tip of the pen ran over the paper smoothly and left no puddle of ink behind. The temptation to press a little too hard, to write a little too slowly was great. There could be much plea-sure in destruction—even of something as simple as a sheet of paper.

She dipped the pen into the ink and left it there, folding her hands neatly in her lap. They still trem-bled. When she'd arrived home, she had blamed the tremors on the cold. Yesterday, she had blamed them on the memories of Michael.

Now she needed to face the truth.

She was shaken by the lack of memory of that night, and the deep sense of violation that filled her. She wished she believed it was as simple as having indulged too much, from having moved from ale to whiskey and downing it with equal speed.

Unfortunately, she'd downed more than her share of whiskey in the past, and she knew what the next morning felt like. There was pain and there was blur—a friend might remark on something Clara could remember only in the faintest outline, but it was there. It was in her mind, even when she couldn't remember the specifics—it was there.

Now there was nothing.

She remembered dinner, and the discomfort of laying to rest Mr. Green's hopes, and Mr. Johnson's visit afterward. She even remembered Mr. Johnson saying he was off to The Dog and Ferret. He'd been shocked at her desire to accompany him, but whether it was the loneliness in her eyes or fear of offending her, he'd said nothing when she'd sent the maid for her cloak, and they'd walked to the tavern in comfortable silence, his horse trailing behind.

Robert was supposed to be stopping by the tavern later in the evening. She'd planned on traveling back with him—which had to mean she wouldn't have overindulged. The whole point of her stay in Aylsham was to prove she could be a proper lady. She would not have flaunted extreme impropriety in his face.

Oh, she knew that going to The Dog was improper in itself, but it was a harmless thing. Robert would have understood—and Lord Darnell would never have heard.

She clenched her hands tighter. She'd arrived at the tavern for a drink expecting that Robert would drive her home after he tilted a tankard or two himself and finished his business with Mr. Johnson.

She hadn't expected to play cards. That had just happened in the way these things do. Someone called to her, she said, "Why not," and that was that.

Only it wasn't. Why did the rest of it vanish?

Why could she not remember the man? She really should have learned his name before she left. It seemed too much like a novel—abducted by the tall, dark stranger.

He'd been the hero from a book, not a real man at all. A real abductor would be short with bad skin and smell of cheese. She snorted at the thought.

No, this man with those near black eyes and strong jaw had resembled a footman. She might have said an actor or a soldier, but the majority of footmen were better-looking than the men who trod the boards at Drury Lane or fought for His Majesty. The man might even have been qualified to be one of Lady Smythe-Burke's footmen. The lady might be old, but that didn't interfere with her eyesight, and she'd be the first to say so.

Her hands relaxed as she thought of the stranger again. She'd felt safe when she was with him. It was a strange thing to say, but true nonetheless. When he'd held her wrist to untie the bonds, it had been with the gentleness he'd hold a newly hatched chick. His grasp had been so warm and safe—no, *safe* was not the correct term, those tingles of heat that had run through her belly at his touch were not safe.

This was not productive. She should not be dreaming of a man who thought she'd stolen his watch. She couldn't even imagine where he'd gotten that idea. Why hadn't she asked him when she had the chance? Well, it was too late now. She'd probably never see him again.

Her fascination was nothing more than relief from the monotony of country life.

She stood and paced once across the room. The rain continued to pour down heavily as it had since the previous morning, pounding against the windows with every sudden gust of wind. It was not a day for marching off her frustrations in the fields.

Needlework? It would not hold her, and she didn't care for it anyway.

Correspondence? It had already failed her.

A book? Perhaps one of those novels filled with impossible heroes? No, it would only make her think of *him* more.

Maybe she should sort through her wardrobe? Given the stranger's glance at her dress's faded seams, it was clear that not all her gowns were up to par even for the country. Her maid, Molly, would help, and that would lead to lively conversation and gossip. It was a distinct poss—

"Clara, we have a caller. Didn't you hear the knocker?" Robert poked his head around the door.

"A caller? In this?" She turned her head to the window as another gust sent a splatter of rain hard against the pane.

Robert chuckled. "I know it's difficult to believe, but apparently some gentleman from Town is stuck at The Dog. The roads out of town are flooded and you know how bad the mud can get."

"So he decides to come visiting?" A sense of cold dread was building low in her stomach. Had she been wrong about the man? Was there more to her forgotten night than imbibing too much and a misunderstanding over a watch?

But perhaps it wasn't he, and everything was as simple as it seemed.

Robert entered the room and walked to her desk, tapping his finger against the top of her pen. "He claims he was without entertainment at The Dog and asked who lived in the area. When he heard your name, he decided that he must visit." Robert smiled broadly at Clara and then continued, "Apparently you're friends with his sister and he's heard only the best about me."

"His sister? I can't think who he could possibly be." Clara ran through names in her mind, trying to tie all the pieces into some type of order, but drew a blank. She shook out skirts with some force, brushing at imaginary wrinkles. "I imagine that the beds at The Dog are lumpy and damp and he hopes we will extend our hospitality for the length of his forced stay. It will probably turn out that he is mistaken in the acquaintance, but we will be forced to house him until the rains relent if not longer."

Robert grinned like a schoolboy. "The weather is making you grumpy, although I am sure you are correct. If we're not careful he'll still be here next Christmas."

"Given that it's only just March, I am afraid to even imagine such a happening."

"As long as he's not like Uncle Timothy sending all the upstairs maids running and squealing."

Clara rubbed her hip. "I can assure you nobody pinches like Uncle Timothy." She stood. "Now I suppose we should greet our guest. Maybe he does desire company for a single afternoon. He must be used to muddy roads to be traveling at all during this season."

"And he probably has pressing business to be about at all." Robert clearly desired reassurance.

"I would have thought you would welcome company." Clara walked to the door. "You're always complaining of how dull it is here."

Robert turned and preceded her down the stairs. "You know I just say that. I am much happier here than in Town. It is one of the things that makes Jennie so perfect for me."

Clara placed a hand upon his sleeve. "I will do whatever I can to help. I would speak to Lord Darnell, but I fear I would not help your cause."

Robert turned, his position on the stairs forcing him to look up at her. "I know you would and I appreciate the effort you have made in coming home. I do understand that it is difficult for you to be here."

"Not as difficult as I feared."

"I am glad to hear it. I know I don't always understand what drives you to do the things you do, but I know you want only the best for me. It has not always been easy allowing you your freedom."

Allow? Clara swallowed her reply. Michael had left her plenty of funds of her own, and she resented the implication that her life was anybody's responsibility save her own.

There was a cough from the bottom of the stairs.

It was *he*.

She had known that it would be, and still it seemed impossible. He seemed impossible.

Why was he here? What did he want?

His hair looked nearly black in the dim light, all its fire dimmed by the water that slicked it back. He stared up at her with no more expression than a three-day-old fish. She could feel his appraisal raking over her. She knew she was pale after the previous nights, and under his gaze she felt a hundred years old. She'd noticed the first fine lines about her eyes in the last months, and now she feared that anxiety had deepened them to crevices.

It was nonsense. Her own mirror had assured her that, other than lack of color, she was little changed, but still he made her feel— Why was she allowing him to make her feel anything?

It would be his turn to explain himself. It was too much of a coincidence that he turned up at her home after the events of that night.

She tapped a finger once.

She was in control of herself. No man allowed her anything, hadn't she just been thinking that when he appeared?

"Lord Westington, I must presume." His voice was lower than she had remembered. He addressed Robert, but his eyes never left her. "Forgive my ungracious behavior in arriving at your home without invitation."

"Not ungracious at all." Robert strode down the steps and extended his hand. "I assure you that if we'd known any relation of one of Lady Westington's friends was in Aylsham we'd have sent a rider to The Dog and Ferret insisting you stay with us. I fear that it is we who have been ungracious in our ignorance."

She was going to murder her stepson. One moment he was alone with her protesting any desire to have a guest, and now he extended the invitation without any consultation or consideration of her thoughts. Granted, he couldn't know of her history with said gentleman, but— And she still didn't know said gentleman's name. How many times could introductions pass by so sloppily?

Enough was enough. It was time she got answers to her questions. "As my stepson seems a little lackadaisical in his introductions, I fear I must depend upon myself, Lady Westington." She nodded, praying he would not give away the events of *that* evening—but why else could he be here, save to torture her? Damn, why was he here? Did he mean to tell Robert the whole sorry saga and demand restitution? She prepared herself for the worst.

"You need no introduction. I would know you anywhere from the many descriptions I have received." He reached out and took her hand, bringing it to his lips, his hot breath warming her chilled fingers. For a moment she thought he would presume upon the evening's intimacy and actually kiss her hand, but he held back his lips a fraction above her skin, pausing for a moment, his eyes looking up at her. He knew exactly what she wondered, what she feared.

"You must tell me what you have heard. I had not believed my reputation to be so widely spread." She dared him on, unable to hold herself back. Running from her own fears had never been her way.

Robert coughed loudly. She hoped he was regretting his impulsive invitation.

"My sister has described both your beauty and your spirited nature."

"And what would you know of my nature on such brief acquaintance?" What was she doing? The words left her mouth before she could stop them. Was she daring him to mention the previous evening?

"I merely saw your expression at Lord Westington's comments. I can assure you that my sister has gifted me with many such expressions when I spoke of *allowing* her to do anything. I might disagree with her sentiment, but I do recognize it." Gads, the man sounded so pompous. Somehow he made her feel like a scolded schoolgirl.

"Ah, the mysterious sister. Lord Westington mentioned she was a dear friend. I must admit I cannot place her. Or perhaps it is that I cannot place you."

"My sister and I have not shared a name for many years, since before her first marriage, so it may be that you simply have not made the connection."

"It would be hard to do so when you have not gifted me with your name." Clara smiled at him sweetly and then swept past him into the parlor.

"Have I not? I find that hard to believe." She couldn't see his face, but she imagined it from his tone—nose in the air, lips tightly pressed, but eyes letting her know that he damn well hadn't told her his name and wasn't sure he was going to.

Robert caught something of the tension between them and spoke up. "Don't mind Lady Westington. She is merely having a bit of fun. It's only been a matter of moments, and as Clara said, the fault is mine for not taking the responsibilities of a host seriously."

"I am sure Lady Westington meant no such thing." The man sounded even more pompous than before.

"I can speak for myself." Her smile could only be described as saccharine.

"No disrespect intended, my lady," the man said. It seemed unbelievable that she still didn't know his name.

Robert merely rolled his eyes. She should have walloped him when he was younger.

"None taken." If her expression grew any sweeter she'd get a toothache.

They all stood there in silence. Was she going to have to ask his name again? She turned to Robert and cocked an eyebrow.

He looked at her blankly for a moment and then grinned. "Lady Westington, do let me present Mr. Jonathan Masters. Mr. Masters, I believe you have already made the acquaintance of Lady Westington."

"Masters? The name does sound familiar." It was there, tickling just beyond reach. And then it hit—no wonder he had looked familiar. "Who do I— Violet. You are Violet Carrington's brother."

Chapter 4

Masters saw the moment she put all the pieces together. One moment, her eyes were clouded with confusion, and the next, they sharpened with a cold, clear understanding.

"I should have known. It all makes such sense now." She spoke to herself, but there was no mistaking the edge of ire in her tone. He could see her mind go through the steps—Violet's marriages, his plans to marry Isabella to Colonel Foxworthy, the rumors surrounding Foxworthy's death. Her eyes narrowed with each consideration. "You are searching for Isabella, trying to bring her home."

"Yes, of course I am. It is my responsibility. What else would I be doing?" He sounded more defensive and bitter than he ought. Damn. He hated it when his guilt and insecurity showed through. He didn't know why he felt the desire to explain, anyway. It was no business of hers why he had chosen the paths he had.

"You're Lady Carrington's brother. I confess you're correct I had not put the names together." Lord Westington stepped into the gap of social awkwardness. "How is your sister? Lady Westington was just telling me she had not heard from her recently."

"She is doing well. I last saw her at the baptism of the Marquess of Wimberley's daughter this past Christmas. It was a most joyous occasion and I have rarely seen her happier."

"You do not know her well, then," Lady Westington spoke the words so softly that he was not sure he heard them. It was clear Westington had not. She stepped toward him, and he could feel the air stir as she moved.

He continued as if she had not spoken. "But you know Lady Wimberley as well, do you not? It is a pity that you were not in attendance at the christening of her daughter. We could have become acquainted at that time. It might have made things much simpler."

She opened her mouth and then snapped it shut, her soft pink lips quivering. It was good to see her at a loss for words. He had never been fond of women who couldn't be quiet.

Her eyes still flashed with emotion though. They were speaking the words that would not come to her lips. In the dim light of the afternoon they looked like fine topazes. He could see the darker rim of soft brown that ringed their golden centers.

He should not be thinking about her eyes. He turned quickly toward her brother—no, that wasn't right, her stepson. It was impossible to picture them as mother and son. Even in a few moments' time he could see that the bond they shared was that of siblings or close friends. There was a playfulness in the expressions that passed between them that was totally lacking in parental authority.

He'd always wished he'd shared that with his sisters. No. That was not right either. He had the relationship with his sisters that necessity demanded. He would not wish for things that could not be.

The clock in the hall chimed, causing Westington to jump.

Lady Westington was still staring at him, her eyes burning with emotion. He wondered what secrets his sister had shared with her. What did she know of Isabella and the circumstances of her departure? Violet must have said something. She had never been known for her discretion. What woman was?

"Perhaps you'd like to be seated and I shall call for refreshments." Lady Westington had pasted a smile on her face as she spoke. "Tea? Or would you prefer some port? Or even a brandy, given the chill."

"Yes, there is a distinct chill in the air, is there not?" He spread his own best smile across his cheeks.

"I don't know what the two of you are talking about," Westington said. "I find it quite stuffy in here with the drapes drawn and the fire burning high. You must forgive me, however. The clock has reminded me that I promised my stable manager

·I'd stop by before dinner. I've a mare about to foal, and I am concerned." He turned to his stepmother. "Forgive me."

"Of course." Her tone did not sound forgiving in the least.

Masters could almost hear her counting the seconds until Westington left the room.

"What on earth are you doing here? Do you have no purpose but to plague me?" Her words were exactly the response he had expected.

"Actually, I came to return your belongings. It seemed only proper to do so."

"My belongings?"

"Yes, a cloak, two shoes, and a single stocking. I felt quite ashamed when I realized you had left without your shoes. I'd brought them to my coach the night before to prevent your departure."

"You feel ashamed for hiding my shoes, but not for tying me to your bed—or accusing me of stealing your watch?" She phrased it as a question, but clearly it was not intended as such.

"Perhaps I should not have returned your belongings. I am sure a woman of your means could have managed without them. Forgive my desire to help." He walked away from the fire. "I can manage quite well without refreshment. I will return to the tavern to await the roads drying. And as for my watch, I recovered it from you, so I am content."

Lady Westington paused for a moment. She glanced at the door and then back to him as if measuring how many paces it would take him to leave. Her desire for his departure was clear. He watched her pull a deep breath in, the movement of her chest clear even beneath her thick wool gown and shawl.

"I am being rude," she said, moving to a chair beside the fire. "Pointing out another's faults can be so easy, do you not find it so? And as for your watch"—she repeated his words with clear deliberation—"you have still never told me why you believe I tried to steal it."

He resisted remarking on the lack of courtesy in that remark; instead, he merely nodded stiffly and took the seat across from her, letting her question of the watch slide by. It would only increase the conflict between them to discuss it now.

She narrowed her eyes. "I do of course appreciate your bringing my belongings. May I have them?"

"I am afraid they are still in my coach. I was not sure that I would find you alone to present them, and it would have seemed ungracious to arrive with a bag as if planning to stay."

"But you are planning to stay, aren't you? You heard my brother's invitation. Only a fool would stay at The Dog when he could be lodged here with all the comforts available."

He refrained from asking what comforts those were. She clearly was set on provoking him and he would not have it—would not let her know how her closeness affected him. He was here to leave her belongings and to assure himself that she was not regularly given to thievery. With those two goals accomplished, he could pursue his sister with an easy conscience. "No, I don't believe I will avail myself of your comforts."

He indulged in letting his gaze rove over her as he spoke, being sure to pause at all the most delightful bits. She really was quite splendid to look at, despite the shrewish temper. He felt how soft she was when he'd put her to bed. She'd been so warm—so warm and soft. Awake, she was neither warm nor soft.

Her back was stiff. He was sure if he took out a ruler he would find it a perfect inch and a half from the brocade back of the chair. She pulled herself even straighter with that magic only true ladies possessed. "I will accept that last comment at face value and not have the maids freshen a chamber. I believe it is time we come to the real purpose of your visit. I am sure you could have found someone lurking about The Dog's stables who could have brought me my cloak without raising an uproar. Perhaps I had just forgotten it."

"That would be the truth."

"Yes. It would be."

"Your shoes and stockings would have presented more of a problem."

She quirked a brow. "If you say so."

She made it seem as if she was questioning his intellect. He would like to know how she would have managed it. But he didn't really want to hear her reply.

She leaned over and rang the bell on the table. The maid appeared instantly, shining with a desire to please. "Mary, would you please have Cook send out some tidbits and a bottle of Robert's port. I'll have a glass of the dry sherry myself." The maid turned to leave, and, as if on an afterthought, Lady Westington added, "Oh, and Mr. Masters mentioned leaving a package in his carriage, a gift for me from his sister." She turned to him. "You did say it was in the brown leather bag."

"No, a green brocade satchel just under the front bench."

She turned back to the maid. "Ask one of the grooms if they can find it. I would love to see what secrets Violet sent me."

The maid left.

"And what do you think of the secrets she has sent so far?" He leaned toward her and let his low voice surround her.

Her glance met his, and then her eyes dropped to his lips. She swallowed deeply and shook herself. Turning her face away, she answered, her voice carefully flat, "We are both aware she did not send you. You made her life a misery and she would never have forced you on mine."

"Where did that come from?" He was surprised by her sudden vehemence. "I thought we were playing with manners."

"Only in front of Robert and the staff. After last evening it seems a bit late for manners between the two of us." She brushed at her skirts as if trying to brush all trace of him away. He could not tell if she succeeded.

She turned her face back to him. "Now why are you here?"

"I have come to assure myself both of your welfare—don't raise that brow at me—it is true. I am not used to sending shoeless, cloakless women out into the streets. And I wished to assure myself that no harm had befallen you."

She considered his words, her brow clenched—and then relaxed. Yes, she could see the truth of that. "And your other reason?"

"You will not be as charmed by this one. I merely sought further reassurance that I was not letting a master thief loose on the county. I am aware that you have decided that I never intended to summon the magistrate. I admit that I didn't want to take the time away from my quest that would have been necessary to pursue a prosecution. I intended that fright would do the job for me."

"Only I don't frighten easily."

"No, you don't. I would have thought awakening tied to a strange man's bed would have been a cause for alarm."

Lady Westington slid back in her chair, making herself comfortable. At the same time, her very comfort highlighted the curves of her body. "That might have been true if it had been the first bed I had awoken tied to. I was more distressed by being tied fully dressed than I would have been bare as a newborn babe. Then I would have understood the rules by which we played." Her smile grew catlike, and he found himself focused on her lips, waiting for her tongue to caress them.

There was a scratch at the door, and a maid came in with a tray of drinks. She poured them quickly and then vanished like a shadow.

Masters shook his head, breaking Clara's spell. She'd done this before at the tavern with the bacon, one smile, one grin, one bite, and all his thoughts fled to his trousers. It was an art she clearly wielded with great precision.

He was no innocent boy to be taken in by such games. He forced his glance up to her eyes. They did not portray the confidence of the rest of her expression.

She caught his glance and he could see her eyes harden and grow more calculating, giving the impression that she knew exactly what she did and why she did it. Her tongue did dart out then, but he ignored its invitation.

He coughed. "It is clear that I am not as familiar with these games as you. I have always considered myself a country gentleman despite my recent time in London. I might never have spent more than a fortnight there were it not for my sisters—and my bankers."

"Violet did say the estate was a shambles when you inherited."

"And she did not know the half of it." He leaned back, resting his head on the high back of the chair. It sometimes felt as if he had the entire world to worry about instead of only two sisters and an estate that, after more than a decade, was finally paying for itself. He wished he could close his eyes and sleep before the fire. His head was beginning to pound. The quiet of the house was inviting with the rain pattering outside and only the distant noises of chattering maids to disturb him.

Of course, the quiet could not last. "Why didn't you share your problems with Violet—forgive me if I call her that, I have never thought of her as Lady Carrington. Your sister cannot be but a few years younger, and she would have given her all to help."

He sat up, letting the veil of disapproval fall about him. "It is really none of your business. All I will say is that she did help."

"By marrying a man more than five decades older. I am not sure that was the type of help she would have chosen."

He turned his head to look at her fully. She was stiffly upright, leaning slightly toward him, fully focused on his face. His answer was evidently of great importance to her. "It was the only help possible."

She leaned closer. Although her voice was quiet, the force of her sentiment was unmistakable. "That's easy to say when you weren't the one paying the price."

"I've never understood why my sister and now you must harp on the issue. It is over and done with." He fought the urge to rub his temples. A dull pain was building, pressing ever stronger in his temples. At least she did not remark on the rumors that had come last year with Isabella's disappearance. "Don't look at me like that. I know that marriage to a seventy-plus-year-old is not every girl's dream, but Dratton was a good man and he cared for her. Do you imagine her life would have been better penniless, without a home? Who would have wed her then?"

"But what of love?" Her voice was softer, more inquiring.

"Love. I don't know that it even exists. I am sure it does not exist when one is starving and cold. My sister has the life she has because of the choices I made."

"They should have been her choices."

"You sound just like her." He stood and walked away from her. His head was pounding now. "I am so tired of opinionated women. Can you never just trust a man to take care of you?"

"There is no reason for us to. We can take care of ourselves."

He turned back to her. "By flirting and flaunting your body. By depending on your sexuality to get you what you want. Is that what you call love?"

There was a momentary stillness to her features. Life normally filled her in a way he had never before seen, and then in one instant it was gone. Until he experienced its lack, he had not realized its importance.

He saw her shake herself, although she made no movement. "No, that is not what I call love. I would be a fool to say that sex is not part of love, but love is not dependent on it."

"Then what do you call love?"

* * *

Her soul hurt. His simple question of her flirtation had caught her unawares, and now she felt ripped open. She was not normally so fragile, but the desolation of not remembering *that night* was still with her, and his question struck at it.

At least she could relax her suspicions of him again. Violet might not care for her brother, but she had spoken of him as honest. She might not like what he did, but he never hid his actions.

That did not make his words less painful now. Clara did flirt. She did smile and flaunt and use every bit of her feminine wiles to control a situation.

It was the only way to survive.

She wished it were not so. Women who managed to survive without using those tarnished resources earned her greatest admiration. There were so few of them.

Men criticized a woman for using her femininity and punished her for not. It was the way of the world.

"Do you have no answer for me? I thought women could spend days talking of the wonder of love. You rebuke me for forcing my sister to marriage—a marriage she never once complained of to me until it was over—and then you can't even tell me what this magical love is."

She drew every inch of that feminine power to her and she smiled up at him. She relaxed the muscles around her eyes, making them soft and young. Her chin lowered, making her peer up at him through her thick, sooty lashes. And she smiled. Not the smile of a schoolgirl. Not the smile one gives when presented with an unexpected surprise.

This was a woman's smile full of knowledge and mystery, a smile of full lower lips, of darting tongue, of knowledge of just what a mouth can do. "Yes, I know what love is. I know it in all its aspects. I know the parts of it that draw and tempt a man to do things he would never do otherwise. I know the parts of it that grow and flourish as man and woman know each other with ever increasing intimacy.

"I know what it is to lie night after night wrapped in the same lover's arms, never wanting to be anywhere else. I know the pain of being away from your love for even a moment and the joy of each reunion. I have been delighted by my husband's smile and felt the pain of each disappointment more sharply than he.

"I remember the delight in the simplest of tasks because he was there with me. Walking across a field with him on a blustery autumn day was a far greater joy than the grandest of London balls.

"And I know love's pain." She let the smile fall from her face—this was something she did not speak of—lest this man, this near stranger, see the pain that she never revealed. "I know what it is to lose it all and to wonder if it was real. There is a pain in love, in always wondering if one is enough, if one does enough, if one is ever loved as much as one loves. And when one loses love, those questions never fade. One always remembers, and wonders."

She dropped her face into her hands, not crying, but unable to face him and see the reflection of her emotion. The reflections of herself that she saw in others were always the most painful. It was easier to hide in a mirror than in the open eyes of another.

"You speak of your marriage." His tone was flat, and she was thankful. Sympathy had never been her desire.

"Yes."

"I am sorry. I've heard little of your life with Lord Westington beyond that he was a good man."

"He was the best." She still did not look at him. "I know that his goodness is forgotten in my actions after his death."

"But only by others, never by you."

"No, never by me." She did look up then, letting him see the full irony of her expression. "Would you believe that everything I have done since then is because of him? That I live my life the way I do in his memory?"

His brows drew together, emphasizing the leanness of his features. "I can accept that it is so, but would confess no understanding." He raised a hand and rubbed his temple.

She was glad of the gesture. It freed her from the temptation to explain. "You are in pain."

"It is nothing."

"You should rest. I will have the maid freshen a bed, and you should lie down for a few hours." She issued the invitation before she could think—and was then left with too many thoughts. Had she wanted him to stay? Or had she only been acting with proper kindness?

"No. I did not mean to stay. I truly only came to bring your things." His brows had not relaxed, and she wondered if his expression was caused by the ache in his head rather than her own revelations.

She picked up the bell and rang it sharply. "That matters little now. You cannot go out in this weather when you are not your best." She gestured to the window, where the rain was now pouring by barrels not buckets. "And if you will not think of yourself, think of your poor coachman. He'll drown before you make it back to town."

The maid arrived, and she gave direction without further ado, leaving him little choice. They did not speak again until the maid returned and led him away. She should perhaps have shown him to his room, but the desire to be alone was growing upon her.

She heard one muttered comment about managing women as he left, but it was not enough to bring even the hint of a smile to her face.

"The gentleman is burning with fever, my lady." The maid's voice filled the quiet room.

Clara glanced over at Robert, before carefully putting her wine down. He grimaced, and she could sense the words behind the expression. After their earlier comments that their visitor would find a way to prolong their hospitality, the irony of the situation seemed rife.

"Are you sure?" Clara could not resist the question.

The maid hesitated before answering. "Yes, I went to wake him as you asked, and I found him still sleeping and flushed. I tried to rouse him, but he only grumbled at me. There was no mistaking the heat rising off his person."

Robert put his own half-full glass beside hers and headed for the door. "I suppose I must check on him. He will have to stay, of course."

"Of course," Clara answered, but she was already speaking to herself. She picked up her wine and downed it in a single swig. She considered Robert's brandy before repeating the gesture.

Masters had been sent her to bedevil her. There could be no other explanation. She was being called to task for all the misdeeds of her life. There was no other reason he should leave her so unsettled—cause those strange tingles of awareness that so distracted her.

A loud crackle of thunder shook the floors, and she resisted the urge to stamp her foot in answer. Instead, she placed Robert's now empty glass beside her own and went to advise the cook that dinner would be delayed.

She had only just returned when Robert entered.

"The maid is correct," he said. "He has clearly taken a chill. I'll have the physician summoned, but I am sure either of us could guess the outcome: rest, liquids, a dose of willow tea, and a good measure of hope." He picked up his empty glass, stared at it a moment, shrugged, and placed it back on the table.

"I'll have his coachman advised that they'll be spending the night. I am sure he won't regret not traveling in this weather." She walked back to the door, eager to escape as she examined her own emotions.

She was not distressed by illness, and not because it required his stay. No, this distress lay deeper, and she feared to examine the reason. Her emotions were raw enough without this added complication.

She could only wonder what would happen if she was forced to interact with the blasted man on a prolonged basis.

Chapter 5

Masters wondered if she'd ever take that step into his bedchamber. Everything he'd ever heard of her daring reputation seemed counteracted by the toes that never inched over the threshold—not in all the seeming eternity of the days he'd been stuck in this bed. The siren that all London had spoken of would never have been held by the bounds of strict propriety, but Lady Westington never took that single step. Only the sharpness of her gaze and the occasional undertone to her voice ever betrayed the woman he was convinced she hid within.

"Aren't you going to feel my brow?" he asked. "How will you know if I am progressing?"

Lady Westington stood in the doorway and lowered her chin. "I can tell from the glint in your eye that you are doing well. The feverish look is gone. And your voice no longer sounds like you've a throat full of rusty nails. You may even be allowed out of bed tomorrow."

"But what of today? If I stare at the bed's canopy even a moment longer I will enter a state of madness and you may never be rid of me." He tried to inject humor into his voice, but was afraid he merely sounded peckish. He was sick of being in bed now that he again felt human, tired of being waylaid from his quest to find Isabella and her secrets. He needed to be up and moving.

"You sound like a child." She spoke without the tinge of sarcasm he had come to expect. "I'd offer to have you moved to the library to sit by the fire, but I fancy you'd object to having the footmen carry you down the stairs, and I would not wish you to become dizzy and fall."

"I do believe I can manage a flight of stairs without assistance. I have been walking for a few years now."

She smiled with absolute kindness. The expression caught his breath. Where was the temptress of the first day? The woman who could make him grow hard while eating a slice of bacon? The woman who would peer at him so knowingly from under her lashes before slicing him down with her words? The woman who stood here now was neither of those. She was soft and feminine in the extreme, but her eyes offered nothing but comfort and solace.

And she wouldn't step into his room.

What trick was she about?

It was impossible to ask her about that or anything when she stood where anybody might hear. Perhaps that was her plan.

It was maddening.

She stepped into the hall, and for a moment he feared she was gone. Instead, he heard her call for a maid and ask that the fire in the library be stoked.

"I shall probably regret this," she said as she stepped back to the threshold. "You will need to let me go first on the stairs in case you should become dizzy."

He examined her from the rounded toes of her slippers, up past the slight if well-rounded hips, over the slender ribs and perfect bosoms, finally ending on her slim shoulders. He could not imagine what she thought she'd do if he did fall. Most likely he'd sweep them both down the steps.

The words were on the tip of his tongue when he stopped. She was chewing on her lower lip and was not convinced that she was doing the correct thing. If he said anything she was likely to change her mind and leave him staring at the ceiling

If he could get her alone in a room he might begin to question, to find out what she was about.

He nodded. "I promise." He started to swing his legs over the edge of the bed. "Is my robe here? I notice that my own nightshirt has miraculously appeared."

"I had your driver fetch some of your belongings from The Dog while you were not quite yourself. Your valet has apparently arrived in the village and should be making his way here by the end of the day when he has put your trunks to rights. It appears that you suffered from the same illness as he. Hopefully, that means that you also will be up and about soon."

She glanced up, mouth agape, as his bare calves made an appearance from beneath the covers and his bare feet slid to the floor. "Stop, I'll get somebody to help."

"I am quite capable of getting out of bed. Of course, if you think I need help, you're more than welcome to give me an arm." He hated that his legs wobbled as he stood.

She actually took that daring step into the room, hand extended toward him. Then he took another step, this one firmer.

She turned, her skirts spinning about her, and stepped back into the hall. "I'll be right here if you need help. The robe you were inquiring about is hanging in the wardrobe. I am sure you can find it—or do you want me to call the maid?"

"I'll manage." It gave him a moment to walk unobserved to the cabinet. He pulled a pair of trousers up under his nightshirt and then yanked out the deep red velvet robe. The lush fabric had been a Christmas present from Violet, and he'd never known quite what to make of it. Was it a gift of warmth and color, or a comment on the stark way he chose to live his life?

"That's beautiful." She was looking at him with admiration.

His chest puffed like a cock on the walk. He'd never known a woman to have this effect on him.

She continued, "You didn't choose it, did you?"

"I gave the fabric to my tailor."

"But you didn't choose the fabric." She said it as a flat statement, expressing not the slightest doubt.

He shrugged and began the slow walk toward
her. He had been in bed for only three days, no
matter how long it seemed. How could he be so
weak?

She waited until he was almost upon her before
turning and beginning the walk down the hall
toward the stair. He focused on the soft sway of
her hips to distract from the effort of each step. He
was glad she could not see his face and realize the
effort this short walk cost him.

She stopped at the head of the stairs and
waited. She did not turn back to look at him, and
he wondered if she was granting him this small
privacy.

The stairs seemed immense and long as they
descended before her. He knew they could not be
longer than the steps in his own home in Dover.
The polished banister that ran down the side was
the only blessing.

He placed his hand firmly upon it as he drew
near to her. She still had not moved. Again he
inhaled the rich scent of cinnamon. Truly, in all
his years he had never known so tantalizing a
scent to linger about a woman. It combined the
deep, musky, and womanly with the memory of
a young boy's joy. It was no wonder he wanted to
bite her.

She had never been so aware of a man. His phys-
icality surrounded her in ways no other had, even
at the most intimate of moments. Stepping away
should have been easy, automatic, but instead, she

lingered, trapped by the sensations that arose in her body.

He was still pale from his illness. Lavender shadows lay heavy under his eyes and stubble darkened his chin. The threat he presented should have been lessened by his state, but it was not. She was as conscious as ever of the strength of his body as his arm slid past her to grasp the rail.

She drew in a deep breath, her chest filling. She held it for a moment, feeling the pressure build within her. She was vulnerable to no man.

She moved away from him, descending a couple of steps before pausing and waiting for him to move. He seemed as frozen as she had been. He hesitated, then took the first step down. And then the second. His legs wobbled slightly on the third, but she pretended not to notice.

She moved farther down the flight, waiting for him to follow.

She should call for a footman. It had been unwise to allow him to attempt this feat, but she had seen the boredom in his face as he stared blankly about the room and had wanted to grant this small mercy. And if she could get him alone in a room, perhaps she could further question him about that night. She still needed to find out why he was convinced she was a thief.

If Robert had not warned her, she would have questioned Masters in his chamber, but she would not go against her stepson's wishes in his own home. It was still important that Lord Darnell believed she was reformed.

She smiled to herself. Wouldn't they all be shocked if they knew that her reformation was real, that she never again intended to play wild games? All she wanted now was to find a peaceful, gracious life of her own—to find her own form of pleasure and joy. If she could just clear up this mess with Masters, that might even be possible.

"Do you want to go back?" she asked softly, her mood mellowed by her thoughts. "I can have a book sent up to you if you but let me know your taste."

"No." His voice was quite forceful despite the hesitation that was evident in his step. "It is getting out of the bedchamber that is the draw, not the thought of a book."

A flash of disappointment hit her, and she realized that she had hoped she was the draw. Fool. It served as a reminder that she had no business thinking such thoughts. She was a new woman, or would be as soon as Robert was wed and she got back to London. It was important that she not forget the risk Masters still posed to her.

Somehow Robert had not heard of her adventures at The Dog and Ferret, and she wished to keep it that way. It was surprising that no one had mentioned her night of ale and cards. Mr. Johnson, at the very least, should have said something to him, but Robert had said not one word.

She peered over her shoulder at Masters. Could she trust him, or was it only his illness that had stilled his tongue? If she explained the situation to him, would he hold her secrets tight? She tried to remember the things Violet had said about her brother. Many of them had not been kind, but Violet had said that he was a man of his word—too much so in some instances.

Even as she wondered, she heard a slight gasp behind her and felt his arm brush by her as he grabbed for the railing again. His fingers caught hold and held it tight. He tilted forward, and she stepped back, using her body to brace him. She turned toward him as his other hand came down on her shoulder, her breasts pressing tight into his chest.

His grasp was strong. The pads of his fingers bit into her flesh. She held back a whimper as she saw the strain upon his face. His mouth formed a curse she was well familiar with, but he released no sound.

Then he caught himself. His body straightened and his face grew expressionless. No, there was a definite expression; it was just not one of pain or dismay. His eyes focused first on her lips and then moved down to where their bodies pressed tight together.

He swallowed. She watched the Adam's apple bob in his throat, and her mouth grew dry. She should step back. He was in control again, and there was no danger he would fall.

"You're hurting me." She turned her glance away from him and looked down to where his fingers were still locked about her shoulder, tanned flesh against the forest green of her shawl.

It took a moment longer than it should have for him to loosen his grasp, and even then he did not release her. His thumb swept up, pushing her shawl aside, stroking the bare flesh above her neckline.

The thumb was calloused. She had not taken him for a man to ride without gloves, but the darkened skin of his hands and the rough calluses on his fingers betrayed him. He did not follow every social nicety.

His thumb stroked again, running a line just above her collarbone.

She shivered. And her eyes rose to meet his. They were so dark. She had thought them so dark a blue as to be nearly black, now they appeared the black of obsidian—deepest pitch with only an iridescence of blue reflecting off the surface. Those eyes devoured her.

She didn't think she had ever seen such want, such need.

He hesitated and she thought he would pull back. A cool breath of air passed between where their bodies met.

He swallowed again, the movement more felt than seen as she found herself lost in his desire. His hand moved from her shoulder, up and around the back of her neck, cupping the nape.

He pulled her closer, drawing her toward him. He bent forward. It was an endless moment as his lips descended. She had a hundred heartbeats to pull away, a thousand flaps of a butterfly's wing.

She knew she should. She had acted unwisely in the past, but nothing compared to the foolishness of this kiss. He did not like her. She did not like him. They had nothing in common. Discord lay in their future.

She rose on her toes, moving toward him, as caught in the impossibility of need as he.

The first touch was soft. She had expected to be devoured by his hunger, but found the stroke of rose petals. His mouth brushed across hers, a caress as much of the imagination as of reality. It gave a hint of possibility, but nothing more.

She pushed higher, wanting more, needing to feel the firm pressure of command.

He drew back so that only his breath caressed her.

A world of possibility existed in that breath.

Just as she wondered if he would desert her, his lips descended. Again the kiss was soft and gentle, but now it grew deeper, the pressure greater.

Their mouths were still closed, but there was knowing in the simple movement of skin against skin. Her eyes drifted closed. It should have felt like the innocent kiss of a first love, but no bumbling boy's kiss had ever made her long for so much more.

There was more want and desire in the basic pressing of lips than in the deepest kiss she had ever shared.

Together they were caught in a moment that could not last. She could step back or press forward.

Retreating had never been an option.

She opened her lips beneath his, issuing invitation. He stilled slightly at her movement and then his tongue swept across the gap. It did not seek entrance, but teased and played.

He tasted of licorice. Cook must have placed something in his last draught. Her own tongue darted out, seeking more, wanting more.

Her skin tingled as his hand slipped from her neck and trailed down her back, coming to rest at her waist. His other hand joined it, pulling her closer, their bodies resting fully together.

His position above her on the stairs caused some awkwardness and Clara stepped up, coming to stand between his legs. She slipped her hands inside the soft velvet of his robe, only the thin linen of his nightshirt separating her from his flesh. His fever had faded, but still he gave off waves of heat, encasing her in warmth and comfort—safety.

Could passion be safe?

The thought flickered through her mind. Passion and safety. It was a strange combination. The two should have been unable to exist together, but now combined in perfect unity.

Then his tongue flicked across her lips again and any semblance of thought was lost. This time the tip swept again and again against the space between her lips before seeking entrance.

She prepared herself for the onslaught. Men's passions were unchecked once released. Yet he surprised her. He explored rather than ravished. And each playful sweep of his tongue invited her to join him.

For a woman who'd always strived for control, the invitation was irresistible. She found herself pressing toward him, her body, her mouth, each seeking closer, more intimate contact. It was her tongue that deepened the contact, delving into his mouth in an endless dance. It was her fingers that caressed his firm muscles and sought the openings in the fabric that would allow her to feel the silk of his skin. It was her body that pressed closer, pushing against his growing hardness.

She moaned with the pleasure of it, of him.

It had been far too long since she'd felt this way. She could not remember ever feeling this way.

His hands squeezed tighter at her waist, attempting to lift her to an even better position, to nest his erection at the apex of her thighs.

She felt him quiver.

Power and desire mixed and grew until they were her whole world.

She felt him shake—and curse.

He folded backward on the stairs, pulling her with him until she lay sprawled across his lap.

She hoped it had been a gesture of passion, a gesture of ardor uncontrolled and willing.

He swore again.

No, it had not been passion.

She pulled herself back, staring down at his flushed face, his brow marked with sweat. Frustration lay clearly across his features, but whether from interrupted passion or his own powerlessness, she could not say.

She slid off his lap and sat beside him on the stairs. His eyes were closed and she could sense his internal struggle. Watching him helped her to quiet her own demons; she was unused to unindulged desires. She could not remember a circumstance where completion had been so entirely denied. Her body burned with the need for his.

Her voice dipped as she spoke. "Are you injured?"

"No, I only need a moment." He gasped slightly as he answered.

She rose to her feet, straightening her skirts and checking her fastenings. Miraculously, they all seemed undisturbed. Her hair had escaped, however, and she quickly finger-combed it into place. "I'll fetch help. We will soon get you back to your room." The moment away would give her a chance to collect herself.

"No," he said, preventing her from leaving.

"But   "

"I said no. I am perfectly able on my own." He did not look at her, and his voice was filled with ice. Pushing himself up, he stood with some effort. "Now do you wish to proceed or should I go on my own? I do not mean to allow some foolishness to prevent my escape from confinement."

She wasn't sure whether he referred to his infirmity or to what had happened between them. He was a man who would regard his own physical weakness as foolish, but it seemed more likely that he referred to the kiss.

It had been foolish—but still his words felt like

a slap, reminding her of her resolve only moments before to become a new woman. The kiss had been a grave mistake.

She tried again. "Please allow me to summon help. I do not wish you to injure yourself."

"No, I do not need your help—not of any kind."

"If you will not let me summon help, it would perhaps be best if you returned to your room. I was wrong to suggest that you might arise." She knew displeasure was clear in her tone, and could only hope the hurt was not evident as well. She felt as if she had been slapped, hard.

He stood still and then took a careful step down the steps. His knuckles were pale on the balustrade, but he moved with steady precision. As he approached, she was forced to step forward and lead him down the stairs. She could have held her ground, but his face was so remote, without hint of warmth, that she did not want to risk further contact.

She walked ahead of him, step by careful step, until they reached the door to the library. She did not turn once but her every sense was aware of him behind him. With each step she waited for him to falter—he did not.

The door was partially open and she pushed it further. The fire had been set and the room was more than temperate. After debating whether to help him to his chair, instead she stood aside and let him enter.

He walked to the high leather wing chair near

the fire and sat, lifting his feet to the footrest in front of him. Only once he was seated did the strain leave his body. His shoulders relaxed back against the soft leather and his eyes closed. He turned his head from her as if he did not wish her to see his weariness.

"I'll take tea. Lemon, no milk," he commanded.

First he sat in her chair, then he ordered her like a maid. They were petty things, but they felt of great importance. A distinct lack of respect was shown in his actions. After the kiss he was probably thinking her the harlot he'd always believed her.

If he hadn't lost what little color he'd had, she would have fought. Instead, she left the room to call for refreshment.

Outside the door, away from his view, she let her own shoulders slump. The kiss had been unimaginable. Her lips still stung from the slight bristle of his beard, and her mouth was still filled with his flavor.

She wanted to shout and scream. The truth was hard to face. In the years since her husband's death, she'd had many lovers—far fewer than public opinion would believe, but in her own mind she qualified it as many. It was far easier than counting and being forced to remember each face, each man. Indeed, had there been only one she would have called it many for the sake of the anonymity that provided. She'd had many lovers, had done many things with them, and not one of them had ever made her feel as that kiss had.

It had made her feel fresh and new and full of possibility. Each soft caress of his lips had made her feel valued, something to be cherished.

Not even her husband had ever made her feel like that. Michael had awoken depths of passion in her, but it had always been earthy. They had known what was between them and enjoyed it to its fullest—with Michael the act had always been about enjoyment.

With Masters there had been more.

Damnation. She should not have given in. He was temptation sent to keep her from her plans of respectability.

"My lady, did you want help with something?" The maid's voice startled her.

She was standing motionless in the front hall, staring into space; no wonder the maid stared at her as if she were possessed. Her thoughts were so scattered and erratic it was a miracle she could find an answer. "No—I mean yes, some tea please for the gentleman. Give him some of Lord Westington's blend."

It was a petty revenge.

"And for you, my lady?" the maid asked.

Clara would have dearly loved a cup of her own blend, but could not think of a way to have two pots without causing him to question. She couldn't picture a man who liked lemon in his tea choosing a smoky blend.

Leaving the door open half a foot, she returned to the room and chose a chair a slight distance from Masters and sat, not saying a word as she picked up her much despised needlework. She did not have it in her to begin the discussion she knew they must have. If he wanted to talk he could choose the topic of conversation.

The fire crackled and gave off small bursts of sparks. The wood must have been damp when set. At least it did not smoke.

"Do you have any sonnets?" he asked at last.

"Sonnets?"

"Yes, sonnets—poetry, anything but Byron."

"You don't seem a man for poetry. Are you sure you wouldn't care for something more intellectual? Perhaps an economic or agricultural text?"

He appraised her with those dark eyes. "Don't you believe poetry to be an exercise of the intellect?"

"Well, yes, I do. I would not have thought you would."

Leaning back in the chair, he stretched his legs closer to the fire. "There is much we don't know of each other."

"That is true," she answered cautiously.

"Much of what my sister has told you is no doubt correct. However, I imagine the portrait she painted was a trifle one-dimensional."

Violet had described her brother as an ogre who had forced her into marriage with not one, but two old men—and there had been all those rumors when Isabella ran off and Lord Foxworthy was murdered. It was true that over the most recent months Violet's tone had changed. She'd seemed more ready to look at Masters's actions with understanding, but Clara had assumed that was because Violet was in love and looking at the whole world in a new light.

Now she was not so sure. "Violet has never mentioned your taste in literature. She was much more interested in discussing your taste in matrimonial partners."

"I assume we are speaking of her first two husbands."

"And your own lack of a bride."

He let his head fall back, and stared up at the ceiling. "From almost any other woman I would take that as the beginning of a flirtation."

"It is not and you are changing the subject."

"Perhaps I do not choose to discuss the way I raised my sisters and the decisions I was forced to make."

"That is your prerogative, but then you leave me free to believe what I wish about you. There was much gossip when your younger sister ran off—and then there was Colonel Foxworthy's death."

"Yes—think what you will, you would do so anyway—as I do about you."

So he did think her a harlot—and a thief. She must not forget that. She should ask him again about the watch—about *that night*, but her emotions felt so on edge after the kiss, she was not sure she was ready to hear him verbalize his clear opinion.

Instead, she sat straight, determined that the subject of his sister's marriages and the gossip about Isabella not merely be avoided. He could refuse to discuss it, but she would have it be a true decision, not just a turn of conversation. "So you have no desire to explain why you forced your seventeen-year-old sister to marry a man well over seventy?"

Chapter 6

Masters looked away for a moment. He was still unsettled from the kiss, his body still demanding more. He knew he had sounded brusque there on the stairs, but what was a man to do when his body screamed with frustration?

It was clear that Clara suffered no such difficulties. She was probably accustomed to such flirtation, and could throw off heady desire without a thought.

The kiss might have been a tool to relax his guard.

No, he did not really think that. It had caught them both by surprise, that was all.

But her question about Violet, that was another matter.

That required a moment's thought.

He had known it would come to this from the first moment that he'd realized her identity. He filled his lungs with air and slowly exhaled. What was he willing to tell her? He had answered partially before, and she had not seemed satisfied. Saying more would imply a level of intimacy that he was not certain he wished to encourage.

A kiss was one thing, even a kiss such as they had shared. A kiss was physical, easily dismissed, if not forgotten. The sharing of histories, of minds—that was something else.

It was hard to know what to do. He could still feel the softness of her lips beneath his, tempting him on. But that is what she was, a temptress—and a thief. He must not forget it, no matter how delicious her lips, no matter how sweet her smile. His mother's smile had been sweet on occasion, as well.

Even as he thought this, she stood.

He had waited too long to speak.

Her body was taut with emotion as she paced once across the room and back, almost vibrating with unsaid words. "If you don't wish to discuss it, I can go. We really do not need to converse. The maid will bring your tea."

She stopped by a shelf and grabbed a book. "Here, the latest of Wordsworth's *Lyrical Ballads*. Not precisely sonnets, but perhaps you will find it entertaining."

The book was heavy, but she held it out to him with her arm fully extended. He left her there, holding it, a moment before taking it and dropping it carelessly in his lap. Wordsworth had never been a favorite and offered no temptation now.

Her lips drew tight as she stared down at him. He could see that there was much more she wanted to say. An impulse to reach up and draw a finger across her narrowed lips took him. He sensed that even in her darkest moments it would be easy to soften her, to bring out unwilling smiles.

Instead, he held firm, watching as she turned, and while she did not stomp out of the room, she gave every impression of doing so.

He waited until she was a step beyond the door to speak, one small step from being too far to hear. He did not speak loudly, as if testing the fates to see if she would answer. He was not yet sure what he meant to tell her. "Do you really wish to understand what happened all those years ago? To understand why things happened as they did?"

His words stopped her, but she did not turn. Her back stayed stiff and straight. She was as motionless as he had ever seen her.

When she did turn it was a toy dancer's pirouette, her whole body moving as a solid piece. He was again reminded of the porcelain doll he imagined when first he saw her. Her lips were too pink against her pallid skin to be unpainted and her eyes glowed like glass jewels, echoing the bronze satin of her dress. It was only the faint lines of much laughter about her eyes that spoke of her humanity. For once he could not determine her thoughts.

She stepped toward him, back through the library's doorway. "Mr. Masters." Her voice was cool, but flowed smoothly like a brook. "I am not in the mood for games."

"Nor am I."

"Then what would you call this? You knew you were going to speak, but waited to see if I would relent before you were forced to." She was more direct than any woman he had ever met. "What has happened between us the last days is most out of the ordinary. No, do not make some insinuating comment about whether anything can be out of the ordinary for one such as I. You know and understand me as little as I you. If you wish to explain your past actions, which have left me with a less than generous opinion of your character, then do so. I am as you find me and I do not feel the need to make excuses—not to anyone."

The doorway framed her with light from the great windows of the hall. It was hard to discern her exact expression, but again he knew she would not surrender. He could play by her rules or not at all.

Before he could answer, the maid appeared behind her, a small figure of a girl encumbered by a great tray. Clara stepped forward and moved some small statuary about on the table to clear a place for the tray. She waved the maid away with the gentlest words, the ice of her temper contained.

When the maid had left, Clara's glance caught on the two delicate Spode creamware cups. She stared at them for a moment. "These were a gift for my wedding. We do not normally use them." Her voice was low, as if she spoke to herself and not to him.

She picked up the pot and filled his cup. She placed a sliver of lemon on the saucer and handed it to him. He took it from her, but held it without drinking. He stared at her still empty cup.

The decision was hers. Would she pour?

"You are sitting in my chair." She continued to look at the empty cup and not at him. He wondered at her petty comment. It was out of context with what he knew of her. When she was mad, the storms brewed in her eyes. She did not play nursery games.

"I am sorry. I did not know." He made no move to stand up.

"I realize that, but being a gentleman you should have waited for me to sit first."

"And you would have placed me here, in the seat nearest to the fire, would you not?"

She lifted her glance to him then. "Given your health, yes."

She still did not pour her tea.

"Would you like me to move?" It was a delicate balancing act between them. He did not wish her to leave, but was unsure how far he would go to make her stay.

"No. It was most impolite of me to mention it."

"As it was impolite of me to sit first." He relented slightly, sharing what he would never have shared with any other. "The truth is I was not sure my legs would hold me longer. I thought only of not having a footman summoned to be of assistance."

"You have too much pride." She said it flatly, leaving off the sting.

"Perhaps so."

The silence was awkward as it had seldom been before. She shifted slightly from foot to foot, still unable to contain her nervous energy.

He was reminded of their first encounter when he held his tongue, waiting for her to speak. It was his turn. "Will you please take a seat?" He gestured to the low cushioned chair next to the tea table.

"Forgive my temper. I am afraid I am still unsettled by—earlier events."

"The kiss." Perhaps if the word was said the emotions could be laid at rest.

"Yes. It was out of character."

Not from what he'd heard. He saw her catch his glance and her fingers trembled. It was clear she'd understood his thought.

She bit her lip, and then her chin jutted out with firm determination.

There was still doubt spread across her face, but she sat and, concentrating on the table in front of him, poured herself a cup, dousing it liberally with milk and sugar. She poured deftly, despite the tremor of her fingers, as if she had done so many times. Undoubtedly she had, although it did not fit with what he knew of her character.

He picked up his cup from the saucer and, after a squeeze of the lemon, lifted it to his lips. It was hard to keep his expression still. He felt like he'd stuck his head over the fire openmouthed. Not even the fresh taste of the lemon could cover the taste of burnt leaves.

"It's my stepson's favorite blend." Her mouth hooked up at one corner, and he knew his expression had not fooled her. He noticed she did not sip, but placed the saucer back on the table.

"It is most unusual." He took another sip. Really, it was not so bad. He could begin to understand the attraction. He allowed a small grimace to pass his lips anyway. He would grant her the small victory. She deserved it for staying.

"You were going to speak of your sister," she replied. "You know Violet is most dear to my heart."

He wondered how little he could tell her. As long as her questions focused on Violet and not Isabella and Foxworthy, he was safe. He could tell no one the full story. He sensed that she would not be so easy to deter this time. "I know. From what she has said, I know she reciprocates the emotion."

"I was not aware that you were in frequent communication with your sister. I cannot believe that I am an important topic of conversation."

"You would be surprised. My sister holds you in high esteem and uses you as a frequent example of what a woman can be."

A faint flush of color rose on her cheeks at the compliment. "But you do not."

"I do not know you."

"But that has not kept you from judging."

That was hard to answer. Such discussion always reminded him of his mother, and that could only lead a foul taste in his mouth. "I would admit to not liking what I have heard. I have never been fond of licentious behavior."

"Licentious. It is as good a word as any other, I suppose." She picked up her tea and took the smallest of swallows. "It is much better with milk and sugar than lemon. But we are supposed to be talking of you and your relations, not mine," she concluded.

He took another sip, then leaned back, staring at the ceiling. He closed his eyes. "I was seventeen when my parents died."

With his eyes closed he could still see them as they'd looked that last day. His mother had worn crimson velvet, a dress she'd been particularly fond of based on the number of times he could remember her wearing it. She'd looked beautiful, but tired, as she'd prepared for another night's revels. His father's eyes had been shadowed as he'd said his farewells and donned his hat. He'd lost weight over the past months and his suit had hung a little loose. Other than that there had been nothing different from any other evening.

Nothing different until the knock on the door hours later, after which his parents' bodies were carried in. His mother had still breathed and she'd called for his father again and again, each call quieter than the last. At the very last she'd grasped his hand tight and whispered, "I am so sorry." He'd never even been sure if the comment had been meant for him.

His shock had only grown greater over the following days as the few details came forth. His parents had been shot returning from a ball—their carriage stopped by masked men. That was all anyone knew. There was talk of brigands and highwaymen, of a lover's anger, but no true fact ever emerged.

He was left with nothing. No knowledge. No single fact that could explain the devastation of the life he had always known.

He was left with nothing. Only two sisters. Two sisters and endless bills—and that final secret, his father's treason.

"My parents died when I was seventeen," he repeated the words. This time he opened his eyes and stared up at the elaborate frieze on the ceiling. It was better than seeing his mother's beautiful face laughing in the candlelight as she left that final night. He hated that he'd loved her despite everything.

Clara answered softly. "You were much too young—not that there is ever a right age."

"What has Violet told you of their deaths?"

"Only that she was not there. She spent the night with a friend and returned the next day to find the maids draping the house in black."

"Isabella was still little more than three or four. I don't believe she even remembers their deaths or them."

"How did they die? Violet has never said."

"They were shot." He waited for her to ask questions. She stayed silent. He lowered his head and looked at her.

She stared straight at him. Her eyes were honey now, soft and glowing, but filled with sadness. Still she did not speak.

"They were returning from a ball. It was one of those things that never happen. Men with guns stopped the carriage. The driver and the grooms could do nothing to prevent the attack. The driver survived, injured. The groom did not. That is all that is known." He closed his eyes again.

He felt a gentle pressure on his knee, felt her delicate fingers grip him. He didn't know if she sought reassurance or offered it.

"My life changed in a minute. One moment I was thinking of university and of mischief with my friends and the next I was alone and didn't know how to proceed."

"When Michael, Lord Westington died, the feeling was the same." Her voice was halting. "I remember being angry that he was late returning from his ride. He'd wanted me to go with him and I was sure it was a petty revenge."

"But you were not left penniless with two sisters to raise, one still in the nursery. I do not mean to sound irreverent, but I do not see that you can know what I faced."

"No, Robert was almost eighteen and had already learned much of what he needed to know about running the estates. I still felt so alone. I knew Robert had just lost his father, but all I could feel was my own pain, that a piece of me had been lost."

"It was the same with Violet. I knew she grieved, but I was too preoccupied with my own mourning—my own mourning and the creditors. They scarcely gave me a day before they appeared in droves." He could not believe he was discussing this with her. One never discussed such things—not even with family—and Lady Westington was certainly not family.

"Perhaps that is what you never allowed Violet to understand—your need to deal with your own pain before you could see hers. Perhaps I am lucky that Robert and I never had such problems."

He dropped his glance to the small hand that still gripped his knee. He wondered if she had forgotten it. Her thumb moved rhythmically across the thick velvet of his robe, sending small tingles up his leg.

Ignoring the desires her touch woke, he answered. "I am not sure that Violet and I did either until the matter of her marriage arose."

Her finger gripped him once tight and then relaxed. He placed his own hand over hers. The unfamiliar intimacy felt both awkward and comforting.

"Ah, yes, her marriage. When you forced her to marry a man in his seventies."

He started to defend himself, and stopped. He was telling her far more than he had ever intended. This whole matter was none of her business. The thought shook him and almost had him pushing her hand away. He was not about to share the closest-held details of his life with a near stranger, no matter how she drew him in. She hadn't even given him permission to use her Christian name despite the increased intimacy between them.

He brushed her hand off, then he swung his feet off the ottoman. He rose hurriedly and turned from her, afraid that his face said too much.

"I cannot do this."

"I didn't suppose you could." Clara held her disappointment to herself. For a moment she had doubted all her thoughts about this man, had thought that he could open up, could treat her as his equal, as a person.

Licentious.

The word stood between them.

He had kissed her every bit as much as she had kissed him. Perhaps if she had not felt so judged she would have taken his withdrawal with more grace.

She placed her teacup and saucer back on the tray with deliberate precision. She brushed imagined crumbs off her skirts before standing with easy grace. "I will leave you to the books. If you do not care for the Wordsworth, I am sure that you can find something else to your liking on those lower shelves." She pointed to a long shelf of slim embossed volumes.

"My thanks, Lady Westington. I shall choose a few volumes and then retire. I do find that I am weary, and I must regain my energy before I can begin my journey again."

She stopped in the process of summoning the maid to clear the tray. "You seek Isabella?"

"I believe that we have already discussed the purpose of my travels. It is my responsibility to find her." He was so crisp and proper. He did not betray how he felt about his search for his sister.

"Yes, we have. I merely wondered that you still search after all this time," she said. She longed to ask about the gossip that had followed Isabella's disappearance. "Do you believe her to be in Norfolk?"

He was quiet, and she wondered if he could see her real questions reflected in her face. Had even thinking about the rumors breached some invisible wall?

He walked to the fire and stood warming his hands as if fighting the cold of his long journey. "While I was in Coventry I heard rumors that she might be employed with Lord Connortan."

She debated, but then answered fairly. "I may be able to help you then. I can certainly make inquiries. The earl's wife was a close acquaintance in my schoolroom days. I will pen a note and have it sent over."

"That would be most helpful, Lady Westington."

He sounded so stuffy—so unlike the man on the stairs. But perhaps that was for the best. She was still determined to begin fresh when she returned to London, and a man who drew her to kissing him on the stairs where anyone could see them was far from what she needed.

She needed to think reasonably.

At least he had not refused her help. She still did not fully understand what had prompted his sudden ending of their earlier conversation. She could see that it was painful for him, but then he should never have begun. She had been surprised that he had been willing to broach the subject—even with her pushing—but even more startled by his sudden stop.

It should not have been important to her, but it had become so—for reasons she could not understand, he had become important. Damnation Her shaky emotions were playing her for a fool.

She needed to regain her sense of power.

"I will leave you to your selection then." She took a step toward the door and then turned, dropping her voice to a low husky purr. "And you really must call me Clara. I only kiss men I am familiar with."

She looked at him from under her lashes for the briefest of moments, letting him see she was not just speaking of their past kiss.

The expression on his face caused her to chuckle, a deep laugh that filled the room. It was a small victory to keep him off guard, but still it helped to restore her sense of balance. She'd have to make it a point to poke at him whenever he grew prim.

It had been five days since she had spoken to him. Masters dropped the book to his lap and watched the flickering flames of the fire. At least he was allowed down the stairs on his own now—and the Wordsworth had actually proved engrossing.

He turned from the fire and glanced at the window. Spatters of rain still marked it. It seemed never to stop raining for more than an hour at a time, making the continuation of his journey impossible.

Now if only Clara would deign to grace him with her presence. He should not have missed her. Aggravating, dominating, spoiled, vexing did not begin to describe her. Clara, Lady Westington was not the type of woman that a man needed in his life. She was everything he should avoid.

But still he missed her.

Robert had provided good company, visiting him on several occasions and sharing rich tales of country life. Masters had to confess that he'd listened to every description of Clara that had sneaked into those stories. When Robert spoke of her she did not sound like the woman that gossip had described.

He rubbed his temple.

If it had not been for the kiss, he might have wondered if society had made a mistake—that kiss had told its own story, however. She was a woman of heady passion, just as had been described.

His mother's face flashed into his mind. She was a prime example of how a woman's unchecked passion could lead only to ruin.

How did the warm, caring woman that Robert described—that he himself had seen—reconcile with the wanton tendencies he had also experienced?

"Do you have everything you need? Should I have a blanket fetched? It is quite cold today." As if in answer to his thoughts, Clara entered the room, the soft, gentle Clara.

"I am fine," he replied, picking up his book again. He would not betray his eagerness for her company.

"I have decided I cannot avoid you longer." She spoke with complete honesty.

"I did not think you would admit to avoiding me."

"I have never seen reason to misstate the obvious. I have avoided you since the awkwardness of our kiss and the following conversation." Her eyes dipped and then rose again to meet his. "I do not like being unsure of my actions, and you left me feeling both most unsure and impolite."

"And yet you are here now."

"Yes." She moved and sat across from him, leaning forward as if to share a secret. The scent of cinnamon was mixed with something else. Vanilla. The woman was a veritable bakeshop, complete temptation.

"Why?"

"I have questions, and only you can answer them."

"I cannot think of what I would know that others would not—unless you mean to discuss my sisters again." His tone clearly stated that his sisters were one subject he would not discuss.

"No, I have realized you have said all you will say. I need to know about that night."

"That night?"

"You know exactly which night to which I refer, the night at The Dog and Ferret. I need to know what happened." She paused. "And I also need to thank you for your discretion. It would have been a nightmare for me—and for Robert—if the story had gotten out."

"Of course. I am a gentleman. I would never have dreamed of spreading such tales. I do not understand what you need to know. You were there. Why should I know any differently than you?"

She paled slightly at his words, and her teeth worried at her lower lip. He saw her lungs fill with a deep breath before she spoke. "I don't remember anything of that night from just after I arrived at the tavern. I don't remember meeting you at all until I awoke the next morning."

"You don't remember anything?" It seemed preposterous, but why should she lie now? If she had lied that morning at The Dog, it would have made sense that she was trying to excuse her crime. Now, when she knew he was not going to pursue the theft, it was senseless.

"Nothing. There is not even a hint of memory. It is as if nothing exists from the time that I arrived until the next morning." Her voice shook as she spoke, and he could see that even speaking of the experience unnerved her.

It made him feel incredibly protective. Whatever she had done in the past, it was not right that anything had made her so vulnerable. "Tell me what you do remember."

She dropped her eyes to her hands as she began to recount her tale. She began by talking of her dinner with Mr. Green. She blushed as she honestly revealed how she had refused his suit, explaining that she had not been looking for a new lover and that Mr. Green would not have fit the bill even if she had.

Masters did not know what prompted her complete candor, but he did not halt her words until she described Mr. Green and explained why his slight build and light hair would never have drawn her.

"Was he wearing a green coat with brass buttons?" he asked.

Her eyes clouded as she tried to recall. "Yes, he was. Why do you ask?"

"He was there later, at The Dog and Ferret. He sat beside you and brought you ale. You did not seem so indifferent to him then."

She paled. "I do not remember."

"Tell me what you do recall."

She recounted the rest of her tale, scant though it was, and then sat quietly.

"It is not much," he said after a while.

"No, and it does not explain why you think I stole your watch. I have never been given to thievery and do not see why I should have chosen to begin that night, no matter my state."

He leaned back, away from her. "I don't know what to say. I came and joined the card game after about an hour of sitting in the bar watching. You did not win a single hand. Mr. Green was getting closer and closer to you. He refilled your mug several times. I won two hands before you stood with some difficulty and said you were ready to leave—you claimed to be extremely weary. You swept your cloak about you in a grand, if slightly inebriated, manner, and in doing so my watch fell from its folds. You must have stolen it from my pocket."

"I cannot believe I would have done such a thing."

"It was most gracefully done and I almost did not believe it myself. I thought you were faking your drunkenness. I debated for a moment whether to confront you, and during that time it became quite clear that you truly were not in a good state. Mr. Green was trying to help you out to his carriage to take you home. You said you needed to take a brief stop before leaving. When you went into the back hall I stopped you, wanting a confrontation. When you could not answer coherently I became set on my plan to give you a good fright when you awoke. I paid one of the stable boys to report back to Mr. Green that you were walking home."

"And you bundled me upstairs and I know the rest of the story."

"Yes, and I saw my watch fall from your cloak, so there can be no doubt that you had taken it." As he spoke he pulled the weighty gold watch from his pocket and laid it on the table. He had always liked the simplicity of the design, heavy and plain. It was designed to last. He had purchased it from a prestigious jeweler after his first successful harvest on his estates. It had been the solitary indulgence he had allowed himself. He rubbed his thumb across its smooth cover.

He glanced up and saw her staring at the watch. The remaining pink leached from her cheeks as he stared. Even her lips lost their color, looking almost gray in the firelight. She reached out and he withdrew his hand, allowing her to stroke the watch.

"This is the watch I am supposed to have stolen?" she asked.

"Yes." He did not understand the purpose of her question.

"Have you opened the back?"

"Not in days. I don't understand what—"

"Open it. Open it, now."

Still not understanding, he pried open the backing and stared. It was his turn to pale.

"*To Michael, with all the love in the world. May all your days have rainbows. Clara,*" she recited the words even as he read them. Her eyes closed as if a great weight held them down. "I gave it to him on our wedding. I had not even noticed it was gone. I've carried it always since his death and I did not even know it was gone."

All Masters could do was swallow again and again, trying to wet his mouth enough to speak. She had not stolen his watch. Indeed, he had stolen hers.

He had called her a thief and she had been blameless. He had caused this whole mess. "I am so sorry," was all he could find to say.

As if sensing his distress for the first time, she opened her eyes. "I know you only did what you thought was right. I imagine you have the same watch."

"Yes. I must not have had it with me. My valet was absent, and I was unused to dressing myself. When I saw you drop it—"

"You assumed it was yours. It was a natural mistake."

"I am not sure why the mistake was not discovered when my valet returned. There is no excuse." He stood hurriedly. If she was not a thief, what else could he have been wrong about? He needed time to think. "Please forgive me. I fear my illness has left me weakened. I must rest."

He left the room, not waiting for her reply.

Chapter 7

Masters was leaving. Robert had said so. Clara considered that as she scooped the warm center out of the soft-boiled egg. She should have been pleased. He had accused her wrongly of theft and nearly caused her great embarrassment.

If anyone had found out about that night, her plans would all have been ruined. She would have faced disgrace, and none of it would have been her fault. She should be furious with him.

Instead, all she could remember was his face when he'd realized his mistake. He'd been more devastated than she. It had hurt her to see his pain.

Still, it had been almost a fortnight since his arrival, and she should be ready for him to leave. He had brought nothing but discontent into her life. She had felt prickly ever since he had arrived, and she did not like it.

How was she ever going to find peace and comfort when she was always jumpy and unsure? She never knew when she would enter a room and find him there.

Only he was never there. In two days since she'd found out the truth of that night, he had avoided her completely. He had taken to his bed again, or at least pretended to, and she'd not seen him without at least two servants and Robert in attendance.

She tapped her spoon against the shell of the egg, not hard enough to break it, but just enough to make a slight noise. It was a pointless gesture, but somehow it brought her satisfaction.

A solitary breakfast was a thing to be desired. It allowed one time to plan for the day, but today she found no pleasure. She tapped the spoon again.

He was leaving.

Masters was leaving.

Jonathan was leaving.

She smiled as she thought the last. He still addressed her as Lady Westington. Sometimes she gave him that special smile and hoped he might slip and call her Clara, but he had not. She had yet to call him Jonathan outside her mind. It was something she was saving for that perfect moment.

Only would that moment come? He was leaving.

And what was she doing even thinking of a perfect moment? He was insufferable, everything she did not need in a man. He had no place in the life she planned for herself.

The attraction she felt for him must be put aside, a thing to be taken out only late at night and mooned upon.

She was no longer the woman who acted on her desires without thought.

She tapped the shell one last time, then scooped the last bite of creamy egg into her mouth. She closed her eyes and savored the rich flavor, flicking the last crumb from her lower lip.

She opened her eyes and—he was there. Masters's gaze was firmly glued to her lower lip. For good measure she ran her tongue across it a second time, puckering her lips slightly at the end.

He froze.

It was difficult for her not to smile. Should she lick again? No, that would be too much. Instead, she leaned forward and plucked a piece of toast from the holder, her eyes never leaving his. It was a pity her morning gown was not lower cut, but the strand of garnet beads she'd chosen to wear did slip below the neckline, drawing attention to . . . oh yes, he'd noticed.

His eyes dropped and stayed.

She waited a minute and then shifted, leaning back in her chair and nibbling at the toast.

"Are you going to sit?" she asked. "Or did you have a tray in your room? I was not aware you were well enough to leave your chamber." She said the last with definite sarcasm.

Masters pulled back a chair and sat stiffly. She softened the line of her back even more in response until she slouched against the chair.

She took another nibble. "Have you given up speaking to me altogether?"

"No. I merely assumed your question was rhetorical. I am sure you know everything that happens in this house."

That drew a smile from her. "I am not sure if that is a compliment or not. Am I a good hostess or incurably nosy? I'll have to ponder that for a while."

"I assure you I meant only the best." His eyes were focused on her mouth again.

He made it so hard to be good. She wanted him to see her for what she was, to see her as his equal, to know that she could hold control. She wanted him to understand the power of her actions, to understand that a little fun was not an evil thing. It was tempting to honey her toast just so that she could lick the drips off her fingers. She hadn't tried that one, and she could only imagine his response.

She could allow a little honey to drip on the skin above her bodice. If she slowly drew a finger over her chest, letting him wonder at the feel, the texture, and then brought the honey to her lips, letting it spread across them, daring him to taste, to savor, what would he do? Would he finally be drawn beyond that icy control that had not once slipped since the kiss on the stairs? Finding out she was not a thief seemed to have left him colder, if anything. Or would he stand and leave? She sensed he'd come close to it on occasion when she pushed too far.

He did not want her to push beyond his boundaries.

She worried at her lip as she considered. And discovered that was more than enough. His focus was so complete he had not even noticed the footman who stood to his side waiting to fill his plate.

"I understand you wish to leave?" she asked, not even bothering to bend toward him.

"Yes. It is time that I did. If not for the weather I would not have stayed after I found out my mistake. I can only say again that I am sorry."

A few moments ago she had been thinking of the great troubles his mistake could have caused her. She only said, "It's nothing."

"That is not true. I could have caused you great harm. It is time that I leave anyway."

She asked, "Is it because of the post I received from Lady Connortan?"

"It does sound like the woman that she described might be Isabella."

"I still have a hard time picturing any sister of yours and Violet's serving as a governess." She put her half-finished slice of toast down on the plate. "I have never seen Isabella, but young, slim, and redheaded does sound like rather a general description. I do hope you have not traveled the country following every female with red hair you have heard of. Oh dear, you have."

"I have limited myself to those who entered service in the half year." He looked away from her and gestured for the footman, who was still standing patiently, to fill his plate. "I know that each lead I follow is unlikely, but this one sounds possible. Lady Connortan is an acquaintance of Lady Smythe-Burke, who wrote Isabella her references. And said lady directed me away from Norfolk. I realize now it should have been the first place that I looked."

Clara imagined Lady Smythe-Burke standing perfectly straight in her twenty-year-old corset and had to agree. The older doyenne undoubtedly had a penchant for deceit. It would be more surprising if in fact the lady had directed him correctly. "So you will go to London following them."

"It is most inconvenient that they left for Town on the very day that Lady Connortan received your letter."

She loved the way he pouted. It was endearing to see that proud brow furrow and his lips draw tight. He looked like a small boy deprived of a sweet. "Yes, most inconvenient. I am sure you will be greatly troubled to return to Town instead of continuing to travel about the country on muddy roads."

"I must find my sister." He spoke with some vehemence.

"Of course you must." She did not understand why he felt the need to defend himself. Isabella could be little more than twenty, perhaps less. While Clara would defend to her last breath any woman's right to make her own decisions, she would certainly not have wanted to be on her own at twenty. The world did not tend to be kind to such women.

The footman stepped forward to refill her cup, and she waved him from the room. There were some moments one did not want the servants around.

Masters picked up a piece of bacon and bit into it with some gusto. She could not resist eyeing it and then glancing up at him with a smile, her lips forming a full curve.

He almost dropped the bacon as he caught her look. "Must you always attempt seduction over breakfast?"

That brought her laugh—it rose within her, filling her chest before spilling past her lips. "I would never have believed you would actually say it." She paused to fill her lungs. "It will spoil my fun if you admit to it. It is ever so much more delightful when you merely throw me sour looks. And . . ." She paused to consider. "I can't say I've ever attempted seduction over breakfast before you. Seduction before breakfast, or even in lieu of breakfast, but never during."

She leaned forward and snagged a piece of bacon from his plate with her fork. She held it up and examined it with some consideration. "It is hard to see the innate attraction of such a food. Although"—she brought it to her lips—"the flavor does make up for the appearance—and the smell." She took a small bite off the edge and watched as his eyes darkened.

"You are doing it again."

"Am I?" She took another nibble and closed her

eyes, savoring the rich flavor. The whole thing was irresistible. Why should she not have one last bit of joy before turning over her new leaf? "If I were really trying to seduce you, I reckon we'd be sharing our breakfast in bed."

"Do you think me so easy?" He sounded offended.

She couldn't help laughing again. "Oh, don't look so glum. No, I don't think you are easy—not by any measure." She put down the fork and turned serious. "What I do think is that you are attracted, as am I. The sensation is most uncomfortable and undesired, but it cannot be denied. I want you and you have great desire for me," she finished.

He stared at her. Some other response would have been more effective, more advantageous, but all he could do was stare. He only hoped his mouth did not gape.

If she had been surprised by his blatant talk of her attempted seduction, he was even more shocked by the frankness of her discussion. It was not exactly taboo, but he had never known a lady to talk in such a fashion.

He dropped his eyes and stared at his rapidly cooling breakfast. Even the food spread across his plate reminded him of her. He swallowed and looked up again.

He could see the laugh hiding in her eyes. A part of him wanted her to let it out—when its joyous sound filled the room, it was impossible to resist. But resist he must.

"You presume much." He toiled to keep his tone flat.

"Do I? I wish that it were so." Her words were forlorn, but her eyes still danced.

"How do you presume to know what I desire?" It was increasingly hard not to give in to her.

She sighed softly. "Do you really want me to tell you how I know?" She leaned toward him again. He could not help his gaze dropping to the tantalizing hint of bosom the gesture again revealed. "Do you really want me to describe how your eyes darken when I am near, how much more pronounced your swallow becomes, how muscles go tense as if awaiting my softening touch?" She placed her hand upon his wrist. "Do you want me to describe how I feel your pulse begin to race, how even without touching I know your heart beats fast within your chest when I approach?"

He wanted to look away, but it was impossible. She was a witch, with each word she drew him further under her spell.

"Or should I talk of myself?" she continued. "Should I talk of that kiss upon the stairs we have so often ignored? Should I tell you how my lips longed for yours for days afterward, how my breasts still swell at the very thought of your touch? You accuse me of seduction over breakfast, but I still see the look of passion in your eyes whenever my maid brings the morning tray. I cannot even drink tea without thinking of you, of your lips. Is this what you want to hear?"

With each word the desire to touch her grew. Her soft fingers wrapped about his wrist and he could feel her blood speeding within them. That was the trap of her words, that she admitted her own entrapment. She offered no defense.

He turned his hand so that hers lay within his palm. He closed his fingers about it, forming a cage. Her fingers fluttered like a small bird, but did not attempt escape.

He drew her hand up to his lips, blowing between his fingers. She fluttered more.

She had spoken of his eyes darkening; her pupils had grown so large and deep they reflected the whole room within them. He could see himself within her, feel the traps that drew them both. He should release her. He should stand and go.

He blew again.

A quiver wafted through her. The lace edging on her bodice shook and then drew still, as if she no longer breathed.

Almost of its own accord, his other hand rose and drew a line along that edge of lace. She gasped in one large gulp of air.

He slipped his finger under the edge of lace, feeling the velvet of her skin. Her heart was pounding in her chest. He flattened his hand, the fingers slipping deeper. Her open desire was more alluring than anything he had ever known.

His fingers slipped around her breast, beneath it until they lay flat atop that beating heart. He wanted to still it, to soothe it, to comfort her, to take her. That last thought filled him.

To take her.

He could take her here, in her breakfast room, and she would not resist. He knew that as surely as he knew from the strong pulse of her heart that she lived.

His fingers slipped higher. He teased the delicate nipple, pinching lightly and drawing a nail across the top.

She inhaled suddenly, her whole body drawing toward him. The hand he still held within his own clenched, the nails drawing across his skin.

He teased again. She swallowed, her tongue dampening her lower lip.

His own desires were almost out of control. His pants were tight, and it was only with supreme will that he kept from pulling her into his arms and tossing up her skirts.

She could see his wants within his eyes. She watched as the hand that held hers clenched and relaxed. He was a man of restraint.

The fingers that stroked her breast moved again, and her whole body responded. She heard the gasp that passed her lips as if it were from somebody else. The hand he did not hold caught the edge of the table and squeezed it tight.

His actions were so small and her response so great.

She was ready to let him take her here, on the breakfast table.

She knew she should not. This was against everything she was determined to be. But how could she not? She might be determined to live a more sedate life, but she refused to give up joy and spontaneity.

She pressed closer, wanting more contact than those teasing fingers allowed. Her eyes dropped to his mouth and she imagined it on her breasts. His lips parted as if he read her mind.

She eased from her chair, slipping sideways so as to not break contact, and came toward him.

He made no move, but stared at her, straight into her. It felt as if he looked for her soul. The desire she saw in him was so powerful, but it was not all she saw.

She bent toward him, bringing her lips down on his, closing her eyes as she did so. She did not want to see his eyes anymore, did not want to acknowledge the expectations and beliefs she saw there.

Instead, she kissed him, softly and then more deeply. She let her tongue and lips speak all the words that she could not, dared not.

He met her kiss full-on, sought control, seized it, lost it, seized it. She would not let him win. This was her kiss. She pressed closer, ran her tongue between lips and teeth, teased and played, lured him to her. She could not reach victory through force, only through persuasion.

His hand finally released hers as it swept down her torso, her thighs, her calves, seeking the hem of her skirt.

She pulled back, panting. "No."

"Yes."

She closed her eyes again, seeking to avoid the look in his. "I mean not here. I will not spread myself between the toast and eggs. And it is already a wonder the footman has not returned."

"Where then?" His impatience was clear. He thought this some further tease. "Your room?"

She needed to find calm, to consider. "No, this is Robert's house and that will only cause talk. We will take further refreshment in the south parlor. There is a beautiful rug I really should show you."

She turned and tried stepping away from him. He resisted for a moment, his fingers tight about her breast, but then relented. It took only the slightest tug to right her bodice. At least her hair remained unmussed.

She walked from the room with confidence, allowing a gentle sway to her hips. The belief that a man would follow was the surest way to make him do so.

She suppressed the desire to turn and give him that one lingering look that assured he knew the sparks between them still burned hot. It was time he learned how powerful anticipation was.

It took but a moment to ask for refreshment. Another to walk the hall, slowly but not too much so, and enter the parlor. She didn't use the room often. Heavy shrubbery blocked the windows and did not allow for much light. She'd always had a preference for sunlight.

A roaring fire had already been set. She had not been sure it would be, given how infrequently the room was used, but someone must have thought it in need of a drying after the heavy rains of the last days. She hummed in pleasure at the warmth.

Turning, she watched as he stalked into the room after her. There was always the possibility that interrupting pleasure would give too much time for thought and sense. His stance spoke clearly that such worries were groundless.

She granted him one smile as she sat near the fire, spreading her skirts about her. "The maid will be here momentarily. Perhaps you'd like to come and examine the rug? My late husband found it during his travels. I've always found it much softer than it looks. Come tell me what you think."

He did not like taking direction. He wanted control no matter how trivial the consequence. If he had stalked before, he stomped now.

"Oh, don't look at me like that." She felt like laughing. It was all so delicious—his scowl, the warm fire, the pleasure that was to come. Anticipation. It was almost too much.

She let her eyes feast on him. He stood before her so proud and strong, his dark eyes flashing. She'd never realized quite how strong he was before, but now she could see the width of his shoulders and the narrowness of his hips.

He turned and looked at her, still scowling. "I don't understand why you called for the maid now. Surely it would have been—"

"Better to be interrupted in fifteen minutes when she knocked to see if we required anything? My staff is well trained and would not enter a closed room, but even the fact that the door is closed will cause comment. They are used to my habits. Once I have a warm drink I can linger for hours. They will assume that we merely sit and talk and will leave us undisturbed."

"You are well experienced in these matters."

It should not have cut deeply, but it did. She wanted to flash a sarcastic smile and stride from the room, the perfect retort on her lips. But there were better ways to punish him. "And are you not? Experienced, that is?"

"I have the normal experience of a man."

"A phrase that says much and little at the same time. Would you like to hear of my experiences? Since the day we met you have mentioned them frequently. Is it curiosity or voyeurism? Do you have your own particular fancies? You have already tied me to a bed." She pouted her lips as she spoke, letting her eyes roam free again. She began with his boots, such polished fine boots embracing his muscled calves. Then her glance moved up along lean thighs and thin hips. She paused there for a moment—he was still aroused—but only for a moment; subtlety was to be desired. A glance accomplished so much more than a stare—she peeked back—yes, her goal was definitely growing.

He stepped impatiently to the side, trying to shift her attention. She would not be moved. She enjoyed letting her gaze move up a button at a time. "Your coat is beautiful. It is so well fitted, there are clearly no pads."

"Of course not." The poor man was distinctly disgruntled.

She pushed out of the chair with a full laugh, glancing at the door before laying the lightest of kisses across his firm lips. "Shh, be patient. It can only be a few minutes longer. Perhaps we will be lucky and Cook will add scones and jam. It is much too soon after breakfast, but one never knows. There are so many wonderful things one can do with jam."

She could not contain the giggle that bubbled from her lips.

Damn that laugh. He wanted to leave. He knew he should leave. He had no place here, but how could he leave when that magic sound filled the room, that sound that spoke of a joy in living so deep as to be endless? It filled him, sneaking into tiny crevices he had not known were there.

Passion might be suppressible, that laugh was not.

He'd felt stripped when she examined him. He stood there fully clothed in jacket and cravat, and she made him feel naked as a newborn babe.

He was a man, not a boy to be toyed with. How did he let her weave this web of desire—desire and joy? He tapped his toe into the deep plush of the carpet she had so admired.

Damn her. He caught her glance and smirk—her

gaze had finally moved to his face—and held it. He
let her see the power of his passion, but also his
dislike of that power. He might be its prisoner, but
not a willing one.

And even prisoners could fight back. He stepped
toward her until the distance separating them was
barely proper. He ran a finger across her cheek and
down along her chin line. His thumb brushed upon
her lips.

She was caught unawares by his movement—still
thinking herself the general controlling the action.
He ran his thumb across her lips again, feeling the
warm breath within. His eyes never left hers. They
shone like warm melted honey now.

Listening for the sound of steps, he stole his own
sweet kiss—his longer and more demanding than
hers had been. It was always important to show
your foe that you would go one step farther.

Finally, he heard the maid. He stepped back, but
only by a few inches. He lifted one of her hands in
his and stroked his thumb across her palm as the
maid settled the heavy tray.

"What a beautiful chocolate set." He drew a
little circle along her wrist. "And what delicate
scones, and the color of that jam. It must be raspberry. I do love a good raspberry jam. I can eat it
on most anything."

He waited until the maid's back was turned
and then dipped the tip of a finger in the jam. He
brought it to his lips, tasting it first with his tongue
and then bringing it into his mouth with great
suggestion.

He had no time for subtlety.

Her eyes followed the movement of his fingers as he sought to remove every last morsel of the sweet jam. He dipped it again and brought it to her lips. "It's nice and tart."

She resisted for a second, and then gave in, allowing his finger access. He smeared a good quantity on her lips before letting his finger be sucked inside. She gave as good as she was given. Her mouth worked his finger hard, and other, lower parts of his body responded in turn.

It was impossible to tell who was winning.

She stood and stepped away, releasing his finger, and walked to the door. She pushed it shut the remaining inches, and after some slight consideration turned the key within the lock. "Raising suspicion is better than actually being caught."

He turned and settled into the chair, legs splayed. He allowed his head to fall back as he appraised her.

Clara watched him settle; he gave every appearance of comfort, but she knew better. She could feel the tension in his thighs, knew how hard his muscles would be beneath her fingers. Her hands clenched in anticipation.

She met his gaze head on. He was trying her trick, letting his eyes speak his thoughts, his desires.

She stepped toward him. This next part required planning. If she'd known how the morning would play out she would have worn a different dress, one that did not require help with the laces. She worried at her lip, considering—but never releasing his gaze.

Then she let the wide seductive smile spread across her face. She didn't walk toward him, she sauntered, hips swaying and drawing his gaze lower. When she reached him, she turned gracefully and sank to her knees before him, head tilted forward, gracing him with the full curve of her back.

It should have been the ultimate gesture of submission, the kneeling slave girl before the master, but she knew it was a gesture of strength, of confidence. She was so assured of her own power that the outward manifestation of submission did not matter.

His fingers tickled the back of her neck, then clasped it. Her vulnerability was clear as his fingers wrapped completely around. She relaxed her shoulders and bowed her head further, uncowed. His fingers tightened for a moment and then relaxed, trailing down her back to the top of her dress, toying with the knot that held the laces tight.

Her dress fell loose almost before she felt the first pull of the knot. His lips brushed along the trail his fingers had left. With unerring skill he found that exact, small spot on her nape—the spot that had always been her favorite.

She could not suppress a gasp as he nipped, then laved the small injury, leaving his mark. She shivered as his hands slipped between her dress and chemise, moving forward to cup her breasts. His fingers swept beneath her nipples without touching them.

Oh, she wanted his touch. She was glad he could not see her face. She feared her expression was close to begging.

She pressed back against him. The one aspect of her position she had not considered was her inability to touch him. She edged farther back and tried to think as his fingers began to softly knead, working their way toward the tender peaks.

Control. That was the key. She schooled her features carefully, wiping her face clean of all entreaty. She bit her lips, causing the blood to rush to them, and then let her head fall back, pillowing it in his lap.

She knew her eyes were dark with desire, but his were darker. He was not unmoved by her actions. She rubbed her head back and forth against him, feeling his shaft swell. No, not unmoved at all.

His fingers gripped tighter, his needs more urgent. She rubbed again. Licking her lips with great intent, she turned her head to the side, letting the heat of her breath sink through his trousers. His hands still played, but his eyes were locked on her lips.

She pursed her lips and blew, feeling his body spasm. As he fought for his own control, she turned within his arms, bringing her face full against him.

It was amazing how one move could shift the balance.

She blew again as his now empty hands tangled in her hair. They pulled her back and then pushed her forward. She slipped her hands up his legs, running a finger inside the top of his boots before moving up over his knees and along his thighs. His fingers now gripped her head tight, holding her still.

But her hands still moved. Up and up, her fingers sweeping wide as they approached the crucial territory. She stopped, her fingers framing him. She pushed up, freeing her head from his grasp, bringing her face even with his. He groaned at the sudden pressure of her weight and then groaned again as her lips crushed against his.

This kiss bore no relation to their others. This was all hot fire, need and demand. Tongues dueled and tangled. Lips pushed and pressed. Teeth, oh yes, there were teeth.

She had never been kissed like this before—kissed as if the room could burn around them and still the kiss would go on. Her fingers worked quickly at the fastening of his trousers as his arms swept around her, supporting her.

Then she held him, hot, firm velvet. His hands moved lower, clasping her buttocks and lifting her until she was seated across his knees. God, the man was strong.

And still the kiss went on, mindless, endless—earth shattering. She'd always thought the expression melodramatic, but this was—there weren't even words.

She felt her skirts lifted, his fingers now trac-

ing the tender skin of her inner thighs, his thumbs
caressing the soft, moist flesh where leg and torso
met, sweeping ever closer to her cleft.

She wrapped her fingers tight around his erection, moving along the hot skin in rhythm to his
fingers. They moved closer, positioned themselves.
His fingers pressed her soft flesh, opening her to
him. She shifted, his tip rubbing hard against her,
sending a thousand spears of passion up her torso.

She pushed her body down, unable to withstand
it any longer. He was in her, filling her, completing
her.

She pressed her legs tight against him, giving
herself leverage as they began to move. Her head
fell back, breaking the kiss. His lips moved to her
neck, sucking, marking.

She rode hard, seeking, searching for that final
ending. The fires grew. The tension became unbearable. She ground down hard, needing more,
helpless as she sought release.

He jerked against her hard, bringing their upper
torsos into full contact. This was the moment.

She heard his cry and let herself go, the whole
world a kaleidoscope of bright color.

It was over. The thought grew in his mind as
she burrowed against him. His body felt limp and
spent, as if it might never move again.

He shook his head, trying to draw the blood
back to his brain. It was over. He had done what
he shouldn't have and would not regret it.

Only he did regret it. Sitting in the south parlor,

not even undressed, with a wilted woman in his lap, was not where he wanted to be. He did not want to face the things that must be said and done.

She was not a thief, but that did not mean she could ever be for him. The rumors of her past were still real.

He closed his eyes to resist looking at her. Even now she was nothing but temptation, the representation of all he denied himself in life. She stirred, purring against his shirt.

He was still in his jacket, his waistcoat, even his boots. Such behavior was not he, was not proper or respectful.

She moved again, her face rubbing against him. She tensed. Awareness was returning to her as well. He felt her lift, separating them. She slid her feet to the floor and stood. Her skirts brushed against him as she turned.

"Please do up my laces." It was softly said.

He opened his eyes and stared at her smooth back. She was more clearly muscled than the women of his acquaintance. There were red indents just above her corset. It must have shifted during their—

He didn't know what to call it. They had not made love. Of that he was sure. But . . . sex. *Sex* seemed such a paltry word for what had happened between them. *Fuck*. The word should have fit but it did not.

Passion. That was what had been between them.

He swallowed hard as he thought the word. *Passion.*

To distract himself, he picked up her laces and began to tighten them. He used great care, prolonging the moment when she would turn and he must face her.

He'd once spent a drunken night with a prostitute. He'd felt less dread awakening on her dirty sheets than he did now. At least on that occasion he'd had drink to blame. He had never drunk so much again.

He could not blame the bottle now.

The forces that overcame him had been a power in their own right. *Passion.* There was that word again. He had been overcome with passion more surely than a growing lad noticing the dairymaid for the first time.

He pulled the knot tight. He saw her square her shoulders, felt the slight jiggle that told him she fixed her bodice. Still she did not turn.

He counted ten full breaths before she moved.

Even then she did not turn. She walked to the door, turning the key and easing it open a few inches.

He feared she would leave. He did not want to face her, but how much worse would it be if she left without a word?

He counted another fifteen breaths as she stood at the door with her back to him.

Then, finally, she turned. Her face was flat, curiously devoid of emotion. "So, you leave this afternoon? That is what Robert said this morning before you arrived. He said you were desirous of returning to your quest to find Isabella."

"Yes, I am leaving. I have one task I need to complete and then I will be gone." He had worried for nothing. There was nothing else to say—and only one more thing to do—one task, and he could leave with his conscience at ease.

"You did what?" Clara could not believe what she had heard. From the moment Mr. Green had entered, his head hung low and looking distinctly greenish about the gills, there had been a strange quality of unreality about the whole morning.

Her head was pounding after a sleepless night. Dreams of Masters had filled her head. It was hard to believe that he had left only yesterday—it felt like a lifetime since their encounter.

She lifted her head from her hands and stared straight at Mr. Green, awaiting his answer. Was it possible it could all be so simple?

"I dosed your ale with laudanum." Mr. Green looked only at his boots. There was a large smear of mud—at least she hoped it was mud—across one toe, but it did not seem worthy of such intense scrutiny. His hands shook and he wrapped his fingers tight together.

"I still cannot believe I am hearing you correctly. Why ever would you do such a thing?" She stood and paced across the room, trying to make sense of his words. She should have been more upset, but her mind could not yet comprehend all the pieces.

"I hadn't planned on it. I'd picked up the bottle earlier in the day. My mother has been having megrims and the apothecary had offered to make her up a potion." Mr. Green continued to stare at his boots, but began to wring his trembling hands. His nervousness was palpable.

"I still don't see—"

"Please let me finish. I promised I'd tell you immediately and I must keep my promise or—" He stopped there for a moment, letting the words hang. It was impossible to miss the fear in his face as he spoke the soft words. He raised his eyes to her for the first time and continued, "It was when you turned me down and then I saw you at The Dog and Ferret. I hadn't planned it before. It just seemed like fate was finally smiling on me. I'd heard that if you got a woman relaxed she might be more amenable. I didn't know how much to give you, though. I only wanted to make you a little friendlier. My brother said you should give a woman whiskey, but I knew you'd taste the whiskey. This didn't seem that different."

She was going to be ill. She wasn't sure which was worse, wondering what had happened that night or this. No, that was not true. She would much rather know.

She sank into her chair. It was too much to take. "Why do you tell me this now?"

Mr. Green looked even more nervous. He pulled his hands apart and clenched them into fists so tight she thought the knuckles would pop through the skin. "Mr. Masters told me I had to."

"Mr. Masters?" How had he known?

"Yes, he came to see me yesterday, just before leaving for London. He told me that if I didn't tell you, he'd write and tell Lord Westington. He'd lock me up if he found out." Mr. Green's glance dropped again as he spoke, and he turned his face away. For the first time she noticed the faint outline of a bruise along his jaw—a bruise that bore a remarkable resemblance to a man's hand.

"Mr. Masters simply told you to?"

Mr. Green answered, "Yes," but there was clear hesitation in the word. The meeting between the men had not been as simple as Mr. Green depicted.

Clara turned and walked to the window, staring out across the fields. Norfolk had always been so safe. It still did not seem possible that this had happened.

She chose her words with care. "I think it might be best if Lord Westington were told. I would not want to think that this might happen to another woman—one who did not have my luck."

"Oh please, my lady." He was crying, large droplets streaming down his face to land on his muddy boots. "I would never do it again. I truly hadn't understood what I was doing. Now that I understand I would never do it again."

Clara squeezed her eyes shut. A dull throbbing was beginning in her temples. She should tell Robert, regardless of how pitiful Mr. Green might now be. She wasn't exactly sure what the crime was, but surely there was one.

She turned back to Mr. Green and froze him with an icy glare. "I will not tell Lord Westington at present, but I do not promise for the future. I may change my mind at any time. Do you understand?"

"Yes," Mr. Green gulped out. He stared back down at his boots.

"You may go now." She put on her haughtiest countess voice. "And be sure that I do not catch sight of you for some time."

"That won't be a problem, my lady. Mr. Masters advised that if you did not choose to prosecute I should consider a term abroad. He mentioned that I might care to join a regiment in—in India. He promised to help with the arrangements." More tears joined the first, but Clara could not find herself moved.

She would never forget the violation of not remembering her own actions.

She nodded, and then turned away from Mr. Green. He began to leave without another word.

"One last question." Her words stopped him in his tracks. "How did Masters know what you had done?"

Mr. Green shrugged without looking up. "I don't know. I imagine he must have seen me. He didn't know what I'd used, but he seemed confident in what I had done. May I go now?"

"Please." Clara leaned back in her chair, unsure what she was feeling.

Masters had not seen Mr. Green pour the draught in her ale. Of that she was sure. He would have said something if he had.

Somehow he had puzzled it out and then confronted Mr. Green with his suspicions.

Masters should have talked to her first. He was once again making decisions for others.

Still, she sat up and stared toward the window. It was nice to have someone who cared—and beyond that, someone who tried to protect her. Michael had always been the one who needed caring for. He had wanted to play and have good times. When it came to actual responsibility, he had always turned to her. She had run his estates then, as she did now for Robert.

With Masters it was different.

Sinking into her chair before the fire, she considered. He could only have *visited* with Mr. Green after their own encounter in the south parlor. He might not have said anything much when she left the room, but perhaps he was letting his actions speak for him.

He had taken action to protect her. First, physical action—if that cheek was anything to judge by—and then he'd formed a plan to move Mr. Green far from her world.

Now she owed him. She owed Masters far more than she cared to. She'd never liked carrying a debt, and now he'd left her no choice.

She'd have to find a fitting way to repay him.

It was not a party she would normally have attended. The Marquess of Wimberley was known to throw a most elegant ball, but elegance had not been her priority in past years.

Now she felt changed. In truth the change had begun long before Robert had asked—she refused to consider it a command—her to come home to Norfolk. The thought of wild late nights held little appeal. She'd planned to begin a new life, and this was the moment it started.

She waited for the couple ahead of her to enter the ballroom and wondered why she had chosen this as the place to start. Marguerite, the marquess's wife, had become a friend over the past years, but not so close that Clara's presence would have been missed this evening. It was unlikely they even knew she was in Town.

The couple moved ahead finally, leaving her in the doorway to the grand room. People were crowded tight, and the light of candles shone upon their brightly colored evening dress. It was exactly what she had been looking for—festive gaiety.

"Clara, I didn't know you were back. Has the evil stepson finally released his hold?" There was no mistaking that soft, husky voice.

"Violet, I didn't know you'd be here," she replied. "And you do know that Robert could never be considered even wicked, much less evil."

"I am only teasing." Violet stepped forward. Her gown was incredibly daring, the low scoop neckline showing all her assets to their best advantage. And the color—Clara had never thought a redhead could wear that bright a fuchsia, but on Violet it looked perfect.

"I know you are. I am still surprised to see you. I didn't think you cared for this type of affair."

"No more than you. But Peter is Wimberley's brother, so this is a command performance. Besides, Peter loves showing me that respectable society won't turn us aside—and I adore letting him reassure me."

Clara chuckled. "I won't even ask how he accomplishes that. I can see from your expression that some things should not be mentioned in polite company."

"And where would I find polite company?"

Clara laughed again, and hooked her arm through Violet's. "Come and bring me to that charming fiancé of yours. A party is always brighter for his presence."

"Don't let him hear you say that." Violet was laughing now too. "He's full enough of himself already."

"Have you set a wedding date? Lord Darnell has finally approved a late summer date for Robert and Jennie."

Violet sobered at the question just as they approached Peter. Clara smiled wistfully at the look that passed between them. Despite the difference in age—Violet was a shocking seven years older—and stature, they so clearly belonged together.

Peter lifted Violet's fingers in a gesture that was both proper and surprisingly intimate. Clara did not miss the way his thumb passed across Violet's gloved palm or the way she closed her fingers around it.

"Are you asking her about a date?" Peter asked. "I can tell just from her expression." He leaned toward Clara and whispered, "She really wants to be married, but I think she wishes it were already passed. I may have to start playing hard to get if she doesn't relent soon."

Violet swatted him with her fan. "Don't even think of trying that. You've tried it already, and I don't believe I'd call you the winner."

"Ah, but you didn't win either." Peter grabbed the fan and held it tight.

Clara had been treated to long letters from Violet describing the situation between the two of them as Peter sought to persuade Violet to matrimony. He'd finally won her agreement, but that had been more than a year previously, and they still had not made it to the altar. She wondered what caused the delay, but there were some questions even close friends could not ask.

Turning away from the couple, she looked over the crush. "Your brother certainly knows how to host an affair. I think I count at least two dukes and six earls in the crowd. Is there anybody who declined the invitation?"

Violet turned from Peter and perused the crowd herself. "I know of only three, and one of them had died the day before the invitations were issued. You'd have to ask Marguerite to be sure, though."

"I am surprised she was up to entertaining so soon after—"

"The birth of her daughter. It has been several months now." Violet finished the sentence. "Don't be so shy, Clara. I am well past discomfort at my own childless state. I've discovered I am quite happy as an aunt. I do love babies, but I equally love leaving them behind at the end of the evening. Peter and I have stayed with Marguerite and Wimberley for both of her confinements, and I can assure you there are many aspects of the process I do not miss at all."

Clara glanced at Peter and was surprised at his level of comfort with such an intimate discussion. For a moment, another face flashed before her eyes, a man who would not have been comfortable with such discussion. She pushed it back, roughly. She smiled at her friend. "I am so happy for you, for both of you. I know I've said it before, but every time I am with you two, you remind me of how much is possible."

It was Peter's turn to answer. "You flatter us, and I can assure you there are many moments when we do not act with such accord."

"But those are the moments that prove how strong you are together," Clara responded. "I can remember from my own marriage. When Michael and I fought, I always knew that no matter how strong the disagreement, it did not affect the soundness of our relationship. I see that with you."

"You are—" Violet began before a voice from behind interrupted.

"Violet, I am so pleased to see you. St. Johns, Lady Westington, it is a most delightful affair."

Clara felt a thousand butterflies rise and take flight as Masters's deep voice wrapped tight about her. He stepped from behind Peter's broad frame.

"Mr. Masters." Clara nodded to him, afraid that her voice would break.

"Brother, I am surprised to see you," Violet answered, her back so stiff she might have been an iron pole. Her welcome was not warm, but neither did she turn away.

"I found myself desiring company now that I have returned," Masters replied. He addressed Violet, but his gaze had returned to Clara.

Clara watched as Violet started to say more, to ask about Masters's trip, and then Violet caught his stare. She followed the line of his gaze to Clara.

Violet's glance sharpened. She could tell something was not quite as it appeared. She was clearly trying to figure out the relationship. It must mean that the strain between them was clear.

Clara dropped her gaze to her hands. He looked as awkward as he had that last morning. She had never felt her actions tawdry before that morning. Now those same feelings washed over her.

With an effort, she relaxed each clenched finger, one by one. She strove to focus on nothing, save that her hands should look at ease and relaxed. This accomplished, she proceeded to adjust her breathing—smooth, even. Her shoulders were next. Her face was hardest. She relaxed her brow, letting the lines between her eyes smooth out.

The smile was even more difficult. It must not look forced. She lifted her head. "I was not aware you were in Town."

He looked away when he spoke. "My task was

more difficult than I imagined. There have been delays. I will perhaps be forced to travel again."

Clara turned to Violet. "I met your brother in Norfolk while he was looking for Isabella. He returned to London, believing her to be here."

Violet allowed her attention to be distracted. "But she was not. I did get that report." She nodded at Masters. Her tone was bitter.

Masters drew his shoulders back. This time his eyes were on Violet, although he addressed his words to Clara. Clara could almost feel his unspoken desire for his sister's understanding. "As I said, the task was more difficult than expected. I'd heard rumor of a red-haired governess. Your inquiries, Lady Westington, appeared to be bearing fruit, and I followed the family after they had moved to London for the Season."

"But nothing came of it." Violet was clearly unmoved by her brother's silent entreaty.

"You are correct," Masters answered. "It took my agent several weeks to confirm that the girl was not Isabella."

Violet would not be stilled. "Did you even bother to check yourself?"

Masters was clearly uncomfortable. He'd become even stiffer than usual. "Yes."

There was a pause, and Clara was not sure he would proceed, even though it was clear that Violet was ready to shake him if he did not. Peter stood back. Plainly he understood that Violet could fend for herself and would not welcome his help.

Finally, Masters began again. "I waited for several hours, for two days running. The governess did not keep to a proper schedule in taking the children out. On the second day, I spied the girl. It was not Isabella."

Violet's face grew grim at his words. "And yet you are still here, enjoying company, not off searching again."

Masters turned to address her fully, but spoke softly. "I am well aware of my responsibilities and I will be off again as soon as I have a direction to follow."

"See that you are. If you had not—"

"I am well aware of what I did." Masters closed his lips tight.

Violet looked as if she wanted to say more.

Peter reached out and placed a hand on her shoulder. "Come, let me get you some refreshment. I believe a glass of punch would not be amiss."

Placing her hand over his, Violet turned to him. "Am I to understand you have a flask in your pocket?"

Peter just smiled.

Violet turned back to her brother as Peter, after a brief nod to each of them, began to lead her away. "She cannot simply have disappeared. Find her."

Masters stared across the room as he answered, not meeting anyone's gaze. "I will return to Coventry where I last heard of her." He turned and stared at Violet. "It would be most helpful if you could

persuade Lady Smythe-Burke to talk. I cannot believe that she has no idea which of all her recom-
mendations Isabella intended to take."

Violet stepped away, following Peter. "It is not
hard to get Lady Smythe-Burke to talk—the problem is getting her to answer."

Then they were gone, melted into the crowd.

Clara was alone with Masters—as alone as one
could be in a crowded ballroom.

"You did not need to tell her that we had met."
Masters did not hesitate to speak.

"It was unavoidable. Did not you catch her
glance? She knew at once that there was something
we were not telling her."

"But she would never have asked."

Clara tittered. She was so nervous she actually
tittered. If she had not wanted to run from the
room before, she did now. "Perhaps she would not
have asked you. The strain between you is evident.
But I assure you, it would have been mere moments
before she tore a hem and needed my assistance in
the withdrawing room. She would have been questioning me in great detail before five minutes had
passed."

"Women." The word was filled with more description than a hundred sentences.

Clara did not answer. There really was nothing
to say—about anything.

"I am sorry that I left without saying farewell."
The words came from his lips, but it did not seem
that he had spoken them.

She still did not answer, but she did raise a brow.

He looked out over the crowd again. "I would admit I was not sorry at the time, but later I came to believe that it was poorly done."

She snorted. First she tittered and now she snorted. He truly had the most ill effect on her. The man actually considered that an apology. That did demand reply. She might not believe that he actually owed her an apology after his actions with Mr. Green, but that was not the point. "You are sorry that your manners were poor. Is that what you are saying?"

"Yes." It was clear he still did not understand there was anything wrong with his statement. He did not look at her.

"I am showing poor manners myself. I should not have let you apologize. I can never thank you enough for what you did with Mr. Green. He came and told me the full story."

He still did not turn to her. "I only did what any man would have done. It was nothing."

"It certainly was not nothing. I was most distressed at first to learn the truth. And I would confess some slight anger that you had not consulted me before confronting him, but over time I have come to fully appreciate your actions. I know there was far more involved than either Mr. Green or you would admit to."

"Again I say, it was nothing." His voice revealed nothing.

It was time that he looked at her. He might not share the details of his actions, but she would not be avoided. Shrugging her shoulders, she let her dress slip slightly lower. The deep burgundy silk was only a shade away from crimson. She was surprised he had not remarked on the fact—naming her a scarlet woman.

He caught her movement. She felt his eyes shift toward her and then stick as if glued to the pale flesh her gesture had revealed. She placed a single gloved finger high on his shoulder, granting him a better look. He did not fail her.

"It was something," she said. "I can only offer my gratitude—and no, I do not mean in that fashion. I mean it with deep sincerity."

His eyes remained on her bosom as he answered. "If you say so."

She was not sure he had even heard her, so fixed was his gaze.

It was tempting to sigh, *Men,* adopting his earlier intonation, but it would have been a cheap retort. She was better than that. Well, not much better. She shifted from foot to foot causing her breasts to jiggle slightly within her dress. "Why are you here, Mr. Masters?"

His eyes jumped up to her face. For a moment he looked confused, her question escaping him. She could see his eyes focus as he gathered his wits. "You know why I am here. I have just finished discussing the matter with my sister."

"I meant why are you at this ball? You must have

known you would meet Violet. I can see there are mixed feelings between you and your sister."

He kept staring at her. "I must admit that I considered it a strong possibility we would see each other, but contrary to your beliefs, I actually looked forward to the meeting. There are matters we need to discuss—I should have realized a ball was not the place for that discussion. There were also other priorities."

Her glance had moved to his lips as he spoke and caught there. It was hard to speak. "Are you going to tell me of these priorities or has this become a game?"

"No, no game." His lips remained parted after he finished.

Clara was lost for a moment, remembering how they'd felt, how they'd tasted. Had he had anything to drink this evening? Would he taste of watery lemonade or brandy? She pressed her knees tight together.

"I am here to begin searching for a wife." He turned back to the crowd, his face now directed away from her.

Even without his movement, she would have regained her focus. A wife? "I suppose you want someone young and sweet?"

"Yes, and well-bred." He had clearly missed the sarcasm in her tone.

"What about looks? Do you seek a particular type?" Surely, he could not miss the sharpness with which she spoke.

He turned back to her, his face impassive. He appraised her as he had back on that morning in Aylsham. "Yes, I would prefer a blonde, tall and slender—regal in stature. That is how I have always pictured my children."

Somebody far different than her own dark hair and full curves. She was not short, but she would never be considered tall and slender. "You speak rather coldly about a woman you would seek to marry—rather like you're seeking a new horse at Tattersall's."

"And what is the difficulty in that? It seems to me that more thought and less emotion should be put into these decisions. Do you disagree?"

Clara considered her own marriage. If Michael had been seeking a mare, she would certainly never have been chosen. Michael had chosen her because he wanted her, plain and simple. "I rather believe I do. My own marriage was certainly not based on my abilities as a broodmare."

"I must apologize," he replied softly. "I had meant no statement on your own marriage." He had not meant to hurt her. Masters looked down at her pale features and cursed inwardly. This whole situation was so damn awkward.

It had never occurred to him that she would be here. He had not even known she was back in Town. Indeed, he'd driven by her house that very day and the knocker had been down—but perhaps she merely hadn't wanted company.

"Then what did you mean?" She was not going to let him be.

"I merely meant exactly what I said. I think marriage is a serious matter and should be considered with the intellect and not the heart." There, that should be clear enough.

She was beautiful tonight. The deep red of her gown highlighting her creamy skin and rosy cheeks. He would never have thought red would complement the gold of her eyes, but they seemed to glow, filling her entire face. Or perhaps it was the candlelight. Had he ever seen her lit solely by candles? He must have, but he could not think when.

"I imagine that is why you found Violet's marriages so desirable," Clara interrupted his thoughts. "If the heart does not matter, then what does it matter if your spouse is an octogenarian? Although it does seem to make offspring unlikely—and I believe you indicated they were one of the main priorities in marriage."

"For the man, yes. He must carry on the family name. It is his responsibility. I do not imagine that it matters so much to women."

Damn, he'd done it again. If anything, she'd turned even paler at his words. Could she not understand that he merely spoke sense? There was no harm intended.

She glared up at him. It was a far different glow that shone in her eyes now. "If that is how you feel, I fear we have nothing more to say."

She turned and walked away. Her stiff spine reminded him of that other morning when she had also walked away. It had been what was best then. It was what was best now. He must remind himself of the fact.

He wondered if Peter St. Johns had anything left in his flask. A stiff drink would be most welcome.

Chapter 8

❧

Clara held her spine straight as she walked away. The books her governess had once tried to balance on her head would have stayed there now without a wobble. It was important that she not let him see how much his words had upset her.

A waiter passed, and she grabbed a glass of champagne, drinking half in a single gulp. She refused not to enjoy herself simply because *he* was here.

She would dance and laugh and have fun—but all in a most respectable way. It was only Masters who offered the temptation to stray from the proper path. She could not even manage to thank him without resorting to flirtation.

When one of her past admirers swept up and asked her to dance, she answered with a gracious nod. "I would love to dance. I think it's just what I need."

Only it wasn't. She twirled. She stepped. She smiled. She flirted. She curtsied. She twirled again. It should have been a delight.

It wasn't.

She wasn't even sure whom she had danced with. Each gentleman blended with the next without leaving a firm impression. It was hard to even pretend an interest.

At least she had resisted looking for the blasted man. She did not allow herself to peer through the crowd seeking him. It was enough to know he was here.

Although, maybe he had left. It was still early, but he had not seemed to be overcome with the joy of the evening. He was good at leaving.

She must not think such things. She was here to have fun, and fun she would have.

As if in answer to a silent prayer, Clara spotted Anna Struthers standing alone at the side of the room, the woman's soft brown curls and light green dress fading into the elegant fabric that swathed the wall. Anna had been one of Clara's dearest friends before her marriage, and she was determined that would not change now.

"Anna, I am so glad to see you," Clara said as she walked toward her friend. "I feared that handsome husband of yours would sweep you off to the continent for a wedding trip."

"No, Struthers decided it was best to stay in Town for the season." Anna spoke without her normal joie de vivre.

Clara was unsure of the circumstances surrounding her friend's marriage. Anna had simply mentioned it in a letter as if it had no more importance than buying a new hat. The two women had shared many a proper and many a not-so-proper adventure over the last few years, and Clara could not help wondering at the little information that Anna shared.

"Are you well?" It was a simple question, but Clara hoped for a more forthcoming answer.

"Yes, I am well. And you?" Anna's answer left much to be desired.

Clara considered. She did not like to pry, but neither did she like to see Anna looking so alone. "And Struthers, he is well also?"

"Yes." It was like pulling teeth from a hen.

"I was surprised to hear of your nuptials." She would be more direct. There was clearly no other course open. "I did not even know that you were acquainted with the man. I played cards with him on several occasions and he seemed an—an unusual choice as a spouse."

Anna stilled. Clara could see her choose her words with care. "You mean you charmed him into throwing in his last penny?"

"No, not at all," Clara answered. "I never played a game requiring deep pockets with him. His play was far too serious for me."

"Struthers does take his games seriously. All of them."

Clara could tell that there was much more to be said. Those few words revealed so much and so little. "You still have not mentioned how you met."

For a moment she did not think Anna would answer.

Anna shifted her feet and turned to look at a large potted palm. "We became reacquainted at Brisbane's house party. We had known each other years ago."

Brisbane. That would explain Anna's reticence. Both women had been lovers of the young duke— although not at the same time. There were some things Clara had no desire to experiment with. She had always thought their friendship had been made stronger by the joint experience, but perhaps it was difficult to discuss being introduced to one's husband by a past lover.

"I haven't spoken to Brisbane for months," Clara replied. "His aunt still writes frequently."

"Does she fit as many words into her correspondence as her conversation?" Anna was clearly glad for the chance to steer the conversation away from her marriage.

Clara lifted a brow and gave her a clear look. "You know Lady Smythe-Burke. What do you think?"

Another couple joined them, and the conversation drifted to general talk of the season and the coming year. Clara smiled and nodded and made the appropriate comments before drifting away. Social discourse had never been difficult, but neither had it been a favorite pastime.

She smiled and nodded more as she made her way across the floor. A waltz had begun, and she had to step quickly through a doorway to avoid being asked to partake. She was not in the mood to be held, no matter how gently and politely.

Standing halfway into the next room, she looked back at the dance floor. Violet and Peter were dancing the waltz in perfect time. Their eyes locked on each other. She could almost see the small world that existed for only the two of them.

It was bittersweet to watch them when she stood so alone.

She stepped back farther into the room. It was a small sitting room, and she was surprised to find it deserted. Glancing carefully around, she checked every corner. She did not wish to interrupt anyone who had come here seeking quiet—or seeking anything else.

There was no one here.

She sat in the half light—she had left the door open a crack—and wished she were home.

She gave herself five minutes. She counted the seconds.

Then she stood, fluffed her skirt, and turned back to the door. She would dance three more dances and make one more round of the floor, wish Wimberley and Marguerite well, and then she would leave.

She wondered if her staff had put the knocker back on the door. If they hadn't, she might leave it off for days and pretend she'd never been here.

The energy that had filled her for the last weeks was seeping away and did not feel as if it would ever return.

She placed her palm against the door, took one deep breath, and . . .

His voice carried through the wood panel. "Social frivolity is nice, but one should always have two ready conversations before attending any affair."

Masters must be standing on the other side of the door.

A soft feminine murmur answered.

He spoke again. "No, I do not believe that knowing what the weather was like yesterday counts as a subject of conversation."

Another quiet reply.

"But you must have read a book in the last months, seen an exhibition . . ." His voice trailed off.

Clara was not sure whether he had stepped away or was debating what other activity his partner might have engaged in. Unable to help herself, Clara edged to the side of the door and peered out.

All she could see of Masters was a gesturing hand. He had not stepped away.

The girl, however . . . Clara did not believe that she herself had ever been that young. The girl barely reached his shoulder and was buried in a dress of endless pink ruffles. She was blond, very blond, and definitely slender. Perhaps Masters was hoping she would still grow.

"Gothic novels"—he was speaking again—"are fine as a topic if one has something to compare them to. I myself have even skimmed through those . . . books . . . published by the Minerva Press. I am ready to discuss their value as entertainment and their lackings as literature."

Was this how Masters proposed to conduct a courtship? The poor man had no idea. The hapless girl's eyes were glazed, and it was clear that she had no thought but of escape.

Clara considered for only the briefest of seconds. She pulled the door open and stepped through.

Perhaps she would be able to even the debt she owed to Masters, after all.

Where did that blasted woman keep coming from? Masters watched as she stepped through the door, the red of her gown vivid even against the dark wood. It was bad enough that she was here at all, but now she was interrupting his interview with Miss Pink—and just when it had been going so well. The sweet girl had been so enrapt in his conversation that she'd had little of her own to add. He turned to her with an approving smile.

Why had she dressed in that gown? It was not the first time he'd had the thought that evening. Indeed, every time he addressed her, he found himself wondering. If they ever did proceed with a courtship, he would have to give her some advice on fashion. He did not normally have strong opinions on the subject, but there were some standards that must be maintained. He knew Miss Pink would be delighted to have someone to offer such valuable advice.

Clara cleared her throat, drawing his attention to the delicate lines of her neck. He could see her pulse beating rapidly.

He forced his eyes up to her face. "Lady West-ington, what a surprise to see you again."

"I don't see why it should be."

"I suppose I am not used to seeing you coming out of dark rooms—although perhaps I should be." He had not meant to say that last.

Her eyes narrowed as he spoke, and then she smiled. It was not a kind smile. "Mr. Masters, you must introduce me to your charming companion."

"Lady Westington, let me make you known to Miss Pink. Miss Pink, Lady Westington."

"Miss Pink." There was nothing but politeness in Clara's tone, but Masters could not miss the devils that danced behind her eyes. "Let me say how wonderful it is to make your acquaintance. And wherever did you get that dress? I have never seen quite its like."

"Lady Westington, I am charmed to make your acquaintance. My mother had the dress made. She said that ruffles are all the rage this year."

"I am sure that's true." Clara's words were soft and she spoke with kindness. "Is that your mother there? In the peach satin?"

"However did you know?" Miss Pink asked.

"She is glancing at you with such care and atten-tion," Clara answered.

Masters was sure it had more to do with the peach satin dress, which seemed to be composed of nothing but ruffles, than any maternal glance, but he refrained from comment.

"Mother does always keep an eye on me." Miss

Pink nodded to her mother. "She wants to be sure my behavior is above reproach."

"Well, perhaps then you'd better not mention me by name," Clara teased, with just that bit of a note that said she was serious.

"Does that mean you're scandalous?" Miss Pink asked, her eyes growing wide.

"I am afraid I am."

Miss Pink glanced at her mother nervously and then turned back to Clara with great interest. "Is it fun?"

That caused Clara to throw back her head and loose that full, deep laugh, that laugh that sent vibrations straight through him.

"Scandal should not be admired," he said firmly, trying to pretend that he was not affected.

"Of course not." Miss Pink dropped her eyes and eased away from Clara and toward him. It was good to see she was so malleable. And her movement indicated she already saw him as a protector. He felt his chest puff.

"I think your mother is gesturing for you to return to her," Clara said, waving toward the peach dress.

"I do believe you're right." Miss Pink was gone before he could even say his farewells. She must truly have been frightened by the scandal that Clara might present.

He tapped his toe once on the hardwood floor. "I did not see any gesture."

"I could argue and pretend that you had missed the motion, but what would be the point?" Clara said. "The poor girl was uncomfortable and you only made her more so."

What nonsense. Miss Pink had been fascinated by his discussion. "I don't believe I agree—"

"You don't need to agree, fact is fact. I was afraid she would turn into a great pink puddle on the floor if you commented even once more on how she should behave."

"I don't—"

"Of course, you—"

"If you interrupt me one more time I will sling you over my shoulder and toss you into the garden."

Clara hoped her mouth did not gape open at his words. He was the most proper of proper windbags with everybody else, but the moment she spoke up, he showed a far different side of himself.

It was impossible to know whether to fight back or to laugh.

She laughed. It started deep in her belly and rose, filling her lungs until it just bubbled out. God, it was good to simply enjoy. It would be so easy to be frustrated with the man, but it was so much better to just enjoy the absurdity of the situation.

"You are attracting attention," Masters said, glaring at her.

Or was he staring at her lips?

She hesitated, leaned slightly toward him, then replied, "Now that sounds more like you."

He stiffened, but his eyes stayed on her mouth. That was very interesting. She licked her lips.

"Was that child on your list of possible brides? I would have thought you would prefer someone—someone taller."

"Miss Pink is of excellent social standing. Her mother was the fifth daughter of the Duke of—"

"Daughter of a duke," she chuckled. "That explains the dress. Only the daughter of a duke could be so confident of her own taste to the exclusion of all others."

He did not answer for a moment but stood surveying the room. He turned back to her finally. "I believe we were actually getting along quite well. She seemed most interested in my company."

"Most interested in escape, you mean. Do you really imagine that the way to court a young girl is to provide direction on every aspect of her life?"

"I was not aware I was doing so." A blue fire lit his eyes as he continued to stare at her. "However, yes, I do think she would be grateful for it. Miss Pink seemed quite taken with my speech. She was so absorbed that she felt little need to add to it. The young must be taught how to behave."

"When they are children perhaps, but despite my earlier comment, she is no longer a child, but rather a young lady." She met his glare with one of her own. "Do you not think that you should be interested in finding out who she is, if you intend to make a lifelong commitment to her?"

"I am not sure I see why I should. I would of course want to know that she was well-spoken and knew the proper duties of a wife, but beyond that I do not see why I should take an interest."

Clara stared at him, trying to determine his seriousness. She had never observed in him a great sense of humor, but the speech was so far from her own beliefs as to be impossible to accept—and there was a gleam in his eye. Marriage was a matter of great importance. Masters appeared to place less significance on it than he would on choosing between sausages and kippers for breakfast.

"Tell me then," she said. "Who here do you fancy as a bride?"

He looked about the room, his glance moving from group to group. She watched his eyes sweep up and down several young women. His announced preference might be for slender blondes, but his eyes seemed more drawn to those with curves. There was more than one ample bosom that he paused over.

Her own curves were more than the equal of any of those he lingered over. She pushed the thought away as soon as she had it. Her purpose was not to attract the blasted man.

It was not.

Still—she drew her shoulders back so that her dress pulled tight. There was no problem with letting the man see what he would be missing in the future. Almost on cue, his gaze darted back to her and settled. She smiled widely.

"I believe that either of the Miss Thwaites or Miss Northouse would do," he said as his eyes returned to her face.

"I've always heard that men had a partiality for twins, but I must admit that I would find the matter confusing. As for Miss Northouse, I believe that her nuptials to Mr. Perry will be announced within the week."

"How do women know these things? You must have barely arrived in Town, and already you know the latest gossip." He determinedly turned from her and gazed back at the dance floor.

"It is certainly not the latest gossip, and I keep a regular correspondence with Lady Smythe-Burke. She seems informed on most of society's affairs."

"Affairs." He let the word linger on his lips but did not turn back to her. "Are you interested in society's affairs?"

How to reply to that? Again, she could not read him properly. She normally considered herself a fair judge of people, but suddenly he seemed a cipher to her. "And should I not be interested in society's affairs?"

Answering a question with a question, that was always effective. And she let her own voice deepen at the end, saying much more beyond the words. Would he be the one to take the wordplay a step further?

"Society is always important." His voice was again somber. "Miss Thompson appears well raised." He gestured at an exceptionally tall woman standing near the windows. She had flaxen hair, but was otherwise nondescript.

"I have never heard anything unbecoming about her."

"And you would have?"

"Indeed, I do believe that she is said to be both well mannered and a good conversationalist. Although perhaps you do not require the last."

He turned to her, and again there was that fiery blue glow in his dark eyes. "I would prefer a wife who could ease conversation at dinner."

"I would have thought you were happy to do all the talking."

"It is nice to have someone to agree with one." That time she caught the quirk of his lips.

"Miss Thompson is perhaps not for you then. I do believe that being a good conversationalist requires one to do more than agree."

"Not in my world."

She started to speak, but then closed her lips, refusing the bait.

"You've turned quiet now," he said after a moment. "It was one of the things I liked about you at the start, your ability to be silent. I've found most women talk incessantly."

Her gaze dropped. "I didn't realize you liked anything about me."

He stepped toward her until the distance between them was only barely proper. "There are many things I like about you—even when I do not want to."

She could feel his breath on her forehead, scent the wine he must have had with dinner. The temptation to lean into him was great, to feel just for a second the warmth of his body pressed against hers. Instead, she stepped back. "Have you been introduced to Miss Thompson? I am well acquainted with her mother from my childhood."

He stepped back and grinned. "Do you mean you are of an age with her mother? I had not realized you were so ancient."

"What would you do if I said yes?" She could not resist smiling back at him. "Given that you are several years older than I, that would mean you could be her father."

"I do feel it sometimes."

"As do I."

He stepped away. "I was introduced a few nights past. I shared a country dance with Miss Thompson. I shall go pay my respects now."

"Yes, you should." She watched him walk away.

She should mingle herself. There were many here whose company she enjoyed.

She tried. She really did.

She danced two dances with men whose company she had enjoyed in the past. Neither one held her attention. Instead, her gaze kept straying to Masters and Miss Thompson. He escorted her to a corner table and fetched her a lemonade. Clara could not help noticing how his eyes stayed fastened on Miss Thompson's face. Perhaps that was an advantage to being rather less endowed, men spoke to you and not your breasts.

Damnation. She should be graciously flirting with her partner, not peeking at a man who didn't even like her—although he said there were things about her that he liked.

No, she would not think of that.

Mr. Brimble, her current partner, was a good-looking man. He was only slightly taller than she, but of athletic stature. He spoke well and was often amusing. He should have been an ideal companion.

Good God, she was sounding like Masters.

She turned to Mr. Brimble and forced herself to concentrate. He had kissed her once. It had been several years before, but it had not been a bad kiss. She was not sure why things had not progressed further.

Masters was holding out his hand to Miss Thompson. Was he going to ask her to dance? It was late to take to the floor. No, they were just strolling.

Mr. Brimble was talking again. She really must attend. "I am so sorry, but could you repeat that? The music is a trifle loud."

"Do you really think so? Perhaps you would care to stroll in the gardens." Mr. Brimble shot an eager look toward the glass doors that led outside.

She knew that look. Strolling was not what he had in mind. She debated for half a moment. Or at least she tried to. She was not so fixated on a man she should not even want that she would refuse someone else without thought. "I am so sorry, but I really must excuse myself for a moment."

"Of course." Even before he had finished the two words, Mr. Brimble's head was turning, looking for a new companion.

Men.

Blast all of them.

She nodded once more in the direction of his departing back and turned toward the door that led out and toward the ladies' withdrawing room. She would splash water on her face and gain a few moments' quiet. Then she would make a polite farewell to Wimberley and head off to her peaceful home.

The water in the pitcher was only tepid, but still it felt good to splash it on her hot cheeks. How could they feel so flushed yet look so pale? She was definitely not at her best tonight. The winter had not been a kind one. There were the beginnings of tiny lines at the corners of her eyes, and she feared perhaps there was even a furrow between her brows.

Age had never been something she feared, but she could not help leaning toward the mirror and pulling the skin tight. Perhaps it was but a trick of the candlelight. When she turned her head just so, the line disappeared completely.

She splashed again, wishing the water was cold enough to clear her mind.

"Did you speak with him?" A high, shrill, and very young voice echoed as its owner entered the room. She was petite and very blond. "My mother says that his estate is quite turned around and that soon he'll be considered a catch. She thinks I should cast a lure now for fear in another year he'll be beyond my reach."

"What nonsense. Clearly your mother has not

spent time talking to him." Another girl entered right behind. This one was darker and perhaps even younger. "I can't believe any girl would ever want to spend enough time with him to form an attachment. He rambles on and on, never giving one a chance to speak."

"You are being harsh now." The blond one spoke again as she stepped around Clara. "I only wanted to remark that my mother is becoming quite desperate. I am twenty and still unwed. If I am not careful, she'll be interviewing the footmen to see if any of them have saved their guineas."

The two girls talked through her as if she was not even there. It made her feel frumpy and ancient. The memories of engaging in similar behavior herself, before her marriage to Michael, did not lessen the feeling of age.

"A footman might at least be fun," the dark one answered. You can be sure he would not lecture you on the proper number of dresses for a lady to own. I had only met the man five minutes before and suddenly we were talking of my wardrobe. Can you imagine?"

"Did you really? How improper."

"And not even interesting." The brunette took a position beside Clara and started to smooth her own hair. "If I am going to have an improper discussion, it should include something worth giggling about and not leave me wondering if I should be saving my pin money."

"Like footmen. Have you called upon Lady Smythe-Burke recently? She had a new one, and you should see the way his calves fill out his stockings."

"You should not say such things, Jane."

Jane Burke, that was the blonde's name. Clara wondered if she should finger her own hair smooth. Soft tendrils had escaped to curl about her face.

"Eugenia, you know it is true. And besides, I am only looking. I am sure my mother will find someone suitable and I will flirt a little and that will be that. I just don't need it to be now. Twenty is not too old. I am only just beginning to be allowed to enjoy myself."

"I do know," Eugenia answered. "There is no reason at all you should even consider a man like Mr. Masters. I don't care if his estates grow gold. He would never give you a suitable allowance and would lecture you for every penny that you did spend."

"And he is old. I don't want to marry a man who must be well above thirty. I want somebody who still knows how to dance and have a good time."

Eugenia took Jane's hand and pulled her back toward the door. "Well, Mr. Masters does know how to dance."

"And I imagine his calves look just fine in stockings," Jane answered.

"Or without."

The two girls were giggling away.

Just as they got to the door, Eugenia stopped. "I still wouldn't want to have to talk with him.

I've had enough lectures on how to behave from my father. Nobody else is going to tell me what to do."

Then they were gone.

Clara shook her head, letting the curls spring free about her face.

She knew exactly what she had to do. Her earlier kernel of an idea had been good. She would repay Masters by helping him find a wife.

Chapter 9

❦

"You what?" Masters could not control the shock in his voice. It was bad enough that she had breached the security of his home under pretense of an afternoon call, but this, this was beyond comprehension.

"I want to help you find a wife. It is the perfect way to return the favor you did me with Mr. Green—to make us even." Clara settled herself comfortably in the leather chair before the fire, his chair.

He bet she knew it was his chair. That was why she smiled so smugly. It certainly had nothing to do with this ridiculous idea she was proposing. "I do not need any assistance. I am managing just fine on my own."

"I don't believe you are." She shifted slightly, drawing the blue velvet of her morning dress tight across her chest. He would not look. He would not. It did not matter to him that she had the finest pair of breasts he'd ever seen. His fingers twitched as he remembered the feel of them, the weight of them.

He turned and strode to the window, staring out first at the neat, unassuming plantings that surrounded his grand home and then at the busy street. There were more carriages than usual for this hour of the day—not many more, but still a distinct increase. "I assure you that you are wrong. I had not a single difficulty last night."

The velvet of her skirts crunched as she moved about in the chair. He refused to imagine what the movement was.

She took a sip of her drink and smiled knowingly at him. "And how did you find Miss Jane Burke and Miss Eugenia—I can't even recall her family name. Did they seem pleased with your conversation?"

"Miss Eugenia Banks, I believe. I found them quite delightful. I would consider either one of them, although I do not know enough of Miss Banks's family."

"You met them for no more than five minutes each and you are considering them for marriage and your only concern is family? Or had you met the young ladies on a previous occasion?"

"No, I had never had the pleasure before last evening." He leaned closer to the window. Somebody down the street was clearly receiving a great number of visitors. He could not be sure which house it was. Struthers's, perhaps. "I was, however, favorably impressed by both young women. They were very attentive to my conversation."

"And do you believe the ladies were similarly impressed with you?"

He straightened, but continued to stare out the window. "I have no reason to think that they were not."

The chair creaked, and he heard her soft steps on the carpet. She walked toward him but did not come close. "Then you definitely need my help."

"Because I impressed two young ladies?" He turned around and faced her.

"No, because you did not." He had thought she would grin at her words, but she did not. Her face was still. "They had been told good things about your estates and I believe had some admiration for your calves, but your personality left them unmoved."

He narrowed his eyes and stared straight at her. "And you know this because . . ."

"I know this because the young ladies in question are clearly not known for their discretion."

"You mean you eavesdropped. I would have thought you were better than that."

Oh, she did not like that. As he watched, her chin came up and her lips pursed. He had thought she would turn away, but she did not.

"You mean," she said, "*even* someone like me. You might as well add the word when your inflection says it for you. And I don't know that it would be considered eavesdropping when the conversation was held right through me, as if I weren't there. The young ladies also have much to learn about manners."

He wished he had not turned away from the

window. He wanted time to consider her words without feeling that every movement was judged. "Why don't you just tell me what Miss Burke and Miss Banks said? It is clear that you mean to."

Finally, she turned from him, going to stare at a portrait of his parents that hung high on the wall, above a painting of him and his sisters. He should have removed it years ago. He was glad she did not comment on it. Rather, she too seemed to need the time to think, to gather her words.

"Whatever else you may think of me you should know that I am not a gossip," she said with care. "I would not have ever mentioned the comments were it not that I felt the situation must be addressed. I would never dream of sharing further details that were discussed, no matter how lax the ladies in question were in guarding their privacy."

He drew in a deep breath. Her spine had straightened as she spoke and she looked distinctly prickly. He ran a hand through his hair. "I do believe you. I am sorry that I implied otherwise. I have never heard you mentioned as a gossip and I should have inquired how you came to know of the young ladies' preferences before jumping to conclusions."

She sniffed and did not say anything. His mother's portrait continued to hold her gaze. He wished she would gaze anywhere but there.

It was his turn to walk toward her. "I truly do apologize. It is unlike me to be so unmannerly."

She snorted. She actually snorted. "You forget I know your sister. I have heard otherwise."

"I do not believe any of us would wish to be judged by a younger sibling's recollection."

"Violet was not so young when you forced her to marry that she has faulty remembrance."

"So we are back to that."

"Your mother—it is your mother, isn't it?—is very like Violet. I have never seen eyes of that shade on another."

"Yes, that is my mother."

"It's not just the eyes, though. There is something in the curve of the mouth, a desire to have fun perhaps." She turned to him in question.

She knew she should not have spoken as she watched his eyes ice over. If he had seemed dismissive before, now he seemed ready to physically remove her from his presence.

"Yes." His voice was clipped. "Violet does bear some resemblance to my mother." It did not sound like a compliment.

"Your sister has spoken of her fondly." There could be nothing harmful in saying that.

"I am not surprised."

Clara did not know what to say to that. Perhaps that was his plan. She closed her eyes a second and then tilted her chin down, staring at him from under her lashes. She would let him get away with it—this time. "So what do you think? Will you let me help you find a bride?"

He blinked at that. "I don't see why you should want to."

"I am, to be honest, not sure either, but now

that the thought has struck I find myself most compelled. And it will let me feel less in your debt. A feeling I am not fond of."

His brows drew together. "Let us be seated again and we can discuss the matter. I must admit I do not understand what you propose."

She turned and walked back to the chair before the fire. She had noted his look earlier and knew very well that it was his chair. Spreading her skirts with care, she made herself comfortable. "I am not sure that I have a purpose beyond the stated one—to find you a wife. I only know that watching the fiasco last evening, I was pained on your behalf and wished to offer my services."

He shot her a definite look. She should not have phrased the ending in quite that fashion. She looked down at her hands.

"I do not see that it was a fiasco, but would, after some slight reflection, admit that perhaps it did not proceed as smoothly as I had thought."

It was a great concession coming from him. She raised her head. "Why do you want a wife? Or perhaps I should say why now? You did not consider taking one when Violet married Dratton. No, don't tighten your lips. I do not wish to broach the subject of her marriages, I merely remark that you arranged your sister's marriage almost fifteen years past. Did you never consider taking a bride in all that time?"

He leaned back, staring at the ceiling. "I did consider it at the time, but the world regards men and women very differently in these situations—as

I am sure you are aware. There is a vast difference between a seventeen-year-old girl of some beauty and a man not yet at his majority who is riddled with debt. There was no lady offering vast sums to wed me. I would admit—and only to you—that I did receive one less than honorable offer, but the amount would have done little more than provide bread for the table."

His ears turned red as he spoke. She longed to inquire who had made such an offer. There were several women of her acquaintance who had entered into such relationships offering money for sex, but despite the rumors that had grown up around her, she had never felt any desire to pay for company. If a man did not desire her for herself, what was the point? She held her curiosity back. There were some questions that did not need to be answered. "I will concede the point. I can see that unless a great *tendre* had developed between you and some girl, most families would not have been inclined to marry into debt. And even with an affection it—"

"—marriage might not have been allowed. I am well aware of the facts. I would confess I had never considered marriage before my parents' death— what boy of that age does?" He continued to stare at the ceiling, his eyes seemingly tracing imaginary cracks. "I do not know what Violet has told you of the situation with Colonel Foxworthy a year ago. But I did not feel free to marry until the matter was resolved."

There was temptation to lie, to pretend that she knew all and then lure him into revelation, but the narrow band of trust that grew between them held. She sensed he did not have many people to trust. "She told me only the barest of facts. Foxworthy had some unflattering papers and it was necessary to retrieve them. I know Isabella was involved and that you meant for her to marry Foxworthy. Violet expressed some anger at the time, but then once the matter was concluded she seemed to have reached a truce with you. I know there is still some mystery regarding Foxworthy's death and Isabella's disappearance."

"That is accurate—as far as it goes."

She leaned toward him, hoping he would say more.

He did not.

She sat back, tapped her foot once. "So I understand why you have not married in the past—what has changed your mind?"

"I suppose it is simply time. I have spent the last year hunting for my sister—unsuccessfully. It has made me feel more alone and also made me realize how quickly the world can change. I wish for the stability of a family."

"Are you giving up on finding Isabella?" It was an awkward question, but one that must be asked."

"Give up? No. I still have hope. But you are correct that there is some acceptance of reality in my decision. I have spent so much of my life working toward something and never reaching the goal. I think these past months have made me decide it is time to stop and simply work toward building the life I want. And that life includes a family."

The warmth of the fire radiated against her face and she turned toward it. His words were bittersweet. His dream was not so different from her own; it was what she had hoped for on her return to Town. In the past, he had discussed marriage so coldly, and he still made it sound so simple. Could marriage ever be so easy? she wondered. It did not seem likely. "Are you sure this is what you wish? I do not talk of my own marriage often, but I will say that I cannot imagine the marriage you have described."

"I am not you."

"Must you always say that with such disdain? You know nothing about me and yet you continually use a tone that makes me feel dirty."

"I assure you that I do not mean—"

"Do not lie to me." She stood and walked over to stare up at the portrait of his parents again. "You mean to sound exactly as you do. I don't know why you see fit to judge me, but you do."

"I assure you that you are reading intent where there is none. I merely question why you should think you are able to help me find a wife."

She closed her eyes. No matter how his words reassured, she did not feel any warmth. He continued to disparage her no matter what she said. It made her feel very empty and very old. For years she had not cared what people said of her. There were reasons for her actions. They were not reasons that would make sense to anybody else, but to her they were the world.

When he spoke she did care. His beliefs bit to her core. It made no sense, but when he sneered it made her question every move she had made for years.

She straightened her spine and turned back to him, chin up. "I am suitable because I have been married, quite happily. I am qualified because I know everybody, and I do mean everybody. I can tell you who attends all the correct functions and dresses impeccably in the latest fashion, but is rumored to be running from creditors on all fronts. I can tell you which girl has flirted with the footmen and which has not.

"I know that you think my reputation might prove a hindrance, but I assure you it is not so. While perhaps I would not be seen as an ideal chaperone, and I would probably not choose to host a dinner party for those young and innocent enough to suit your apparent desires, I am well accepted in society. I know which lines I can cross and which I cannot. And I've yet to see a marriage-minded mother turn me away. Having an unwed earl for a stepson makes me most popular." She finished in a rush and waited.

"I will not dispute your words." He did not look persuaded.

It was worth another try. "I can help you choose who is suitable and who would bore you within minutes or spend you to the poorhouse. I can help guide you in the conversation that a young woman—and a young woman's mother—wishes to hear. I am of the impression that you have not spent much time learning the intricacies of society, and I have become an expert"—she flashed him a look from under her lashes—"when I choose to be."

He rose and walked toward her. "I am sure that you can be whatever you choose to be and I do not doubt your talents"—he let the word hang—"at matchmaking, but I am still not sure this is a suitable arrangement, all things considered."

"All things considered." She took a step toward him. "Do you mean because we were intimate? Because one morning we took leave of our senses and did something"—she watched his expression carefully as she continued—"we both regret?"

His gaze held hers steadily. "I was not sure that we would ever speak of it."

She longed to drop her eyes, but was afraid it would be seen as cowardice. "I am not sure that we are even now, but it clearly stands between us, coloring our words and actions."

"Yes."

He had not denied regretting it. Somewhere deep inside she had hoped he would. Despite everything, she realized she did not. Even as she had spoken the words she had known them for a lie. "We were foolish, but we hurt no one. It is over—

perhaps we had some curiosity that we needed to satisfy."

"An itch we needed to scratch." He spoke derisively but his expression was soft.

"Yes, and now that it is done perhaps we can move on. I will not deny that it has created some bond that I did not expect. Perhaps we can be friends." She took the final step toward him and held out her hand.

He hesitated and then took it—palm to palm. His skin was warm, even through her glove. The tingles the contact produced were distinctly not those of a friend. She pressed her legs tight and ignored the tiny shivers.

It was harder to ignore her response as he lifted her hand and placed a light kiss on its back. He lowered it then, but did not release it.

"I have never had a female friend," he said.

"Not even when you were young?" She should step back, withdraw her hand. This was not what she had intended. Instead, her gaze focused on his lips, awaiting his next words.

"No, not even then."

"What of Violet? I have heard her speak fondly of your childhood together. I remember a story of you guiding her pony around in circles for hours."

"I doubt it was hours, and she was likable enough, but I would hardly have considered us friends—but with you, it is different. I continually find myself sharing things I had no intention of speaking—ever. I do not know why, but you always seem so ready to listen. Perhaps that is why I seem so judgmental. I am wary and react defensively." He stared straight into her eyes. "I am doing it again. I can assure you I never meant to think such things, much less say them."

His lips remained slightly parted, and she could see their slight vibration with each breath. They were such firm lips, she could remember how they had felt pressed against her own, how they had asked and commanded all at once.

She forced her gaze back to his eyes, only to find his glance settled on her mouth. Her breath caught, and she became aware of each movement, each swallow. Her tongue darted out nervously as her mouth suddenly felt drier than a desert. His glance followed its movement.

She shivered, sucking in a deep breath, and his glance dropped further. Her dress was not immodest, but it did reveal the top swell of her breasts. She shivered again. She felt her nipples rise to a point and dared not look to see if her dress revealed them. The blue velvet was thick, but fluid, and it was impossible to imagine what cover it provided.

Only it was all too easy to imagine. She wanted to close her eyes against the images that raced through her mind, but it was too heady an experience watching him. His pupils had grown large and she could feel the change in tempo of his breath. It caught and held and then sped. Now it was his tongue that flicked over dry lips.

She found herself leaning into him. Her glance moved between his lips and his eyes. His gaze remained fixed. She pulled in a deep breath, letting her chest expand, and he stopped breathing altogether. She felt so powerful—and yet so weak.

When his eyes finally returned to meet hers, she could feel the spark of fire between them. He moved forward until only a hairbreadth remained between them. When he breathed out, she breathed in the very air that had filled his lungs. His free hand rose and hovered above the skin her neckline bared. He did not touch, but she could feel the heat, the very vibration, of his skin.

It was a second frozen in time, a second that could decide the fate of their worlds. A single breath, a single touch, a single kiss, and things could never be the same.

She moved, a gesture so tiny it hardly seemed to count, and felt the silken skin of his lips against her own. She did not move to press and neither did he. It was enough to touch, to feel that connection with another. Their eyes acknowledging what their words never could.

His fingers brushed her breast, no harder than a butterfly's kiss. She closed her eyes. Her entirety reduced to lips and breast. She felt him shudder, the movement coursing through her as well.

Then he was gone, cold air filling space where warm flesh had been.

Her eyes opened slowly. He had backed away and now stood a good foot from her. His expression was shuttered, but she could see the difficulty he had in holding his expression still. It would be nothing to disturb his hold, to push him to that edge from which there could be no return.

She must not. She could not have defined why, but she knew that only heartbreak could follow such a choice. She turned from him and walked to the window, staring at the crush of carriages down the street. She focused on watching a single groomsman guide a curricle between two older, heavier vehicles. A single wrong pull of the reins and disaster could ensue.

She sucked in the muscles of her stomach, holding them tight until she felt she would pull apart. Her hand shook as she placed it upon the cold glass of the window. She was glad there was no reflection to be seen. She did not need to see herself shaken and haunted. She would imagine only strength.

She turned back to him. He had walked across the room and stood gazing into the fire with the same absorption with which she had addressed the window. "I will take my leave then. I cannot see that there is more to say."

He did not look from the flames as she walked toward the door.

It was only when her hand was upon the handle that he spoke. "I will accept your offer. Help me find a wife. I am clearly in need of one."

Chapter 10

Even four days later, Masters did not know why he had spoken. It would have been by far the wiser move to let her go. But then he continually acted unwisely around her.

If he had just let her go, he would never have found himself in this ridiculous position of riding in circles in the park. She was late. Nothing else she did made life easy, why should something as simple as a stroll in the park be any different?

He rode past the same tree for the fifth time. Soon every newly leafed branch would be engraved in his memory. Where was the blasted woman? The plan was simple—she would walk by with her companion, he would dismount and join them, leading his horse.

Clara had explained that meeting in this way lacked all the pressure of setting an actual appointment to stroll. There would be no expectations and no need to follow the exacting strictures of public courtship.

And she had said with great emphasis, because they would be in public, she would be an acceptable chaperone. She had winked as she said it, letting him know that her standards would allow for a certain permissiveness of behavior.

His mind had immediately been full of hot, hungry kisses behind the pines. It reminded him of being a schoolboy trying to steal a kiss from one of the maids. He could only hope that he met with greater success now than he had on that occasion. There was something deliciously wicked about the whole situation.

He could picture Clara's surprise as he pressed her back against the rough bark of the tree, feel her lips open beneath his in a gasp of surprise, smell the sweet smell of cinnamon wafting from her hair—only it wouldn't be Clara.

It would be Miss Thompson—he believed. It was so impossible to keep the young chits straight. Yesterday, he had met with Clara and Miss Wilkes while shopping and invited them for ices.

Who ate ices in May? He shivered and drew the collar of his coat closer. There was that tree again, six times.

Then last night it had been dancing and polite chatter. He knew he had danced a reel with Miss Thompson. It must be she that he had *planned* to meet.

Then there she was, just as he rounded the next bend of the path. Half her wardrobe must be blue. Today it was the bright blue of a robin's egg fogged slightly by early morning mist. Gads, when had such description begun to enter his mind? Her pelisse was blue. He would leave it at that.

Her hair was brushed high and caught at the crown of her head, elongating the elegant length of her neck. He'd never noticed her neck before, how long and graceful its lines were. A bonnet hung loosely down her back. He didn't think he'd ever seen her wear a proper hat. Clara liked her freedom too much for that.

He allowed his gaze to drop lower. The close-cut lines of her pelisse emphasized every curve. He had known she was luscious in Norfolk, but now she seemed made just for his hands, his lips. If anything, she seemed fuller every day, more ready to fill his eager palms.

"Good day, Mr. Masters. It is wonderful to see you here. It is delightful that the weather has finally seen fit to turn." Clara spoke the lines as if written by her governess. He could hear the lecture now—proper conversation when meeting a gentleman unexpectedly in the park.

He glanced up at the gray sky. "Yes, quite delightful." Her lips were rosy today as if she'd bitten them gently to bring out the color. Violet had once explained such womanly secrets to him when she'd been but a girl. Had Clara bitten her lips just to present him with such temptation?

"You do remember my companion, Miss Pettigrew, do you not, Mr. Masters?" Clara gestured to the girl at her side.

Miss Pettigrew? Masters turned his eyes from Clara and examined the girl. Had he ever met her? There was something familiar in the shape of the jaw. Where was Miss Thompson? He had been sure they were supposed to meet Miss Thompson today. "Of course, it is wonderful to see you again, Miss Pettigrew."

The girl giggled, a high-pitched, shrill tone. That would have to change if he were to wed her. He could not face giggles at breakfast—or lunch or dinner, for that matter. Now, a laugh like Clara's, that was the way to start a day. He didn't think he'd even mind being woken from the deepest slumber by such a sound.

He was just starting to imagine the brush of her soft hair against his face and opening his eyes to her smile when Miss Pettigrew spoke. "What a surprise it is to see you here." She giggled again. "Lady Westington was ever so kind to suggest that we stroll on this lovely afternoon. It is always so pleasant being out of doors."

For a man who had been raised in the country, a London park hardly qualified as out of doors. Indeed, he'd seen hothouses that were wilder than these manicured lawns. "Fresh air is always refreshing. What else was there to say?"

"Oh yes, it is refreshing, most refreshing. I do so love being refreshed. From giggling to gushing.

He wondered if she would repeat each word he said in triplicate. "I do hope the weather holds. I fear the clouds are threatening."

"Oh, don't say such things," Miss Pettigrew replied. "Threatening always sounds so, well, threatening."

Miss Pettigrew repeated that only twice. He caught Clara suppressing a grin. She tried to put on a stern expression as he turned to her, but failed. It was impossible to hide that gleam in her eyes.

"And you, Lady Westington, how do you find the weather?" he asked.

"I truly do find it most delightful. It is warmer than it has been the past days, and of that I can only approve. I have never been one for chilly days. I do not mind a true cold that causes one to bundle up from head to toe, but I dislike that lingering chill that seems to always catch one unprepared. I believe such days are best spent huddled under the covers in bed."

Masters did not doubt the sincerity of her comment, but as he gazed up at the heavily clouded sky and shivered beneath his coat, he could not help wondering that she wasn't in bed right now—and he wouldn't have minded being there with her.

"I see from your look that you wonder that I find this day better than any other. I suppose I am ready for summer to finally take firm hold and will take every sign that it is truly here." Clara turned and stroked a twig. "When I see the green filling the trees, I am convinced the weather will be good. I refuse to believe otherwise. It is probably why I am often caught unprepared when the weather becomes chilled."

"I find myself growing chilled just listening to you speak," Miss Pettigrew spoke up. "Being chilled is so unpleasant and it may lead to one catching a chill."

Did *catching a chill* count the same as *chilled*? He wasn't sure whether to count it as two or three.

He examined Miss Pettigrew's face for any sign that she was hiding a great sense of humor. Could her words really not be deliberate?

He found no sign of anything but earnest attention. It was only as a deep flush rose on her cheeks that he realized how long he had been staring at her. He turned back to Clara, who still had that almost-grin upon her lips. "May I dismount and stroll with you? I cannot think of a more pleasant way to spend an hour than walking with such fair companions."

"Oh, please do. That would be most pleasant." Miss Pettigrew held herself to only one repetition.

"Yes, that would be most pleasant." Clara's eyes sparkled, and it was clear her words were most deliberate.

"Then let us all be pleasant together," he concluded, and swung down from his gelding. He heard Clara's snort even as she attempted to turn it to a cough.

This was not going the way she had expected. Or maybe it was going too much so. Miss Pettigrew was certainly acting perfectly on cue. She smiled and simpered and listened with eager ears to every word that Masters said. If she accepted it as gospel that every word must be either repeated or forgotten, that was hardly her fault. Clara had met the girl's mother and she was exactly the same.

Masters was paying attention to the girl for all that his eyes frequently seemed to slip over to her. Clara slowed her pace, dropping back until she walked a few feet behind them. It was important that Masters concentrate on the task at hand.

Miss Pettigrew might not be the most scintillating of company but she was good-hearted and ready to take direction. She was the sixth daughter of a viscount, with solid bloodlines on her mother's side as well. There was very little not to recommend her. In fact, if she'd been a mare she'd have been bought in a moment.

Damn, she was thinking like him now. Women were not commodities. That was one of the reasons she'd decided to partake in this exercise. It was important that Masters realize he needed to actually know the girl before asking for her hand.

She slowed. The best way for them to get to know each other was to be forced to talk. A fine gray mist was beginning to form, unusual for this time of day. Each droplet slid against her cheek like a tiny tear.

What a morbid thought. She'd always loved a good misting, and this was not the exception. She'd been sincere when she described the weather as improved. She didn't know why her thoughts were suddenly turning to tears.

Masters and Miss Pettigrew were a good dozen yards ahead. Her feet sped up even as she told herself that it was better to leave them alone. She merely wanted to be sure that Masters was not lecturing the poor girl again.

They had developed a special code for her to use when she felt that his pontificating was growing wearisome. She merely needed to use the word *roses*, or *daisies*, or indeed the name of any type of flower, and he would consider his words and change the subject.

Or at least that was the theory. In all honesty, she had to admit that it had been her plan and that he had been quiet in his agreement.

Catching up without appearing hurried was not as easy as it might have been. The mist had left her skirts decidedly dampened and they clung to her legs, making it hard to increase her stride. At least the velvet did not reveal far more than she intended. A muslin might have proved disastrous on such a day.

Or perhaps not—

Masters was striding forcefully ahead, seemingly unmindful of either Miss Pettigrew struggling at his side or Clara herself, still trying to catch up without resorting to a run. She wondered if transparent skirts would have slowed his pace. She rather thought they would have.

The thought had the corners of her mouth turning up just as she finally drew close.

"There really is no need for a woman to read the papers daily. Her husband can inform her of the happenings in the world and those points of interest he believes she should be able to discuss," Masters expounded.

Clara almost stopped to shake her head. He could not really be spouting such nonsense. How was a woman to make her own decisions about what was important if she received information only through a filter, and what if she found things interesting that her husband did not?

She was about to say something when Miss Pettigrew spoke up. Perhaps the girl had more gumption than she'd given her credit for. "Really, Mr. Masters, I find I must disagree. A woman must certainly look at the papers on her own. How else is she to know the latest news?"

"I am sure that her husband will be sure to discuss all the important aspects of the day's news with her." Masters held firm in his opinion.

"I doubt that." Miss Pettigrew was also unpersuaded.

Clara was developing a distinct liking for the girl.

"And what do you think your husband would not share?" Masters used a tone that would have sent any dog running, its tail firmly between its legs.

Clara had to bite her tongue to keep from speaking. It was important that Miss Pettigrew find her own answer.

Miss Pettigrew's shoulders slumped and she looked suitably cowed, but she did answer. "I am sorry, Mr. Masters, but I find that neither my father nor my brothers can ever get the gossip right. They don't seem to understand the importance of whether it's Lord M or Lord N and whether it happened at a soiree or a musicale. Please forgive me if I am wrong."

The scandal sheets. The chit was concerned that

her husband wouldn't pay attention to the scandal sheets. That was what this was about. Now Clara truly had to bite her tongue—so hard that she tasted blood.

"You are not wrong." Surprisingly, Masters looked less disapproving and more pitying. "I rarely even look at such things, and when I do it is only because one of my sisters is convinced the world will end if I do not pay attention to some crucial detail."

"Then you will understand the importance of my staying informed." Miss Pettigrew again sounded confident.

"I assure you my wife will be free to read the gossip sheets all by herself." Masters cast a look over his shoulder at Clara, and she was left wondering if eyes could smirk.

"That's a relief. You had me greatly troubled," Miss Pettigrew added. "I don't mind being told about other countries and wars and the poor, but I would hate to miss any of the important things."

"Be assured I would never force a woman to miss the important things." Masters kept his eyes on Clara as he spoke, and she took a multitude of meanings from his words. She also did not miss the emphasis he placed on repeating the few words of Miss Pettigrew's statement.

"Good, then that is settled." Miss Pettigrew looked as if she were Wellington at Waterloo.

"Yes, it is all very definitely settled." Masters slowed his own steps until he was next to Clara and Miss Pettigrew a few paces ahead. "Don't you agree, Lady Westington, that a gentleman should never keep his bride from the scandal sheets?"

"I am not sure that I think he should keep her from anything." There, that was succinct and did not cast Miss Pettigrew in a poor light.

"Oh, I must disagree. I think there are many subjects unfit for feminine ears." Masters spoke as if she were the only one there. "Surely you do not wish to hear of war and death, or be forced to listen to the minutiae of what happens in Lords each day."

"It is my sons who will go to war and my country that is affected by each decision our government makes. How could I not want to know?" Clara addressed him with great seriousness.

She would have thought he would dismiss her comments. Everything she had seen and heard of this man indicated his low regard for women. Instead, he stopped in his tracks, his horse taking the chance to lower its head and nibble at branches.

He turned and faced her dead-on. "I must confess it seems a simple thought, but I have never thought of it in quite that fashion. I would suppose that a woman had no need of the details, because she could trust her husband or father to protect her interests."

"And why should his interests be the same as hers?" Clara felt fire rising in her belly.

"Because he is her husband. Man and wife are one person and that person is the husband." He spoke with all seriousness.

All she could do was laugh. It began deep within

her, first bubbling and then roaring. She was surprised the whole park did not stop and stare.

Masters's shoulders rolled back and his chin went up. He tried to chill her with his glance, but it only made her laugh harder.

Miss Pettigrew stopped a few yards ahead and stood staring back at her as if Clara were possessed. It made Clara laugh still harder.

"You actually believe that." It was hard to speak while her chest still vibrated, but she forced the words out between laughs. "You think that a woman ceases to exist when she marries."

"I did not say that." Masters pulled up so straight that he appeared to gain several inches.

"Then what did you say?"

"I merely meant that the man is in charge after marriage."

Clara sucked in a deep breath, regaining control. "I don't believe that is what you said, but you may believe what you like."

Masters took a step closer to her. "Don't worry, I will. As will most of society."

She moved nearer. "I think you would be surprised what society believes. And the men that do believe so, do so only because their wives allow them to."

"I don't know what you mean," Masters said. And the poor man probably didn't. His lips pursed as he spoke and she almost reached out to stroke them. There was something about his pontificating and arrogance that she found most attractive—as well as most maddening.

"I am afraid I don't either." Miss Pettigrew did not want to be left out.

They were close enough that Clara could see how his breath disturbed the mist in the air. There was temptation to move closer, but instead, she glanced over at Miss Pettigrew and stepped back. "Do forgive me, Miss Pettigrew. I am forgetting the time. I must return you to your mother."

"But . . ."

"No, my dear, we really must go." She turned back to Masters but moved away as she did so. "I do hope you will forgive us, Mr. Masters. It is important that Miss Pettigrew has time to rest for this evening. She's attending a soiree at the Blakes'. Are you planning to attend?"

That had been more direct than she had intended, but she'd never had a talent for dissembling.

"I was considering it," Masters answered. He, on the other hand, clearly had mastered the art.

"Oh, I do hope I see you there," Miss Pettigrew gushed.

Masters smiled at Miss Pettigrew and then turned to Clara. "And you, Lady Westington, will you be attending?"

She had planned to. Clara attempted a smile as her mind fought for the right words. What was the right thing to do? She needed to be sure that Masters didn't spend the evening lecturing the poor girl on the proper etiquette of a wife, but she also could not afford the temptation he offered whenever she got too close.

"Perhaps," she answered, delaying the decision.

"Oh, I thought you were accompanying me. I am sure Mama has it all arranged," Miss Pettigrew spoke up again.

"Well, if your mama has it all arranged, then of course I will not disappoint." A slight tension began to build at the back of her skull. How could such a simple plan turn so awry?

"Then perhaps I will see you there." Masters nodded at them both and swung back up on his mount.

Perhaps. Was she destined to be aware of every time a word was repeated in conversation?

"Perhaps." It truly was the only possible reply.

She saw his eyes crinkle for a moment, and then he turned the horse away.

He had already danced with two of the prospective brides from Clara's list, one of the Miss Thwaites and Miss Burke. Miss Thompson was not to be seen despite the fact that he had spied both of her parents and her grandmother. Her father admittedly had been hurrying to the card room as quickly as possible, but even so he had stopped to give Masters a quick hello.

Miss Pettigrew had also failed to make an appearance. He found himself glancing around the room in hopes of spotting her. She had said she was coming, and she did not seem a young lady who would go back on her word once given.

Not that it had exactly been a promise—one couldn't place saying one was attending in that category.

He scanned the room again, looking for that ebony hair. No, Miss Pettigrew had strawberry blond hair. He didn't know why he'd been looking for hair so dark it looked black.

Damnation, of course he knew whose hair he was looking for, knew whose presence had made him decide to attend one more of these blasted affairs.

Clara, Lady Westington.

He had to stop thinking of her. He had a purpose here—to find a bride. Clara could never be considered in that category.

Even the thought of Clara and the word *bride* sent an unwelcome shiver running through him. She would make a most dreadful wife, always disagreeing and never giving a man a moment's peace. She'd leave a man most unsettled—not what one desired for a lifetime. Although, desire—there'd certainly be plenty of that. His lower anatomy stirred at the thought.

And then, as if on practiced cue, he heard her low purr behind him. "Why aren't you dancing with one of the chosen few? Or at least conversing over lemonade?"

He turned and there she was. Her hair was swept up in an elaborate knot with soft curls left to caress her cheeks. Diamonds were scattered throughout the waves and curls, looking like stars on the clearest of nights.

And her dress—it must have been sewed on, so tightly did it hug her full curves. It was gray. It should have looked dull and drab, but it was layered in some mysterious way that made a rainbow of color shine through, making her look encased in mist. It made a man dream that if he got close enough he'd see right through it—see through to her.

He swallowed, feeling a lump rise in his throat. He'd never seen her naked, despite all they had done together, and now his eager mind was filling in all the imagined bits.

"You're staring," she said. "I do hope you don't look at Miss Thompson or Miss Pettigrew in such a fashion. It would frighten them right off. A woman does not care to feel that she might be eaten at any moment."

His mind filled with an image of her spread before him, a veritable banquet. He stepped closer, forcing her back against the wall. "Are you sure? Experience has taught me otherwise."

As he watched, her pupils grew large. Her tongue flicked out to moisten dry lips. Like a kitten following a string, his eyes traced the movement.

"I had not taken you for a man of such experience." Her voice cracked slightly as she spoke. She was as affected by their closeness as he.

"Just because my experience is not as varied as your own does not mean—" He stopped midsentence as he watched her face grow shuttered.

She slid to the side and stepped away from the wall. "As I was saying. It is not appropriate to look at a woman in such a manner in a public setting. For all your lectures on decorum, I am sure that you know that to be true. Please do not forget yourself again. I must go and find Miss Pettigrew and inform her that you are here. She is most anxious to find you. Her mother also wishes to converse."

"I am sure she does." It had not escaped his notice that Lady Pettigrew was most eager to find a husband for her daughter. He imagined that with half a dozen husbands to find, a woman would be enthusiastic if the porter expressed interest.

"Do not sound so put upon. It is you who seeks a wife within such a narrow parameter of specifications. If you were to choose to seek a woman that you liked instead of a girl who fit your plans, it would be a much easier task."

"Nonsense. It is planning that enables anything to get done." He couldn't tell if she looked cross or was about to burst into laughter.

"If you say so, my lord." She spoke softly and he still could not catch her tone.

"I am no lord," he replied.

"Your voice says otherwise. You sound almost regal when you speak so solemnly with your chin tilted in such a high-minded fashion."

"You do not seem to be intimidated."

It was clearly a smile now, she was working to suppress it, but there could be no mistaking that upturn of her lips. "But then I have never been an obedient subject—only a loyal one."

There was some message in that last and he struggled to understand. She always left him with the feeling that there was more he should know.

"Were you not looking for Miss Pettigrew?"

Her nose wrinkled. "Yes, Your Majesty, I hurry

to obey." She turned and disappeared into the milling crowd.

He had not meant for her to go. He had meant it only as further banter. The room seemed to dull the moment she was gone.

He closed his eyes and took a moment to regain control. It was better that she was gone. He needed to concentrate on the task at hand.

He turned and looked out over the crowd, glad of the height that let him look over most people.

Chapter 11

❧

"**W**hat are you doing here, Robert?" Clara asked as she entered her parlor. It was not the most gracious of greetings, but then she truly was surprised. She had spent the afternoon shopping with the Miss Thwaites and her mind was numbed. Masters had strolled with them, after a bit, but he had been surprisingly silent and unengaged, a far different man than he had been last night at the Blakes'.

Her stepson grinned at her from his spot near the fire. He'd built it up so high the flames licked at the edge of the stonework. He caught her glance. "It was a cold journey. The bricks weren't properly heated at the last inn and my feet are frozen."

"You didn't ride?" She was falling into his trap of avoiding the issue.

"No, my mare picked up a pebble and I didn't want to lame her." He settled back in his chair, lifting a glass of what had to be her best brandy. "And to answer your other question, I came to find a gift for Jennie. Her birthday is the end of May and I want to get her something that shows how deeply I care."

That probably was the truth. Didn't the boy know that men weren't supposed to care about things like presents except when they were part of a transaction? *See these diamond ear bobs—sleep with me and they're yours. See these emeralds—don't make a fuss that our relationship is over.*

When had she gotten so cynical? She'd never been given such gifts—had always played on an even field.

It must be Masters. It was listening to him talk about finding a wife with as much passion as selecting ham or beef for dinner and considerably less than he'd put into choosing a vintage of wine that had her thinking this way.

She softened her voice. "And what are you thinking of giving her?"

"I am unsure. I would like to give her jewelry, something that can truly be hers instead of a family piece, but I can't think of what would really explain the way I feel. I thought of horses and a phaeton, but I am not sure her father would permit her to drive before we are wed. He finds it unfeminine."

"Your father once gave me a hunter, a great, majestic beast of horse, but I imagine that Lord Darnell would find that even less acceptable."

"Fury," Robert said. "I remember him well. Father took me to look him over before buying. I felt like such a man."

"I loved that horse."

"And yet you sold him."

"After the accident I lost my desire to ride, and it didn't seem fair to keep him stabled. I never loved riding hell-bent-for-leather as your father did."

They were both quiet for a moment. Clara could see in Robert's face that he too was remembering the horrid morning when the grooms had returned with Michael's limp body. He'd still been warm. She could remember holding his hand and thinking that he couldn't be dead.

Of course, he had been.

"Father would not have wanted you to give up riding," Robert said, at last.

"I know. And I haven't. I still go out some mornings early, but my mare is a more gentle beast. I don't feel a need to race the wind anymore."

"He would have thought that didn't count as riding."

She chuckled. Robert was right. Michael would have shaken his head in despair if he'd seen the sedate pace she kept to now. "I know, but the truth is that I've always liked a quiet ride. I won't deny that a good gallop can lighten my heart, but I am happier crossing a smooth field on my mare than jumping fences on a beast that wanted to pull my arms from their sockets."

"That was Father."

"Yes."

Robert opened his mouth to say more, but then closed it again. She was glad. She knew that he wanted to ask her more questions about those years following Michael's death, but luckily he refrained. She was not eager to talk about that time when she had lived as if there were no tomorrow. He was still her stepson for all that he seemed more a brother than a child.

"So no horses for Jennie," Robert said as he turned back to stare into the fire.

"I do hope I haven't discouraged you."

"No, it wasn't the right thing."

Clara picked up a china figurine of a pair of young lovers off the table and ran a finger along the curves of the woman's skirts. "What about a dog? I've seen some of the most delightful creatures recently, some so small you could almost fit them in a reticule."

"Given the temperament of Lord Darnell's hounds, I think that also is a gift that should wait until after the wedding. Although I do think she would love such a fanciful creature."

"I suppose that leaves out a kitten as well. Lady Smithington has a cat with hair as long as my fingers that is due to kitten any day."

"I am afraid not."

Clara placed the statue back on the table. "I am sure something will come to you." She waited until Robert turned back to her before proceeding. "Tell me the rest of why you have come. I cannot believe that you came to London searching for a gift without knowing what it would be. While I will admit you can find almost anything in this city, you can find much of the same closer to home."

Robert shrugged. "I would admit to being worried about you. You left rather suddenly. I was concerned that perhaps you felt unwelcome as Jennie makes herself more at home at the manor."

"Oh, I do hope I did nothing to leave you with such an impression. I merely felt the desire to be about Town. With the season starting it was time for me to be here."

Robert looked doubtful, but accepted her answer. He rose and stretched. "Are there any invitations I should know of? I was fancying a quiet evening at home. But I'd be happy to accompany you if you wish."

Did she wish? Having Robert with her would make her even more desirable company. There was nothing like an unmarried earl to attract every matron in the building. It could be almost comical how quickly the word would spread, that a marriageable man was about. If word of his engagement spread, then a few would disperse, but only a few.

His presence would also help keep things under control with Masters—or at least she hoped it would. On the other hand, Robert might notice the sparks that flew between her and *that man*. Her stepson often saw more than she might wish. "I'll be fine on my own—or perhaps I may even stay home. How would you fancy a light dinner and a few hands of cards before the fire?"

Robert pretended to consider, but she could see he was more than willing. "That would be perfect."

"It's decided then. I'll send my regrets and apologize to Miss Pettigrew that I won't be accompanying her."

It was not Miss Pettigrew who filled her thoughts, however. Masters would not let her be. It was the right decision to leave him on his own for the evening. If he was determined to marry one of the girls they had selected, he needed to talk with them for an evening. Any tolerable marriage would require conversation.

She could not always be there to correct his faults and guide him along the correct path. He must learn to catch himself when his tendency to dominate grew too strong.

She grinned at the thought.

"What has you smiling?" Robert asked. "I haven't seen that look on your face for years."

"Oh, nothing. Just my own fanciful thoughts."

"Well, two of them are out of the running," Masters exclaimed as she entered her study the next morning. The porter had settled him there when he'd arrived before she was fully dressed.

She walked to the settee and stared down at him. "Is that why you are here? You really must stop making them sound like horses. The analogy grows tiresome."

"I'll just say that two of them will not suit then."

"You could still refer to them by name. I do think any woman you consider marrying deserves a name." She sat down beside him, careful to keep a respectful distance between them. He smelled of pine this morning. It must be his soap, but she had an image of him striding through the forest at sunrise.

She shook herself. "And how could you lose two contenders in one evening? Can I not ever leave you by yourself?"

He mumbled something under his breath. She caught the "silly twit" but was not sure if he referred to her or to one of the young misses.

She glanced down at her hands, folding them in a most ladylike fashion. "So tell me what happened."

"It is really quite simple," he said. "I cannot stand to speak to Miss Melinda Thwaite for another moment and therefore do not believe that marriage is an option. If I have to hear one more time about why she chose only a blue bow for her hair while her sister decided to weave their mother's pearls amongst her curls, I will surely become crazed. I can only imagine a lifetime of mornings spent discussing notions and ribbons over breakfast. It could not be borne. I fear that her sister, Belinda, may be the same, but I have not had much chance to speak with her."

"At least now you begin to understand the reasoning behind letting your companion speak. Can you imagine not finding out until after marriage that your wife's conversation begins and ends with discussing Ackermann's fashion plates?"

"You send shivers down my spine." And based on the sudden pallor that had dulled his skin, he spoke only the truth.

"And who is the other that you no longer wish to consider? Miss Thompson? She seems to be able to hold her own in conversation, and is, I believe, rather well read. Miss Wilkes? She is certainly tall, slim, and blond. Her children will be beautiful. Her entire family is. Miss Pettigrew? She seems quite taken with you."

He placed his hand over hers. "Miss Wilkes, I am afraid. She made a point of inviting me to look at the long gallery. I must admit I had hopes that I was gaining in her affections." His thumb stroked the crease between her thumb and fingers. It was all she could do not to open her hand to him. The sensations he evoked were really quite incredible.

"Oh dear, what happened?" She held her voice flat.

"Her affections are engaged by another. She took me aside not for some lovers' interlude, but to tell me that she wished I would not call again. Apparently her other suitor owns no lands and she is afraid that her parents will look unfavorably upon him. It is the first time I have felt my estates too grand."

"You are too modest now. I do believe you ignore your work of the past decade or more." She turned her hand so that his thumb was centered in her palm. "I have heard nothing but good about the growth and upkeep of your lands."

"Why should you have heard anything?"

Could she admit she had asked? She had not meant to, but somehow several recent conversations had turned to the subject of Masters. And it was true, everything she heard had been good. There were rumors of his parents and the near-destitute state they had left the estate in, but now there was only admiration that one man—a boy, really, when it had all begun—could have rescued everything so completely. Even Violet had given grudging praise on the subject.

"One just hears."

The corner of his mouth quirked but he made no comment. He merely continued his slow massage of her hand, the fingers now moving to the thin ruffle of lace at her cuff.

She found herself leaning toward him as his fingers slipped beneath the fabric, his touch so gentle it could have been the merest breath of wind. But no wind had ever affected her as did his stroke.

She lowered her glance from his eyes and stared at the top button of his shirt, barely visible beneath his cravat. There could be nothing attractive about a button. If she focused on nothing but that, surely her thoughts would remain under control. It was mother-of-pearl, the iridescent swirl of blue and purple running through the snowy white as the froth of foam danced upon the ocean's waves.

There, that was a good thought. Now she could speak. "So it is to be Miss Thompson or Miss Pettigrew?"

"Yes, I have been thinking—"

Before he could answer, the door pushed open and Violet entered. It really was the morning for unexpected, uninvited guests.

Clara pulled away from Masters quickly, returning her hands to her lap.

"Oh good, you are here," Violet said.

For a moment, Clara did not understand. Of

course she was here. It was her house. Then she realized that Violet did not address her at all. Violet's eyes were firmly on her brother.

"Why yes, apparently I am," Masters answered. "But how did you know?"

"I heard from your porter."

Masters moved farther from Clara and focused slowly on Violet. "And why should he have told you?"

"Oh, don't take that tone with me," Violet said. "He told me because I asked him to."

Clara would have used that tone herself. As always, it amazed her that Masters did not argue. Instead, he considered the words and answered with reason.

"You must have expressed that the matter was of some importance that he shared my whereabouts with you," he said.

Violet strode over to a hard-backed chair and sat. "Yes, it is most important. That is why I have come."

"And are you going to tell me?" Masters asked, his impatience clear.

This time Clara admitted that she had to take Masters's part. Violet was being remarkably slow in getting to the point.

"Well, yes, it's Isabella," Violet said after a considered look at Clara.

Masters exclaimed, "You've found her."

His whole body tensed as Violet spoke. He might have relaxed his search, but it was clear how important this was to him.

"Well, no," Violet answered. "I really am making a hash of this."

Masters did not answer, but raised a brow. He was trying to act unconcerned, but Clara could not mistake the intensity of his gaze. His fingers shook as he tapped them against his leg.

She could only sit back and watch the interaction between Masters and Violet.

Violet took a settling breath. "I will begin at the beginning. I came to call on you because I wanted to invite you to a small dinner party I am holding."

"You wished to invite me to dinner? Why did you not just send an invitation?" His voice rang with surprise.

Clara could hear all that he did not say. He wondered that Violet wished to invite him to her home and wondered if this was a sign that they were truly reconciled. He longed for this to be true, but could never have said the words. It was easier for him to ignore his first question and move right on to the second.

Violet granted him the favor of answering only the second. "I am not unaware that you have expressed some interest in a certain lady, and I wanted to know if you wished her invited also. I did not desire to put pen to my thoughts and decided it would be pleasant to call upon my brother. Is there some difficulty with that?"

So perhaps Violet was not totally letting him avoid the issue of their relationship. Clara knew her friend well and could sense that Violet's discomfort was as great as Masters's. Whatever stood between them was too great for a simple dinner invitation to repair.

Masters looked taken aback by Violet's words, but answered smoothly, if with some tension. "Of course not. Were you thinking of Miss Thompson or Miss Pettigrew? And what does this have to do with Isabella?" He was clearly impatient to find out about his sister.

Violet shot Clara an exasperated and questioning glance. "I was not thinking of either Miss Thompson or Miss Pettigrew."

Surely Violet didn't think that— No, the very thought was preposterous. Just because Clara and Masters had been seen spending some time together was no reason to think— Clara's mind was spinning with the possibilities. Even with all that had happened between them she had never considered Masters as a possible marriage partner. Why, the very idea was ridiculous. Then why did her mind seem to fix on it?

"—and Isabella. No sooner did I arrive than your agent burst in and asked for you." Violet was talking again, and clearly Clara's wandering mind had missed some crucial detail.

Masters had not missed it, and he leaned toward his sister, his face drawn tight. "My agent? I wasn't expecting to hear from him until the end of the week, and even then only by post." Masters stood and began to pace. "What did he say?"

"He wouldn't tell me much. In fact, he seemed annoyed that I questioned him at all." Violet clearly had been put off by the man.

"Then what did he have to say that sent you here in such a rush?" Masters asked.

"It was more what he didn't say. He clearly had hurried to your home with news to share. And he did tell the porter it was about Isabella—I could not help hearing that. I knew I must find you at once so that you could question him in more detail."

"Well, why didn't you say so immediately?" The tension grew with each word he spoke. "We must be off. Is the man still at my house?" He turned without even looking at Clara.

"I believe so," Violet said, turning her face from her brother. "The porter was doing his best to settle him in the library when I left to find you."

"Then let us be off." With little more than a nod back, Masters grabbed his sister's arm and made for the door.

"You will send word when you know more?" It was all Clara could do to get the words out as Masters grabbed his hat and gloves from the table.

"Of course," he said.

Then they were gone.

Clara sat for a minute, letting the sudden silence close about her. She didn't understand what had just happened. Masters and Violet had seemed more separated by the task of finding Isabella than united. She had always considered adversity a bonding agent, but whatever issue lay between Masters and Violet prevented this.

And yet— Masters had forgotten her the moment his sister's name was mentioned.

She felt wounded.

It was foolish, but true. She examined the feeling for a moment, trying to understand its cause.

She had no reason to be upset. She was glad that there might be news of Isabella. So why did she feel a sudden need to mope?

It was that damn man again. For weeks now they had been coconspirators in his quest to find a bride, and now suddenly she was excluded. One second he was rubbing her wrist and causing butterflies to dance in her belly, and the next she was forgotten.

But then so was his quest. In less than a minute he had forgotten his desire for a bride. There was some satisfaction in that.

What was she thinking? Clara grabbed her needlework from the basket beside her. She chose a bright red floss and stabbed the needle into the fabric.

She would not care about what that man thought or did. She did not need him. She would concentrate on her own life again.

Isabella might be in Richmond. Masters could only stare down at his desktop as the thought circulated through his brain. His sister might be found. After all this time searching, she might be so near.

Should he have searched longer himself?

His hands trembled.

What would he do if he found her? It could as easily lead to heartbreak as resolution. Finding

Isabella would definitely force him to confront his sins.

He picked up a quill and set it down again.

He needed to tell Clara. She would be so pleased. That, at least, was simple. He had seen the concern that marked her face whenever he spoke of his sister and she didn't even know the whole story.

It was this last thought that stopped him cold. No, Clara did not know the whole story, not even Violet did. Why then did he have a sudden urge to share it all with Clara, to open up those dark secrets of his heart that he had so long hidden?

Clara was nothing to him.

Yes, she was helping him find a bride, and yes, there had been the wonder of that one morning, and yes, there was this continued urge to touch her, to feel the rapid beat of her pulse, to—

He should not be thinking such things.

He would not even put to thought the temptations his mind played with. Clara was helping him find a bride, and all else must be forgotten as if it had never been.

He picked up his pen again. He would send a note and explain the need for his absence that night. He would leave it to her to make explanations to Miss Pettigrew and Miss Thompson.

Leaving Clara with such a task would make it clear to her where she stood in his life.

Why did it feel like he was trying to make something clear to himself instead?

* * *

"Clara." She heard Robert's call from the hallway.

Could she never be left with a moment's peace? Since Masters and Violet had rushed out the day before, she'd been constantly trying to find peace. It was hard to admit that it didn't matter whether she was left alone or in company—peace was not to be found.

"Clara!" This time he yelled.

There were some habits it had proved impossible to break him of, and screaming from room to room was definitely one.

She considered a moment, placed a smile on her face, and yelled back, "I am in here."

He came in the room, grinning widely. "If I call loud enough you can always be depended on to holler back. I know that you hate it, but you always do it anyway."

"I do enjoy how it amuses you, but really, couldn't you just learn to ask the porter where I am?"

"And where would be the fun in that?"

"You are impossible," she answered.

"And you love me for it."

It was true, she did. She must have an attraction for impossible men: first Michael, then Robert—if in a certainly different way—and now Masters. Perhaps that was all the attraction was. He was impossible and therefore she found him irresistible.

She looked more closely at Robert. He was still smiling. "What has you in such a good humor? It is clearly more than getting me to scream like a scullery maid."

"I've found it."

"Found what?"

"The perfect gift for Jennie." His voice was filled with pride.

"And whatever did you choose?" It was probably a pretty necklace. Men always ended up with jewelry. Even Michael had given her shiny things more often than not.

"Books and plants."

"You are teasing me."

"No, I am not. I thought about what you said about finding something that she would like. You know there is nothing she likes better than her garden."

"Except perhaps you."

"Well, I might grant you that." His eyes crinkled. "But she loves nothing more than to stick her hands in the earth and make things grow."

Clara had not known that. In fact, she had a hard time imagining the ever-spotless Jennie covered in dirt, but she trusted that Robert knew of what he spoke. She nodded.

"Well, I met Mr. James Wedgewood at Tattersall's. He mentioned the newly chartered Royal Horticulture Society, and, after talking with him, I came up with a list of several books to get Jennie. Plus he's going to arrange for some cuttings so that when Jennie moves into the Abbey, I will have the greenhouses already stocked with some exotic specimens. What do you think?"

Clara thought that was the most wonderful thing she had ever heard. "I am so proud of you,

Robert. You will make Jennie a truly wonderful husband."

He blushed. She sometimes forgot how young he was. It was not a matter of years, but of experience. He had come to London a few times during her marriage and perhaps a dozen times since, but he remained a country boy. Perhaps after his marriage he would come to London for a full season and take up his seat at Lords.

Michael had never done that. He'd considered life too much fun to spend time listening to "dusty old men." At the time she had felt great sympathy for him, but now—having sowed her own wild oats—she wondered if a little more responsibility might have been better.

"You're looking solemn suddenly." Robert interrupted her thoughts. "I do hope it is not about me and Jennie."

"Of course not. I have only smiles when I think of you. No, I was thinking of your father."

"Normally, you smile when you think of him too. You won't always talk about him, but he makes you smile."

"I guess not all memories can bring joy. Even when they are mostly good."

Robert pushed back to his feet. "I am sorry to have brought you low. I only sought to see if you liked my gift for Jennie."

She looked up at him. "It is a perfect gift. It will show her how much you care and bring her hours of delight, perhaps even a lifetime of it."

"I will take my leave then. I promised to meet some fellows at the club and then proceed."

"Do not think I haven't noticed that you do not tell me where. I am sure you're off to Jackson's to pound at each other a bit."

"You will notice I do not answer." He turned to walk toward the door. "I will be leaving for Aylsham in the morning so I will not be out too late."

"We'll wait and see."

She listened to his boots echo down the hall. He was so happy with Jennie. Clara could only be relieved that she had done nothing to ruin their match. She made an even firmer resolve that she would live by society's dictates until they were wed. Lord Darnell would have no reason for complaint.

Chapter 12

❦

*I*sabella is gone from Richmond. I am off to
Cornwall.

Clara supposed she should be happy for any
communication from the man. Masters had at least
not depended on Violet to fill her in on the details
of his search for Isabella.

Well, that was not strictly true. If she wanted details, she would certainly have to apply to Violet. *I
am off to Cornwall* could not be considered detail.
Still, it was something.

She carefully folded the note away. She didn't
really need to look at it anymore. She could see
those two sentences in that strong masculine hand
with her eyes closed.

Three weeks and she received two sentences—
and that had been more than two weeks ago. She
wondered if he'd written to either Miss Pettigrew
or Miss Thompson or if she'd been supposed to
inform them of his whereabouts, as she had when
he went off to Richmond for a day or two at
most.

Three weeks.

She dropped the folded sheet on her dressing table and stared straight into the mirror. Had she changed in three weeks?

It was a silly question on its surface, but she knew that she had changed.

Her hair was still the same, dark and thick with a tendency to curl, but never when it was supposed to. Her skin no longer had the shiny firmness of youth, but it was still smooth and clear, with only a sprinkle of freckles across her nose. She leaned forward, examining the first faint lines that ran from the corners of her eyes. They were always more visible when she'd neglected to wear her bonnet.

She scrunched her nose, exaggerating them. They did not disappear as quickly as they once had, but she did not mind. They were the markers of every smile she'd ever had. She would rather have the lines than have missed the experiences that caused them.

She drew her brows together and released them, running a finger over the two slim furrows that grew between. Those had never been there before Michael's death. It would be easy to wish them away, but even there she was not sure. Would wishing them away be changing the past or only canceling out her emotions?

She sat back, pushing away from the mirror. She was being a twit. She turned thirty-one tomorrow, not a hundred and three. Yes, she had the beginnings of lines, and being a woman she was entitled to fret about them, but this was silly.

Picking up her brush, she ran it through her hair, counting the strokes as if that would blank her mind.

Her eyes were drawn again to the mirror. She imagined herself as she had been on the day of her marriage. She'd been slimmer then, her breasts less full, her waist more willowy. She rather thought her eyes had been more carefree, but less playful at the same time. She was a woman now, a woman ready to deal with whatever cards the world dealt—even this one.

She tossed the brush on the table and rose, pacing across the room and back.

It was good that she was no longer that sweet young girl who had drawn Michael's attention. That girl would be useless now. It was far better to be the woman she had become.

The woman who could face scandal and laugh.

The woman who could smile at the most powerful of men and cast a spell.

The woman who managed her own money, hired her own staff, and never let another take responsibility for her actions.

It was good to be this woman.

Clara walked across the room and stood before her high dresser. She reached up with care and took the ebony and mother-of-pearl box off the top. She turned to her bed and placed it gently on the coverlet.

She took a deep breath before opening it.

Inside were her memories.

First, the badly written poetry that Michael had

slipped into the base of her glove on their second meeting.

Second, a silk scarf he tied around her eyes during some foolish Christmas game, before leading her into a quiet room and kissing all the thoughts out of her head.

Third, a dried flower from her bridal bouquet.

A small book of verse from their first anniversary.

A single pearl on a chain from when she'd told him she was expecting.

There was no marker for the baby that had never come to be. Some memories needed no marker. Her hand fell to her stomach and cradled it.

There was a small piece of black twill cut from her widow's weeds. She'd debated that marker, but somehow it had seemed fitting to include that chapter of her life. She picked up the shred of fabric and rubbed it between her fingers.

Michael was the past. She'd acknowledged that in the past year and felt only bittersweet sadness now. He would have understood what she needed to do.

The fabric dropped back into the box. She reached into her own pocket and with some care pulled out her watch, Michael's watch, the watch that had started this all. She ran her thumb over the case, kissed the warm metal, and then with great care, she added it to the other memories. All these memories were stored on the top shelf of the box. She grabbed it by the edges and lifted it out to reveal the space underneath.

Here was more of a mixture of her life. The medal she'd won by running the fastest at a local fair at the wise old age of twelve. A bit of silk braid from her first real gown. A locket with her parents' pictures.

And then the more recent memories. It was these she pulled out to examine.

There were not many of them. Only three, to be exact.

The world imagined so many more, but there had been only three.

Brisbane, the dashing young duke. She pulled out the flashing green ring. If it had been real, it would have ransomed a king, but it was only paste—the marker of a masquerade that had started her rapid fall from grace. She'd thought she could love the young duke, but he had not been ready for love. And if she was honest, neither had she. Michael had still been too often in her thoughts.

Mr. Winchester. His memento was an ivory gaming marker carved like a fish. It was small and fragile, so unlike the man it represented. He'd been a cit, a self-made man no self-respecting hostess would ever have entertained. His lower-class accent had entertained Clara and made her laugh. Not even Michael had known how to laugh like Jeremy Winchester.

Jeremy had sailed off to America to seek a place that he could call home, far away from the narrow, cold streets he'd grown up on. She'd understood his need and sent him off with a kiss and a letter of introduction to a shipbuilder's daughter. They'd wed within three months and now had four children of their own. She'd been full of delight when she heard, and there had not been even a heartbeat of regret.

Finally, she picked up the large brass button and rolled it between her fingers. She'd been to the vilest of gambling dens with Alex Clarke. He'd been so lost in the horrors of what he'd seen in the muds of Belgium that nothing else could penetrate. She'd done her best, been her gayest, but none of it had mattered. Some men were beyond a woman's abilities to save.

She dropped the button back into the box and returned her other memories as well. The top shelf was firmly fitted into place, and she closed the box with a decisive click. She stared at it for a moment before picking it up and carrying it to the next room. She opened a bottom drawer in a tall dresser and wedged it between a pile of old gloves and an ostrich feather headdress that might have been worn to court by some long-dead relation of Michael.

Shutting the drawer, she stood and walked to the door without turning back. It was time to move forward.

Her hand dropped to her belly for the briefest of moments.

Yes, it was time.

Time to face what the world must be.

She needed to know where Masters was.

Her baby was already three months along, and she needed to make decisions before things progressed further. She had never thought to marry because of a baby, but then life was full of the unexpected.

He was tired, tired to the very bone. It had only been three, nearly four weeks of searching this time, but the lack of success had robbed him of all energy.

He thought he'd accepted that Isabella was gone. Now he had to accept that he could never give up hope—and that the pain would never fade. Finding her might have presented problems of its own, but this was so much worse.

It was not the first time he had failed to find his sister—indeed, this was the first time he was sure beyond a doubt that he was on the right track. She had left behind a scattering of belongings in Richmond, and the small filigree brooch had definitely been Isabella's. He had given it to her for her fourteenth birthday. He hoped it had been abandoned in error and not intentionally. He needed to still hope that he could reconcile with her—if she was ever found—as he mostly had with Violet.

He sagged forward, letting his head rest in his hands. She had been in Richmond, and all the signs were that she had gone on to Cornwall. Only in Cornwall there was no indication that she had ever been there. The family she was reported to work for did not exist. Nobody could remember seeing a girl with bright cinnamon curls. He'd found one driver who might have remembered picking her up in Richmond—Isabella was memorable—but he couldn't remember where she'd left the coach.

Masters rubbed an aching temple. It should have been good to be home, but it didn't feel like a home. The house was so quiet, as it had been for the last year or more, and nothing seemed quite right. Violet had described it as dull and dour, and he feared that she was right.

He longed to hear Clara's laugh filling the halls. Her laughter always made him feel that things were right in the world. And the smile that went with it, when her lips turned up just that little bit at the corners, and—

He would ask Miss Thompson to wed. It was time he had a wife and a home. Being here, in this house, only made that clearer in his mind.

If he wed, he would stop thinking unsuitable thoughts about unsuitable women, or an unsuitable woman. He would marry and take his bride home to Dorchester. He would set up a nursery and lead a peaceful life.

He would visit London on occasion to see Violet, and he could hope that at some point Isabella would be found, but in the meantime, he would let life progress. A sweet young wife, a baby watched over by a nurse, an assured place in society, and the continued success of his estates—this was the life that he wanted, the life that he would have.

He rubbed his temple harder, wishing the pain would leave. It was tempting to take to his bed for the rest of the day, but having made up his mind, he would brook no delays.

He would call upon Miss Thompson and then her father. His natural inclination was to call upon her father first, but he wanted to be sure that nothing in Miss Thompson's affections had changed while he was away.

He would call and ask her if she wished to ride in the park. He might even decide to address her by her first name. He paused for a moment trying to remember what that name might be. Kathryn. That was it.

After he was assured that she received his suit favorably, he would call upon her father. Perhaps they could have a July wedding. It was not much time, but if he remembered Isabella's past ramblings correctly, June was the preferred month for weddings. July must be almost as good.

He was determined to do this right.

And once that was all in place he would visit Clara—Lady Westington—and inform her that his quest was done. He felt both eagerness and dismay wash over him at the thought. It would be good to see her again, to show her that he had not needed her help to accomplish his task. Miss Thompson did not seem put out by his desire to be sure that she understood what he looked for in a proper wife.

No, it was only Clara who seemed to find his wants questionable. Well, not all his wants—some of them she seemed to understand very well. He had a vision of creamy skin and passion-darkened topaz eyes. Her lips would part slightly, the flash of a tongue between. He'd lean closer, feel the heat of her breath upon his neck, taste the sweet salt of her skin as he—

She would never make a biddable wife. She was too full of ideas for that.

He rubbed his temple again. It sometimes felt that he had spent his whole life giving up what he wanted for what he should have. He felt like a child in the nursery, eating eggs with toast soldiers instead of cake.

Damnation. It was all too much for him. He would go upstairs and rest. Then, when his brain had recovered, he would speak to Miss Thompson. He picked up a pen and wrote out a card letting her know of his intention to call.

He rang for the porter to take the card and poured himself a good snifter of brandy.

He took a deep swallow, feeling the burn down his throat. The door creaked behind him.

He held out the card without turning. "Please deliver this to Miss Thompson. I assume you know the direction."

"Why yes, I do." The low, husky voice filled the room. "Do you want me to convey a verbal message as well?"

"What are you doing here?" Masters answered, his eyes taking their fill of the luscious picture Clara presented. There was nothing the least bit daring about the butter yellow silk dress, but somehow it gave the impression of revealing as much as it covered—or perhaps it was simply her shape. He suspected that even burlap would flatter her curvaceous figure.

She laughed softly, drawing his eyes to the long lines of her throat. "Is that the correct way to greet a guest? Didn't I listen to you explain to Miss Northouse how the exact words you used in greeting explained the different levels of relationship?"

"You are hardly a guest."

"What am I then?" She had stepped toward him, her voice growing even huskier. The light odor of vanilla and cinnamon wafted to his nose. How could a smell be so comforting and arousing at the same time?

And what was she to him? He could not think of a single word that described their relationship. "You are simply you."

She gave him a crooked smile that said she understood very well his avoidance. "But, to answer your question—no matter how rudely it was phrased—I am here because it truly is urgent that I speak to you."

"Have you heard something new of Isabella?" He could not stop the hope from sounding in his voice, but even as he spoke he knew that was ridiculous. "No, of course you have not. It must be something else. Miss Thompson or Miss Pettigrew, perhaps?"

She paled slightly at his words. "No. I have no news of them."

"What then?" He knew he sounded abrupt, but he found her pallor most unsettling. "And how did you know I was home? I have not even been here a full day."

Clara stepped back from him and walked to the couch. She sat, her legs shaking. "I did not actually expect to find you here. I merely planned to leave a note asking you to call upon me when you returned. It was only when I knocked that the porter said you were in. I suppose he has come to accept our meetings. I told him I would show myself in."

"That is simple enough." He walked back toward her until he could smell the soothing odor of vanilla again. He stopped as his boot brushed her skirts. There was a curl falling over her cheek, and he had to tense his fingers to keep from brushing it aside. "You still have not said why you are here."

"Yes, well—" She seemed to have difficulty finding the words.

"I suppose it must be one of my young misses."

He watched her neck tighten as she swallowed. "Does it not occur to you that I might—"

For some reason she was having difficulty, and he rushed ahead to help her out. "Before you go on, I should tell you something."

Her hands were twisted into a tight knot in her lap. He had never seen fingers so intertwined. She glanced down at her hands and then forced her eyes up to his. "I really should tell you first that . . ." She paused, and he could see her gulp as she tried to find the words. She licked her lips nervously.

Normally, it would have been the most arousing of gestures, but now he could only feel her distress. He started again, eager to remove her dismay. "No, let me speak. I must tell you that—"

"That what?"

He drew in his own deep breath. "I must tell you that I have decided to marry Miss Thompson."

"Marry Miss Thompson?" her voice faltered. Clara could only drop her hands back to her lap. This was some trick of fate. She had come to tell him that they must marry because of the coming baby, and all he could talk of was Miss Thompson. It had not even occurred to him that her news could be about herself. She had tried to tell him and he had not listened.

"It has become clear to me that she will be a near ideal wife. She is fair to look at, of good conversation, fine breeding, and seems to have a most compatible temperament. I did consider Miss Pettigrew, but I must confess I find her a bit silly."

"A bit silly." She sounded like Miss Pettigrew herself, repeating phrases.

"Yes, I have found it difficult to have a decent conversation that does not involve ribbons, kittens, or her best friend, Betsy. I do desire to discuss at least a few more subjects."

She knew he was attempting humor, but it fell flat. She forced herself to smile. "You want to discuss the newest height of heels for half boots, and whether blue or green is a more conducive color of paint for dining?"

"I don't actually care for dining on paint." His words seemed as strained as her own. While she had never questioned his sense of humor, it had never been the main means of communication between them.

Fighting perhaps, but never poor jokes.

She relaxed her fingers, one by one, and smoothed her skirts. It was hard to understand what she was feeling. There was shock, certainly. A small measure of fear, perhaps. She had certainly never dreamed of being an unmarried mother. But there was no despair or anger.

She would have expected anger.

She stood and walked to the window, resting her face against the cool glass.

"Are you not going to offer felicitations?" His voice sounded right behind her. She had been so caught by her own thoughts that she had not heard him approach.

She blew out a long breath, watching as a circle of mist formed on the window. She lifted a finger and drew a line in the condensation. It seemed a moment for symbolism, but the line remained only a line.

She pulled herself straight and turned. "Of course, I wish you only the best. I merely thought to hold my congratulations until after Miss Thompson had agreed to the match. She has not done so yet, has she?"

"No, she has not."

It was relief she felt. Plain and simple relief. Her mind told her that it was relief at his last answer, relief that he was not yet promised, that she could still tell him and change the future.

Her heart told her differently.

She was relieved that she would not be forced into marriage. He would not be a good husband for her. He was domineering and would expect obedience. He would try to rule her, and with the law on his side, he might succeed. She would lose all the independence she had worked so hard to obtain.

And as a father? She had seen how he raised his sisters, the extremes he had driven them to. If a wife was property, how much more so was a child?

Masters might have made peace with Violet, but he still was not sorry for his actions. He still believed he had done what was right at the time. He could not see that there had been any choice, that he could have given Violet, and then Isabella, a voice in their futures.

In choosing Miss Thompson, Masters had granted Clara another chance at freedom.

It felt as if a massive strain had been lifted from her shoulders. She granted him the first true smile of the day. "I am happy for you. I imagine that Miss Thompson will be just what you need in a wife."

He looked cross for a moment, his brows drawing together tight. "I am sure that she will."

"You sound upset by the thought."

"Of course I am not. It is merely . . ." He let the words trail off.

"Merely what?"

He lifted a hand and rubbed his temple. "I am not sure. I expected a different response, that is all."

She stepped closer toward him. Laid a hand upon his arm. This was the last time she would have the right to touch him; soon he would be promised to another. He let her fingers trail over the thick fabric of his jacket. "What other response? How should I respond other than with well wishes?"

He placed his hand over hers. "I suppose I expected you to argue, to tell me I must spend more time with Miss Thompson, that I should come to know her better."

"Surely you are not upset that I choose not to argue, that I agree she will be a fine wife?"

"Of course not." He did not sound so sure. "How could I be anything but gratified that you agree with me?"

"How could you be?" The heat of his palm warmed her cold fingers, did more than warm them. She could feel her heart begin to speed at the mere brush of his fingers.

She looked straight into his eyes, seeing the answering knowledge there. It was the last time they could touch each other, the last time they could do more than touch. After this afternoon they would never be alone together.

Indeed, they might never see each other again— or at least not for a long while. Clara knew that after this she would leave London and go far away. She didn't have a firm plan, but clearly, staying here would prove impossible.

She slipped her fingers away from his and ran them up his arm and then across his chest. She could feel him shiver beneath her touch.

He did not have a waistcoat beneath his jacket, merely a shirt. She drew a circle around a button and then slipped a finger inside the front, feeling the firm heat of his skin beneath her fingertips.

He sighed. She could see question in his eyes and then acceptance. He slipped a hand about her waist and drew her closer until her hips nestled close between his legs.

"What is this thing between us?" he murmured.

She slid the button undone, slipping her whole hand beneath his shirt and over his heart. "I do not know. I have never felt its like. And do not comment that that is surprising or some other snide words designed to let me know what you think of me. If we do this, let it be honest—a few minutes of stolen pleasure and passion."

He met her gaze and held it steady. "It is honest—as honest as any exchange ever is between man and woman."

She wanted to pull back at that. Instead, she pressed her face against the fine linen of his shirt, hiding her face and her feelings. She had asked for honesty and could not fault him for being himself.

"I can settle for that." She drew open his shirt and watched as the hairs on his chest stirred with her words. She blew softly, finding herself aroused by his response.

He hugged her close for a moment and then set her back. He put a finger under her chin and lifted it until she met his gaze.

For a second, they did nothing but stare. She could see passion to match her own in his gaze, but also cool consideration. She could see him balance doing this against not doing it, balancing the needs of the moment against the needs of a lifetime.

There was knowledge in his glance also, the knowledge that this was the last time they could be together. His hand moved from beneath her chin to cup her face, his thumb stroking down her cheek.

She counted her own breaths and then his.

Whatever they did would be forever.

She turned her face into his hand and laid a kiss across his palm.

Where before there had been harsh passion, now there was warmth and gentleness—but passion still.

She watched his chest expand and fall. He dropped his hand from her face and stepped back, his eyes roving over her.

For a moment, she thought she had lost—that it truly was over—but then he spoke. "Clara, if we are going to do this I want to see you. I do not want some hurried affair in a chair. We have done that and it was wonderful, but it is not what I want. I want to see you—naked."

Chapter 13

He must be insane. It was the only reasonable explanation, but then, so must she be. He had just told her that he planned to marry another and they were going to make love on his rug.

And there was no question but that they were going to.

He might doubt his sanity, but he did not doubt his actions. He would do this and he would not regret it.

She stared at him blankly for a moment after he spoke, and then a slow, wide smile spread across her face. He could see the moment that she also accepted that there was no other possible outcome. "I'll expect you to return the favor. I've a hankering of my own to see those fine legs." She dropped her arms to her sides and turned her back to him, waiting for him to manage her laces.

Her shoulders were creamy white above the sunshine of her dress. He stepped toward her and laid a single kiss above the ruffled edging before lifting his head. His hands slipped about her waist, drawing her close. He pressed his hips into her soft buttocks. There could be no heaven greater than this. He bent his neck and buried his face in her hair, breathing in that magic smell of biscuits.

He could have stayed like that forever.

Only, of course, he couldn't—his body had other desires.

Slowly, he moved his fingers up her sides, lingering to trace an intricate knot of lace here and sleek satin ribbon there. She quivered each time his hands stilled, but made no other move. As he reached the lower curve of her breasts, he granted himself the liberty of sweeping his hand up the front of her dress. It was a soft, gentle sweep, barely brushing the fabric, but even so he felt her soft sigh as his palms moved over her hard nipples.

His hands longed to stop, to caress and fondle, to play until they were both beyond all thought, but he forced his fingers upward. He wanted this long and slow—it would need to last a lifetime.

He stopped moving, closing his eyes tight and drawing in slow, deep breaths. He counted each one, working to think of anything but the willing woman pressed so tight against him.

"Do you need help?" she whispered.

He chuckled softly into her hair. "Don't hurry me. When your voice cracks like that on the low tones, it does do strange things to me, but I think you'll be even happier if you let me progress at my own pace."

"Then do it, but quit dawdling." She pressed even tighter against him, moving her hips slightly until he was nestled in the crevice between her buttocks. His fingers bit into her shoulders, and he wondered that she did not complain. He was surely leaving bruises.

"But you like it when I dawdle." It was more of a gasp than a sentence.

"You don't know what I like."

"All the more reason to go slowly and find out." That sounded steadier. He loosened his fingers and edged up her neck to swirl a finger around the back of her ear. Oh, she liked that—yes, she did.

Bending her neck slightly to the side, he replaced his fingers with his lips, nuzzling and nibbling. He gave one soft bite, followed by a kiss to make it better.

She was moaning now, her body curving back into his.

He nipped again.

This time she straightened but let her head fall forward, exposing the long, lean lines of her neck. He kissed her there, right at the nape. She liked that too—he found himself cataloguing the spot for the future—a future that would never be. It made this moment as painful as it was sweet.

Finally, he let his fingers find the fastenings of her gown, loosening it bit by bit—and with each bit came a kiss. One right there at the slight bump of her spine between her shoulders. One halfway down to the top of her chemise. Another just at the top of the chemise—he ran his tongue along the lace edging with that one. Then a kiss on each shoulder blade, the left one soft and sweet, the right one more demanding—leaving a reddish mark where he'd drawn the blood to the surface.

His fingers were busy now, unlacing her light corset and pushing it aside. His fingers slid along the slick silk of her chemise and around to cup her breasts again; this time his thumbs stopped to play and circle the puckered tips.

He should have known she'd wear silk beneath all; the sheer fabric was no barrier to his eager grasp, the faint weave of the fabric only adding to both their pleasure. He pulled it tight against her breasts, sliding it back and forth along the peaked nipples. He could imagine how it would look damp, and translucent, her areolas showing through. Were they pink or brown or peach?

Suddenly, imagination was not enough. He spun her around in his arms, pushing her dress to her waist as he did.

Her head still hung forward, and he took a moment to raise it to his own. He let his gaze roam over her. This was what he wanted, what he needed. Her eyes were huge and unfocused, the centers dark. Her lips were swollen, awaiting his kiss, her cheeks flushed and full of color. And the rest of her . . .

God had known what he was doing—her narrow shoulders, full breasts rising above the loosened corset . . . Masters was impatient to see them and slipped his fingers beneath the corset to draw them up, resting them on the stiffened edge of the garment. They settled upward, draped only in that maddeningly thin silk.

He was breathing heavily now, panting, if truth be known. It sounded so loud, he was surprised his porter did not come running—although on hearing such a sound, his porter was sensible enough he'd have herded the rest of the staff down to the kitchens or out to the gardens.

He stared again at those taut peaks. This was his moment—he lowered his mouth and drew one into his mouth while his fingers cupped the other, playing, pressing, loving. He sucked deep, drawing as much of the breast as he could into his mouth, his tongue laving at the tip. This was heaven.

He drew back then and took in the artwork he had created. Her nipples were somewhere between peach and brown, a deep, ripe color that was surely made with him in mind. The damp silk revealed as much as it hid.

He moved quickly to the other breast, creating a matching pair. She was the most glorious thing he had ever seen.

Her fingers tangled in his hair now. Her urgency and impatience were clear in every tug and jerk.

He buried his face between her breasts even as his fingers worked at loosening the waist of her dress and sliding it to the floor. Her corset was harder, but with a few good yanks, and only the slight sound of tearing, that joined the dress.

He stepped back then and looked at her. The curves that had been hinted at while she was dressed were now fully revealed by the thin chemise, the narrow waist and ribs, full perfect breasts, and gently sloping hips. He could make out the hint of dark shadow at the juncture of her thighs.

His body grew more impatient, but he forced it to obedience. In this he would rule, both himself and her.

He held out his hand and, when she took it with only slightly quivering fingers, led her to the thick rug before the fire. She slid to her knees with easy grace.

He ran a hand through her hair and down to her shoulder, beginning to push the strap of her chemise aside.

She caught his hand.

He looked at her in question.

"No, you first," she said, her eyes moving along the lines of his body.

He nodded. This he could definitely grant her. He shrugged out of his jacket and began to unbutton those buttons she had not yet touched. When he started to pull his shirt open, he could see further desire flare in her eyes. He slowed his motions, teasing both of them.

He sat then and began to pull at his boots. When he experienced some difficulty, she came and bent over them, giving a good tug; when still this didn't move them, she swung a leg over his, presenting him with the most delectable view of silk-clad buttocks as she pushed and pulled.

She freed the first one.

When she repeated the motion and began on the

second, her silk-clad behind became irresistible. He placed his now bare toes on her and first tickled and then pushed.

She twisted her head back to give him a good glare, but he could see the laughter hiding in her eyes.

The second boot came free, and she slid to the floor along with it. She turned and rose up between his thighs, her eager fingers finding the fastenings of his breeches. He closed his eyes as her fingers slipped inside and wrapped around him.

He knew his eyes were rolling back within his skull, but he could not control them as the sensation of her small fingers overwhelmed him.

This was heaven.

It was not the first time he'd had the thought, but each time it grew stronger in his mind. He had never experienced anything like this—passion and play, emotion and power.

Her fingers were back at the waistband of his breeches and he lifted his hips obligingly as she tugged.

He opened his eyes as she stepped back, breaking contact between them. Her hands were at her shoulders, and she pushed the straps down. The chemise slithered down so slowly that it seemed to take forever and yet be done in an instant. It caught briefly at her still peaked nipples before falling to her waist. A slight shimmy of her hips and it was on the floor, wrapping lightly about her feet like the gentlest of ocean waves.

Only in his dreams had he imagined such a sight.

Her body was all he could desire, but it was not this that held him. It was the look on her face. He could not have put a name to all he beheld there. He knew there was passion and desire, but, more than that, there was warmth, and comfort, a look of full offering. In this moment he felt that he saw all of her, down to the very dark reaches of her soul. She was naked before him, and not merely in a physical sense.

She took a step forward until she stood between his knees, the flesh of her outer thigh brushing him in the briefest of caresses. She leaned in toward him, her breasts falling forward like an offering of the gods, but still it was her face that held him.

Not only did she offer him all, he could see in her eyes that she saw him, and not just the cynical face he presented to the world.

She saw him.

It was a humbling thing.

It was the most powerful experience he could ever remember.

She stood there, staring for a moment.

Then she leaned forward, bringing her lips against his. It began as a gentle kiss, of the kind one might bestow upon a child, soft dry lips brushing soft dry lips. She pressed harder, and he was reminded of the first kiss a parlor maid had bestowed upon him when neither knew the art of the thing. It was a kiss of joy and promise.

Then her lips parted, tentatively, and he felt the first probe of her tongue moving against his mouth, seeking entrance. He opened his mouth and her tongue slipped in. She moved with great care, as if each second, each move, was an experience to be savored.

She settled against him then, her bosom flattening against his chest, the soft weight full of the promise of future pleasure. He wrapped his arms about her, pulling her into him and lifting her to his lap so that he could support her fully.

He took command of the kiss, deepening it from those first tentative tastings to something fuller, deeper, more mature. His tongue thrust and probed, twisting in rhythm with hers.

She grew frantic beneath his onslaught, or maybe it was he who lost control. It became harder to know where one began and the other ended. She moved against him, her body beginning to sway in the dance of man and woman.

Her hips lifted and fell, her breasts swayed against him, first pressing and then falling back.

And her lips. There were not words enough in the dictionary to describe the magic that was her lips, her tongue.

Even when they stilled for a second, the heavy panting of two people who needed to fill their lungs loud between them, he could feel the passion and heat vibrating within her. He cupped her face between his hands and brought their foreheads together. They rested then, her eyes were closed, but the very softness of her face told him secrets he had never dreamed.

He ran his fingers down the long lines of her back, her buttocks, pausing to savor the sweet swell of a hip, as he drew his hand forward. His eager fingers trailing along the soft skin of her inner thigh as they moved upward, seeking their goal.

Her eyes opened at that, her mouth forming an "oh" of surprise. He grazed the soft edge of her lower curls before letting his fingers sweep to their destination. She was moist and hot, her body betraying its urgent needs.

Her whole body clenched as he found the tight knot of nerves. He slipped a finger inside her, his thumb continuing to stroke the point of her desire.

His own body throbbed with the need to replace his fingers. His cock moving of its own accord as it made its desires known. He shifted her weight slightly and her legs fell open.

A low moan escaped his lips as he fought for every ounce of control he had.

He moved his fingers within her, forcing his mind away from his own needs and focusing only on hers. He closed his eyes, refusing to look at the voluptuous bounty spread before him.

He concentrated only on the silk and dampness beneath his fingers, moving, stroking, pinching, loving, only in response to those small movements he felt. Her body was tightening now, he could feel it in the clench around his fingers, the hardening of her muscles against his lap, and her breath— a sudden halting, followed by a deep, sudden inhale.

Her thighs tightened about his arm. He opened his eyes and watched her come apart. Her body clenching and quivering and her eyes—wide and unseeing, filled with pleasure and discovery.

She cried once and then was still, other than the occasional shiver as her body recovered and awareness returned.

She lay still for a moment, then leaned up and kissed him. It was as soft and simple a kiss as the first one, but this was different. There was promise here, both of what had been and what was to come.

She slid off his knees and onto the floor. She slipped back until she lay flat before the fire. Her arms stretched toward the fire as if seeking to grow in length. Her full breasts flattened slightly, but the peaks still reached eagerly toward him, inviting his touch, his taste.

She smiled, a wide, womanly smile that invited him, promised him, told him it was her turn now.

Her feet slid toward her buttocks, raising her knees, opening her fully to him. What a moment before he had only felt, now he saw—the sleek, dark, womanly secrets of her.

He stood, a marionette at the call of her strings.

The light of the fire danced along her body, highlighting and hiding.

She raised her arms to him and waited.

He was beautiful. She had never thought of him as such before. She had seen plenty of beautiful men in her life, but she had never considered him among them. He was too strong-featured and harsh for such a word.

But now, as he stood there proud and naked, every clean line of his body revealed, *beautiful* was the word that came to mind.

She held out her arms, waiting.

He took a step toward her, and her eyes devoured the fire's play of light and shadow across his skin. He came to stand between her feet. She should have felt vulnerable lying spread before him, but instead, she felt incredibly strong. Desire was plain in his gaze, and she could see how his eyes followed her every move.

She opened her hands, gesturing him down. He sank to his knees and then came into her arms, lifting himself on his elbows to look down at her. She didn't think she had ever spent so much time looking into another's eyes.

Even with Michael it had always been fast and full of fun and play. This slow emotional sharing was something new.

She ran her hands down his muscled back. He was not heavily built, but every inch of him was hard and smooth. She reveled in the feel of his satin skin as she rasped her nails along his spine.

He did not move other than to shake slightly as she hit more sensitive spots. She started to move her fingers lower, bringing them forward around his hips to that other area that was so hard and smooth. She could feel him heavy against her thighs and longed to measure his girth with her hands.

He shook his head, stilling her fingers. "Not yet."

"Why? I want to."

"I'll embarrass myself like a schoolboy if you do. Give me a moment to be sure of myself."

She laughed, unafraid that he would take it the wrong way. "I want you now."

"And you shall have me, but you must wait."

"Must I?" She lifted her hips slightly, bringing herself into fuller contact with him. She inched lower until he was right where she wanted him. She could feel his penis moving of its own accord, seeking entrance.

His lips grew tight and he glared at her, but it was not an angry glare.

She laughed again. "Do you really want to wait? Do you really think you can?" She raised and lowered her hips, running her slick folds along his length.

"Damn you," he whispered as he brought his lips down upon hers in a fiery kiss and thrust into her at the same moment.

He filled her so completely—and then he started to move, each jerk of his hips causing the pressure to build within her again. She clenched herself about him tight, fighting both for her own pleasure and his.

He fought back, withdrawing and then surging forward.

It was war between them.

She bit down on her lip, almost tasting blood, as she sought for control—and victory.

Opening her eyes wide, she stared up at him,

seeing the strain that marked his brow, the small beads of sweat appearing there.

"Twelve, eleven, ten, nine—"

She heard the soft whisper and almost cursed him. He was counting backward, seeking to hold on. She tightened every inner muscle she could control about him. Then released. Then tightened again.

His whisper stopped. And then his breath. She watched as his face drew tight, and then with a massive cry he gave in.

But it was too late for her as well—his final thrust forward sent her spinning, her every muscle clenching without her control. Her head fell back and she gave in to her body, finding mindless pleasure.

She screamed his name.

Screamed again.

And then fell back, every muscle limp save for the occasional belated pulse of desire.

He too lay limp, his heavy weight atop her. She could still feel him within her, still moving slowly near the edge of her womb.

She almost told him then.

Told him of the baby, of her own needs, her own wants.

But she bit her lip again, holding back the words.

Nothing had changed.

He was still not the husband for her.

Chapter 14

He shifted his body off hers, knowing he must be too heavy. He turned on his back and stared at the ceiling. Only the curve of their shoulders touched.

It was over.

He wanted to take her in his arms again, to begin again. But he did not.

It was over.

There should be words to say. They almost rose to his lips, but he held them back. This had been a wonderful moment, a moment he had never expected but long desired.

If only life could be filled with such moments—but it was not. There was still duty and propriety. There could be no future between them.

She was everything he did not want.

If he married her—it was the first time he had even allowed the sentiment words—if he married her, there would be talk and scandal. He might have come to know that she was not as worldly as society painted her, but still there would be talk—talk that could not be dismissed.

And she was no longer young—could she even have a child? She had not had one in her first marriage.

And comfort and obedience—his life would have neither of these things if he married her.

He shook his head, trying to clear his thoughts. It was over. It was best that way.

He turned on his side and stared at her. She too stared at the ceiling. She did not turn to look at him, although surely she must have felt his move. Her face was placid, impossible to read. A few minutes before, he had thought he could see her soul, now all he saw was a mask, a polite society mask.

He lay back again, letting his gaze rise upward. There was the beginning of a crack that ran from the corner. He would have to get the plasterers in.

He was silent. In some deep corner of her heart, she had hoped for words, words that would let her know that what she thought was wrong, words that would tell her that he could be the man she needed.

He was silent.

She stared up at the ceiling and planned. Her fingers came to rest across her belly, sheltering the fragile life within.

She could not go back to Norfolk, not now, but perhaps later. She would go somewhere for her confinement, somewhere that she was not known. It would not be hard to find such a spot. She could weave some story for the time that she was there—

a new name, a newly dead husband or a husband who was away at sea.

And when the baby was born?

That was the real question. Did she wish to keep it and raise it? She could never claim it for her own—stories would only hold up while she was away, those who knew her would never believe she had wed again so fast—not with no husband to be seen. And she did not believe she could give up her world—not even for the child.

No, she could not claim the babe, but she could raise it. She could find a new maid who could pose as the mother or she could return to Town alone and have the child arrive later—an old friend or cousin dying and naming her as guardian. It would be an unusual arrangement, but not unheard of. There might be those who would suspect, but she doubted any would pose a direct question.

And Masters?

She turned on her side, staring over at him.

What of his rights? Could she never let him know of the baby? Could she risk running into him at the park and having him see the child and never know? What if he had his own children—undoubtedly he would, and soon, if he followed his current plan— could she imagine having their children playing side by side and never knowing?

He felt her turn and turned also, staring deep into her eyes.

But it was different. The connection that had flowed through them only moments before was gone. Now she saw only deep dark eyes watching her with seeming indifference. She schooled her own features to match his.

"We were not quiet," she said. "Will your servants not suspect?"

"I do not know," he answered. "I have never been in this situation before. I may have a bachelor household, but I have never been one to bring my indulgences home."

An indulgence. That was what she was, an indulgence.

She sat up, not letting him see that his words had hurt her—and confirmed her own thoughts.

There was a moment's temptation to turn to him again and lose another hour in seduction before returning to her life, but that was a dream of fancy.

Instead, she reached over and grabbed her chemise, pulling it over her head and shimmying into it. The silk was cold and slippery as it grazed her warmed skin. She kept her eyes averted from him as she pulled on her corset as well. Several of the side seams were pulled and perhaps even ripped, but she thought it would hold until she arrived home.

She turned her back to him. This time there was no play as his fingers mechanically laced her corset and pulled the laces tight. She did not wish to think about how much practice he must have had to do it with such ease.

He lifted the butter-colored gown and held it out to her. It was badly wrinkled, and she feared no amount of brushing would make it decent. She could only hope her cloak would cover enough of it to hide her until she was home. His servants would surely gossip no more over a few wrinkles than they would over the strange cries that had come from the library.

She yanked the dress over her head and turned sharply to present her back to him this last time. He could at least have shared some words of warmth and comfort with her, expressed some regret that this was the end—and more of an ending than he realized.

He had also dressed, she discovered when she finally turned to face him. His cravat still hung loosely about his neck, but otherwise he looked much as he had when she'd arrived. If anything, he looked even more troubled now.

First an indulgence, then clearly trouble—she needed to leave with haste if she was to have any pride left at the end of this encounter.

Not that she had come here for pride. She had expected to grovel before him and beg that he marry her. She was glad that had not happened. How much better to lose a little face in a meaningless sexual encounter than to have risked the truth and been bound to him forever.

Only it had not been meaningless.

That was what made this so difficult now. A meaningless affair would not have left her wounded, wondering that she could have shared so much and he so little. She had been sure she had seen real emotion in his eyes and in his gestures, but it must have been a trick of the firelight, or perhaps he was a better actor than she gave him credit for—a man who knew what he must do to get what he wanted.

She schooled her face to meet his indifference. "I will be going then. I will trust you to manage your staff so that this afternoon does not become a source of gossip. I have been through much the same before and it would matter little, but I imagine Miss Thompson would be most distressed to learn of the events here this afternoon."

"Is that a threat?" he asked, his brows knitting together.

She forced a light laugh. "Of course not. I wish you all the best with Miss Thompson." She walked to the door. "I can assure you that if I had wanted you—and I mean for more than this"—she gestured toward the rug—"I would have had you and you would never have known it was not your idea."

She sailed through the door, shutting it with the lightest of clicks. She was reminded of that first morning when she had left him at The Dog and Ferret. Only now she was forced to wait, standing at the door as they retrieved her cloak. She could only hope that he did not come out until she had left. She was not sure how long she could hold on to her calm.

Finally, the porter arrived, cloak in hand. His face was absolutely placid, and she could only wonder at what he had heard.

She grabbed her cloak, gave him the briefest nod, and was out the main door as soon as it was open.

Only as she stood in the fresh cold air did she begin to feel her heart slow.

Masters waited two days before calling on Miss Thompson. It had seemed ill-fitting to call on her right after Clara had left, and even the next day it had still not felt appropriate. He had seen Miss Thompson at a soiree and spoken with her with some gaiety. He trusted she did not know how much effort he had put into it. He had promised to call upon her the following afternoon to take her for a drive if the weather was fair, so here he was.

He stopped his high phaeton in front of the Thompson residence. It was a fine house, solid brick with white painted trim. It was easy to imagine the dependable girl who would have grown up in this house, and Miss Thompson personified that girl.

She would be a perfect, amicable wife.

So why did he hesitate?

Perhaps he should speak to the girl's father first? It was the correct thing, the proper thing. But the thought of sitting across a desk from Mr. Thompson was even worse than addressing Miss Thompson. It was undoubtedly because he wanted to be surer of the young lady's feelings before committing himself.

He swung his legs down to the ground and handed the reins to his tiger. He stood looking up at the house and then slowly progressed up the walk.

He knocked once and waited for the porter to open the door.

There was the expected delay as he waited for Miss Thompson to be ready. He spent the time with her sisters, assuring each one that she looked lovely and that the color of her gown particularly suited her. Then there were the similar comments that must be made to Mrs. Thompson. It was a ritual he had completed many times before and would many times again.

Normally it seemed pleasant. Today it was completely lacking in joy. Then Miss Thompson was there and an appropriate round of new compliments must be made.

"Your eyes are shining bright today," he said. "The knowledge that summer has firmly taken hold must be cheering you."

"If that is what you wish to credit it to," Miss Thompson answered. "I might find another source for my pleasure if pressed."

If Clara had spoken that line, it would have been full of play and left him imagining all the possible things she could have meant. From Miss Thompson it merely sounded like the expected flattery.

Maybe that was Clara's secret. She said all the right phrases, but made them sound like so much more. The light in her eyes and that magic laugh imbued her every word with her deep sense of fun.

He would not have to worry about that with Miss Thompson. Her words were always just as she said them, no secret meanings. It would make for simple life. He would never need to guess at what he was missing.

"I am glad that the weather is holding. Are you ready for our drive?" he asked, pushing all other thoughts from his mind. He would think only of how pleasant it would be to take a turn about the park with such a lovely companion.

She was wearing yellow, not the buttercream yellow that Clara had worn, but a deep vibrant yellow, the color of daffodils. It heightened the highlights of her hair, making it much brighter.

It was not normally his way to notice such things, but perhaps Clara's views had influenced his own. He almost snorted. Clara would have lectured him on how little you could tell from a woman's appearance—you needed to understand her personality. He was starting to actually look at his companion as a person in her own right and not just a possible wife.

It was a horrid thought.

He chuckled at himself.

Miss Thompson sent him a questioning look. He could only shrug.

Her expression when they reached his phaeton was almost enough to set him laughing again, but he suppressed the urge.

Her eyes grew large and her skin lost a definite shade or two. "This is yours," she squeaked. "It's not quite what I expected."

"I know. It's really quite something, isn't it? I only recently took possession of it." He could not keep the pride from his voice.

"Perhaps we could just walk."

"What nonsense. It is the perfect day for a drive. Come, my tiger will bring the step and help you up."

She nodded at him, but he could see the tension in her jaw. She'd love it once they were on their way. The light breeze, the potential for speed even if one held back. The vehicle was a true delight.

Miss Thompson placed her foot on the step and with only some slight trembling was helped up to the seat. Her fingers clutched the side so tightly her knuckles whitened.

He had a moment's hesitation, but then walked over to swing up beside her with a calming smile. "Just give it a moment. I am sure you'll find it delightful."

"Of course you are right," she answered through only slightly gritted teeth. "I am sure I will enjoy it immensely."

He picked up the reins and with a flick was off. The streets were crowded and he looked forward to the chance to maneuver through them.

"Is this wonderful? I told you you'd like it." He turned to Miss Thompson, who was staring determinedly ahead, a faint green tinge coloring her skin. Even as he watched, she squeezed her eyes shut.

Deciding to manage on one's own and actually doing it were not the same, or so Clara was discovering. In the few days since she'd said her hurried good-byes to Masters she had accomplished not one thing.

Well, she'd cried a lot, but she put that down to the baby. She'd heard that expectant women were prone to such fits.

That was actually one of the problems. She'd heard limited bits and pieces over the years, but now that she was in need of the knowledge, there was not one person she could talk to. Nobody here could know the truth of her condition. Once she was away she could employ some older woman who would know all the details of such matters, but for now she was on her own.

In the past she might have dared to share the truth with Violet. Her friend had knowledge of many things that Clara did not and had lived a life even more full of potential transgressions than Clara's own. That was, of course, before Violet had met Lord Peter St. Johns and changed her ways. Clara grinned to herself—or at least Violet had changed her ways in public. Clara was very aware that what went on between the unmarried Lady Carrington and Lord Peter could never be described as proper.

But Violet was Masters's sister and there was no way around that.

Clara would have to hold to her own counsel for the moment.

Maybe she should go out tonight. She'd planned on staying in a few more days until she heard the announcement about Miss Thompson and Masters. She was not sure she first wanted to be confronted by the knowledge in public. She might know that she was doing the right thing, but that did not mean her emotions always agreed.

Particularly—she wiped a stray tear from her eye—these days. Damnation, she'd much rather have been sick every morning than be so blasted weepy.

She stood with great determination. Enough of whining and weeping. She would set the maids to packing and have the coachmen prepare for a journey. She didn't know where yet, but that would not be hard.

She had money, and that could solve many problems. All she needed was a quiet cottage and some months away and she would be fine.

As with all great problems, it was merely a matter of taking everything step by step, piece by piece.

And she would go out tonight. She would go out and have a wonderful time—and begin to make her farewell whether spoken or unspoken.

And then tomorrow, or perhaps the next day, she would go—go and start the chapter in her life that must be lived before she could return here. Yes, it would not be too hard if she didn't think beyond the next thing she needed to do.

At least she had not vomited on his boots. That was the best that could be said of the afternoon. Masters stomped up the stairs into the house in an even more hopeless mood than when he had left that morning.

Couldn't the blasted girl have told him that she had a tendency to get sick in carriages and was also afraid of heights? If she had said something, he would never have insisted on taking her in his phaeton. He shuddered as he wondered if the leather would ever come clean. Yes, he had wanted to show it off, but he was not unreasonable. If she had actually said anything, he would have listened.

Blasted women, why could they never just say what they meant? Why did they always expect men to read their minds and then give in to whatever silly thought took their fancy?

Women not saying what they wanted were the bane of his existence.

If either Violet or Isabella had told him she was unwilling to marry, things might have been different, might not have ended so badly. He might have had suspicions of their feelings, but neither one had ever said a word to him—and when he had learned the truth, he had tried to find another way. It was not his fault that it had been too late to avert disaster. No, it was his fault. It had been his job to protect his sisters and he had failed.

He pulled impatiently at his neck cloth.

If only they had been honest with him.

Damn women.

How could they still blame him for something they had never naysayed? He might blame himself, but that was another matter. Why, Violet still blamed him for not giving her choices when she was a girl, but she'd never indicated she wanted them until much later, long after her husband's death.

He didn't even nod to the porter as he strode into the house and straight to the library. He stopped in the doorway and turned back to the stairs. He definitely did not want the library and all that it represented.

Clara, at least, spoke her mind. She let him know each and every time she disagreed with him. He'd never have to worry that she'd blame him for something later. He'd know right away if she was displeased.

It might be most aggravating, but it was certainly better than girls who didn't let you know before they loosed the contents of their stomachs over new carriages.

And he hadn't even asked her to marry him.

The impossibility of the thought had him stopping on the stairs and letting out a positive guffaw. He could just imagine having asked for her hand as she leaned over the edge of the carriage.

He sobered quickly. She probably would still have said yes. And he still had to ask her anyway.

A cold, hard lump formed in the pit of his stomach.

This day could not get any worse.

No, that was the wrong attitude. He wanted to ask Miss Thompson to marry him. She was the perfect bride, and with her he would lead an ideal life, just like the one of which he had dreamed since he was a child.

He would just be sure to never invite her to travel in his curricle. It would be closed carriages for her from now on—and he would ride alongside.

It was time to dress for this evening. He hoped his valet was in a talkative mood. That would keep his mind away from things that could not be changed.

* * *

Clara looked down at her dress. She had worn it before—several times, in fact. She couldn't remember when she had first worn it, but it had been soon after she came out of mourning. At that time she had felt almost naked with the low bodice and sheer fabric of the skirts. Now it seemed like just another dress, if a very becoming one.

It was her happy dress. Whenever she wore it, she promised to have a good time, and so far she had succeeded. It was a matter of mind over mood—and a dress that made her feel like a princess in a child's story.

She twirled slowly before her mirror. The gown was a masterpiece of illusion. The sheer over-layers floated about her when she spun, making the skirt look as full as the dresses of two decades ago, but when she stopped and was still—that was a far different story. She'd once seen a drawing of a painting by a lesser-known Italian artist from centuries ago, a painting of Venus arising from the ocean clothed in foam and mist. When she stopped she became Venus, the dress flowing against her skin closely, almost indecently, every curve revealed.

Or at least that was how it looked. The true illusion of the dress was that there were so many layers of silk required to give the illusion of near nudity, she was more covered than she'd been when presented to the queen.

But it was appearances that counted.

She spun again. It almost appeared that the skirts were going to float away from her, as if she was an Arabian concubine dancing her dance of seven veils. Violet had once shown her a scandalous book of drawings that depicted such a dance— and the way it ended and ended and ended.

One more twirl and that was it. She was sure expectant mothers should not be twirling until they were dizzy.

She stopped and stood staring at herself. She had never looked better—not even when she'd been a much younger woman. Her skin was clear and glowed in an almost ethereal fashion. Her eyes were bright and full of expectation. She'd finally started to gain some weight, but it had only filled in her already full curves, making her look ripe.

Her hands dropped to her belly, pulling the fabric tight. She turned to the side and examined. There was a definite bump. Her belly had always been a little soft and curved, but never with such a definite rise to it. And beneath the softness it was firm, losing some of its accustomed jiggle.

She let the fabric fall loose, glad of the fashions of the day. Not even her maid had yet noticed the changes in her, but it would not be long.

Tonight would be her final performance. She'd been trying to wait until she heard the news about Masters and Miss Thompson, but enough was enough.

She was going to go out tonight, and she was going to dance and twirl and have a delightful time—and then tomorrow she would leave and head north. She didn't have a final destination, although she knew she'd begin by visiting her mother's cousin in Middleham. A good packet of currency and letters from her bankers had already been procured, granting her great freedom of movement.

She hadn't told anyone yet, not even Violet. That could wait until tomorrow. A letter to Robert could also wait. It was a pity she would miss his marriage.

Tonight was about her. She was going to remind herself of why she was doing the right thing, why she didn't need a controlling, domineering husband.

She heard the clatter of hooves as her carriage pulled up in front of the house. The Gadsworths' ball would already be well under way. It was time to go.

Masters spied Miss Thompson across the dance floor. That was an auspicious beginning. He had spent the remainder of the afternoon—after checking that his phaeton had escaped without permanent damage—convincing himself to be of better cheer. He was getting what he wanted tonight.

There was no reason to be glum.

He caught Miss Thompson's smile across the room and nodded back, a nod full of promise.

Tonight would be his night.

Chapter 15

❧⎯◯◯⎯❧

Clara watched him cross the room. Of course he was here. She drew her stomach in, straightening her spine. It was why she had worn the dress. She might have given herself a dozen other reasons, but this was the truth.

She wanted him to remember her in future years and wonder what he might have missed. It was petty. It was childish. It felt so good.

Her hand dropped to her belly. There was so much he would miss.

She turned to her companion, one of the dozen young gentlemen who'd been drawn by her gown. She'd smiled at one and then another, had seen the question in their eyes—were the rumors true? Could she really have done the things they'd heard?

She leaned in toward her chosen companion, gifting him with a look straight down her dress. She paused there, half a space too close, let his eyes find their target and lock, then she stepped even closer and tilted her chin, drawing his eyes to her mouth. And then she smiled, opening her lips slowly—just enough to make him wonder. She flicked her tongue out and ran it over her lush lower lip. She named it lush in her mind, letting her own imagination make it true.

His glance flickered up to her eyes, but quickly fell back down.

She had him.

If only she wanted him. Once she would have, or at least would have told herself that she did. Even now, she could not be sure of everything she had felt during those lost years after Michael's death.

She could not regret them. They were a great part of what had made her who she was today.

She shot one quick glance across the room. Masters had moved to talk with Mr. Thompson, his daughter standing by his side.

She turned back to her companion, drawing in a deep breath. His eyes dropped as expected.

She didn't even know his name. It was Mr. James, or Jims, or Thames. Perhaps he was named after the river. No, that she would have remembered.

Yes, she had him. Now what was she going to do with him? The evening certainly was not going in the fashion that she hoped.

But she didn't wish to hurt him. It was not his fault that she felt the need to prove her femininity. She had not acted this way since those years after Michael's death.

She should be ashamed of herself.

And she was—until she glanced up and caught Masters glaring at her from across the room. Allowing her shoulders to fall back, she turned to the gentleman on her other side and gave him a slow glance, ending with a raised eyebrow.

He took a half step nearer.

Oh dear, she was going to be crushed by eager men if she wasn't careful. She peered back at her first companion.

He was puffing up his chest, ready to protect his territory.

She stepped back, leaving them facing each other. "Really, gentlemen, I think you may want to reconsider your options for the evening." She spoke low and husky, leaving anyone not included in the immediate conversation to wonder what it was about.

Mr. Thames—she still wasn't sure that was right, but she was willing to go with it—was clearly going to be the more difficult of the two. She couldn't even blame him. She had been teasing him and there was no excuse.

The other gentleman shrugged and stepped back.

"I believe you might enjoy discussion with Lady Bulham," Clara said to him, gesturing to a woman descending to the dance floor. "I've heard she has been lonely in recent weeks, although I do not know if you shall suit."

He nodded and walked off, stopping to grab two glasses of champagne from a passing waiter.

"And am I being so dismissed, too?" Mr. Thames asked, not stepping back. She could smell the musk of his cologne. It was not unpleasant, but she found herself longing for the fresh pine of Masters's soap.

"I would not precisely call it a dismissal. I merely would suggest that you consider where you wish to end up this evening," she answered.

"Because it will not be with you? You are very blunt for not actually saying anything." He still did not step back.

Clara made her own move to increase the space between them. Her eyes strayed across the floor again.

Masters was still speaking with Mr. Thompson, and they all looked so cheerful. This must be the moment. Was an announcement going to be made?

There was a moment's temptation to take back her words to Mr. Thames, to ask him to take her from this room and to make her forget everything but the two of them.

Only she doubted he could.

Why was it always at moments like this that one realized one's true feelings? She'd always thought that was the stuff of romantic novels.

But now, only now, as she watched Masters making his plans with Miss Thompson, did she realize how much she cared for him. She wasn't sure it was love. She certainly didn't want it to be love, but watching him about to announce his future happiness hurt far more than she had ever expected.

Not that she fooled herself. She had made the right decision in not telling him. He would have made her a terrible husband. She was not young and malleable and had no desire to be. She would never have accepted his pronouncements as fact and lived her life accordingly.

And parenthood.

She could only imagine the screaming rows they would have had over how the baby would be raised.

And he would have held all the power. He had already said plainly that husband and wife became one in marriage, and that one was the husband. And the law supported him.

No, she had made the right decision.

"You really meant what you said about my finding a different ending for my evening." Mr. Thames's voice interrupted her thoughts.

"What?" was all she could answer.

He straightened up, pulling back from her. "You've been staring across the room for several minutes without hearing a word that I've said. It would have been enough to give a less confident man pause."

She looked at him steadily. "Yes, I did mean it. I am definitely not the company you seek this evening, and I do apologize that I indicated otherwise earlier. It was most unkind of me."

"As long as you promise it is not me," he answered, "but whomever you keep staring at across the dance floor that is the reason for your lack of, shall we say, interest. I do forgive you, on one condition."

"What is it?"

"Well, actually, it is two conditions. First, you must partner me in the waltz I hear starting. I have long admired your dancing, Lady Westington, and if that is all you have to share this evening I will eagerly take it."

"And second?"

"You must tell me who else among your acquaintance has been lonely these past weeks. It seems most unfair that you advised Barton and not me."

She laughed. Why could the rest of life not be so simple? "Of course. I am sure that there must be some lonely heart awaiting you. I will just have to recollect who has mentioned how blue and depressed the slow arrival of summer has left them." She held out her hand to him. "Come, lead me to the floor and I will keep an eye out for the perfect companion for you."

He was about to ask. The words were just forming on his lips, when he heard Clara's laugh across the room. He should not have been able to hear it through the crush, but it echoed about as clear as the rooster's morning cry.

He turned and saw her. He could only hope his jaw had not dropped open. He'd always known she was lovely, but tonight she shone like a goddess, her skin glowing, and her figure—he swore it grew fuller and riper every time he saw her.

He forced his eyes back to Miss Thompson and tried to remember those words he had been about to say—something about a walk in the garden. It was quite cool for the season and they would have some privacy there. Then he could say the words that really needed to be said.

He heard the laugh again, and again he turned.

Clara was smiling fully up at the gentleman now, her lips parted and eyes sparkling. She held out her hand and let him lead her to the floor.

It was a waltz. Of course it was a waltz.

He jerked his head to Mr. Thompson. "I was considering asking your daughter if she'd care to join me in a stroll on the terrace. But, as the evening is chilly, we might find ourselves alone. I do wish to be sure you have no objection to my speaking to her with some privacy for a moment."

Masters could feel himself being measured by Mr. Thompson. The man gave a gruff nod and, taking Masters's hand, gave it a firm shake. "Yes, please go ahead. Mind you don't stray too far. I wouldn't want to have to chase after you."

Miss Thompson blushed a bright pink as he offered his arm and led her toward the door.

His stomach felt lined in lead, but surely that was not an uncommon response in a man about to propose. Giving up one's freedom was never easy.

Clara watched the interplay from across the room. There could be no mistaking that hearty handshake—a deal was about to be finalized.

For a moment she almost faltered. She had assumed it was over and done, never imagining she might actually be forced to bear witness to the whole affair.

Her belly turned and soured for the first time

since she had found out about the baby. She
clenched her lips tight and began a stately dash
toward the ladies' withdrawing room. The only
thing that could make this evening worse would be
to lose the contents of her stomach in public.

All he had to do was say the words. He didn't
even have to worry about the response. That had
been clear, first in her father's handshake and now
in Miss Thompson's eyes.

The terrace was lit by the great windows of the
ballroom, the light falling in long stripes amid the
shadows. He could still see the crowd in all its
gaiety gathered within.

Miss Thompson shivered slightly and moved
closer to him. Her long paisley shawl had not been
designed for the chill of this night. It would perhaps be gentlemanly, under the circumstances, to
wrap an arm about her shoulders.

He found himself strangely reluctant to do so.
Instead, he peered off into the walled garden. In
daylight it was probably possible to see the signs
of lush growth and early summer, but in the full
dusk of the evening, all he could see were silhou-
etted branches and shorn grass. It was decidedly
bleak. Even the paving stones looked unusually
gray. Stones were supposed to be gray, but these
seemed sucked of life.

"Aren't you going to kiss me?" she asked.

Both the suddenness and the content of the question shocked him.

Miss Thompson took an extra step forward into his path and turned to face him, so that they stood face to face. Her chin tilted up in expectation.

As the words had not come before, now his lips seemed loath to cooperate. He lowered them anyway, placing a dry kiss upon her mouth. She leaned into him.

She smelled of something floral and mixed, the smell overly sweet for his senses. Her lips were warm and soft.

It should have been pleasant—wonderful, even.

It was like kissing his sister, his much younger sister.

In fact, he was sure he'd soothed many a scraped knee with just such an innocent kiss—not on the lips to be sure, but this felt little different than kissing a forehead or a cheek.

Even as the thought filled his brain, he pulled back and stared down at her.

She was a child. He didn't know why the thought had never taken him so completely. Clara had certainly joked about it enough times.

Miss Thompson looked up at him in question— and expectation.

He knew what he was supposed to do now. The words were still there, lodged in the back of his throat, but they were no more willing to come out than they had been before the kiss.

"That was nice," she said.

He coughed, hoping to find words to say, if not the perfect words, at least any words.

She was still smiling, her lips unswollen from the kiss, but her eyes filled with coming joy. They would not stay that way for long if he did not speak.

"Yes." Well, that was a word at least.

"I've heard this is difficult for men. I cannot quite imagine why, but I can see that it is so. Would it help to walk a moment more?"

He nodded, and she slipped her arm back through his. They had reached the edge of the terrace, and the only way forward was down into the darkened garden. Taking those steps would be as effective as actually saying the words. As long as they were within sight of the windows, respectability could be pretended, even with the kiss. Once he took that step into the full darkness, his intentions would be set.

He set his shoulders back and prepared to take that step. Miss Thompson huddled even closer.

"And where would you be off to, brother?" Violet's voice called from behind.

He turned to see her standing in the doorway, St. Johns just behind.

He cleared his throat. "Miss Thompson and I thought to take a bit of air."

"How foolish men are," Violet said to Miss Thompson in a stage whisper and then cast a knowing look up at her fiancé. "Lady Smythe-Burke saw me heading out to take a breath myself and warned me of the cold. She mentioned she'd seen you head out yourself and was worried for Miss Thompson. She's dreadfully afraid the poor girl will catch a chill and be taken with consumption. I can see for myself that the child is chilled through and through. Her very lips are turning blue. I would have thought you'd be more careful, Masters."

She said the last with a strange emphasis. It was clear she had guessed his intention, but whether her problem was his proposing in a cold, damp garden or in his proposing at all, he could not say.

"I am sure you are right, Violet," he replied. "We men are foolish creatures."

"I never thought to hear you say it," she murmured, before turning her attention to Miss Thompson. "Now do come with me, dear. There's a nice fire in the drawing room and it will get you right warmed up."

She turned to her fiancé. "And you, my love, you take my brother to Gadsworth's private library and pour him a large brandy. He looks close to frozen himself. I am sure that Lady Smythe-Burke told you right where it was kept. The lady seems to keep the plans to every house in London tucked between her ears. I've even known her to recall rooms the hostess can't."

"Come along now, Miss Thompson."

And just like that, he let himself be managed.

Or at least he pretended he did—because he knew now that the step would never have been taken, the words never spoken.

Even as Violet had called out to him, he had known he could not do it.

He might want a young biddable bride, a slim blonde to give him his preplanned children.

Yes, that might be what he believed he wanted.

It was not, however, what he needed.

He knew exactly what he needed. It had only taken one look from his sister up toward her husband, one look as she teased and managed, one look that told of understanding and comfort for him to see all too clearly what he needed.

It was time to go and find her.

Being sick was not pleasant. Clara had forgotten just how unpleasant. Why had she had beets with dinner? She spat into the basin, glad that she had the room to herself. Picking up the pitcher of water, she poured a glass and swished it around her mouth.

She wished it were brandy.

That would wash away the flavor.

She spat again, before carefully rinsing the basin. There was nothing she could do about the lingering odor.

She stared at herself in the mirror.

Big cat's eyes in a narrow pinched face. Most days she could at least find a glimpse of the beauty others seemed to find there. When she was with Masters, she actually felt the beauty, saw it reflected in his gaze.

Now she just looked tired, tired and dried out. She pinched at her cheeks, trying to draw color into them. A few pink spots appeared, but it would have been a great stretch to call them blooms or roses.

Biting her lips proved slightly more effective. At least they turned red.

She fluffed her hair with her fingers. It sprang obediently into curls. That was good.

She pinched her cheeks again. It would have to do. She would go downstairs and make her farewells. She would explain that she planned to leave on a trip in the morning and that she needed to rise early.

Maybe she wouldn't even explain.

It wasn't as if anybody cared.

God, her mouth tasted awful. The ham tartlets and lemonade had not been pleasant on the way down and were certainly not improved by their upward journey.

She was feeling sorry for herself, a whiny, unpleasant girl.

She smiled wryly. She was hardly a girl.

She was a woman, and it was time she acted as one.

Her decision had been made, and it was unseemly to complain, even to herself, about it.

She would go downstairs, make her farewells, and begin her new life. She had nothing to complain about.

It was all as she had chosen.

She swept out of the room just as two other ladies entered. One shot her a strange look.

Was her recent discomfort plain to see?

She really needed that brandy, just a single swish, one taste to sweeten the evening.

She stopped by the door to Gadsworth's private library.

There was a decanter within. She'd once spent an evening playing chess and laughing with Gadsworth and friends and she knew just where that decanter was.

Opening the door, she stepped in.

She'd have one small toast to her new life.

Chapter 16

"**W**ill you marry me?" The words that had refused to leave his lips earlier positively jumped from them as he saw Clara enter the room.

She stopped still in her tracks. He watched her eyes widen as they caught sight of him, and then grow wider still as his words filtered into her mind.

"Marry you?" she said, her voice quivering. "Is this a farce? Surely, I did not hear you correctly, or perhaps you expected Miss Thompson."

"No, I—my words may have been hasty, but they reached their intended target."

Did her legs shake as she walked and perched on the edge of Gadsworth's desk? She lifted her large eyes to him, the color reflecting gold in the dim light of the single oil lamp.

"Marry you?" she asked again.

"Is it so strange a thought?" he replied. He was himself aghast that he had asked the question in such a fashion, but he could see he was not as dismayed as she.

She didn't reply this time, but just sat staring at him. She licked her lips, and he became aware how pale she was. Her skin lacked its usual vitality and even her lips were almost white.

At first he thought it was his question that had so leached her color, but he realized she had looked peaked from the moment she entered the room.

Oh, she still looked beautiful. He expected she could be a hundred years old, covered in manure, and he would still find her radiant. It was something far beyond her physical appearance that caught and held him each time he saw her.

She licked her lips again. It was not the seductive gesture that it often was, but rather one of nerves and discomfort.

"Would you pour me a finger of brandy?" She gestured with her head toward the cabinet from which St. Johns had so recently filled his own glass.

He rose to do so, then paused and picked his own still half-full glass off the table, bringing it over to her.

As he held it out he could see the memory of that first teacup reflected in her eyes. She hesitated and then took the glass, taking a small sip from it. Her mouth avoided the spot where his own lip print lay.

There was a message in both gestures.

She took another swallow and then looked up at him. "I didn't realize you knew Gadsworth well enough to know where to find the best stash."

"I don't, but St. Johns does. He joined me for a

drink before going off to search out Violet. I stayed behind to finish and have a moment's quiet."

"And then I arrived." She set the glass beside her on the table. "Are you serious in suggesting marriage?"

"Yes, I have never been more so." He had never felt so nervous. He wanted to move closer to her, but something in her glance held him back.

"And what of Miss Thompson? I thought you were planning to ask her, that she was your ideal bride. Did she refuse your suit? Did her father? I know he is a man of high standards, but . . ."

"No, or yes, or—I had intended to ask Miss Thompson, but I found that I could not."

She raised a brow.

He continued, "Her father indicated his approval, and Miss Thompson herself gave me reason to believe that she would agree."

"And how did she do that?"

"Well"—he felt some discomfort now—"she asked me to kiss her."

Clara pursed her lips. "And did you?"

"Yes, it was not a bad kiss."

"I take it this happened this evening?"

"Yes, on the terrace." He should not have told her about the kiss, but it was part of making her understand.

"So, you kiss Miss Thompson on the terrace—not a bad kiss—and within the hour you are proposing to me in the library. Are you that great a libertine, or is there something I have missed?"

Why did she sound so angry? He had always

thought women were supposed to be overcome with joy at the prospect of matrimony. Instead, she looked distinctly sour.

"It wasn't like that."

"Then how was it?" She leaned toward him, and again he was tempted to move closer.

He leaned back and stared at the ceiling. While he had never considered himself a wordsmith, never before had he found himself so unable to form coherent sentences. "I found I couldn't ask her. That is all."

"Not ask your ideal wife to marry you, why ever not?"

"I realized that she was not my ideal—you were." There, that sounded articulate—and flattering.

She laughed. She actually laughed, and not the full, low laugh that did such wonderfully strange things to him. This laugh was tight and strained. "You expect me to believe I am your ideal? I begin to fear that you are having some type of fun with me, that it is a farce after all."

"I assure you I am not."

She lifted a hand to her hair. "I am not blond."

"I find perhaps my tastes have changed."

"I am of far from slender build."

"Have I ever seemed to mind that?"

She was still for a moment and then slipped off the desk. Stepping toward him, her fingers curled into white fists at her sides, her eyes almost flat. "I have never borne a living child. I do not know that I will ever deliver a healthy baby."

That brought him to his feet. "Never borne a

living—" Comprehension filled him. "Oh, Clara, I did not know. I am so sorry."

She turned her face from him toward the darkened window. "And now that you do know?"

"My heart goes out to you. Although Violet has never spoken to me of it, I know that she has faced some of the same pain. She once had a child who lived for only hours, and even months later, I could see the pain of it in her face."

He reached out to soothe her, but she stepped away.

"That is not what I meant." She shook her head as if to clear it. "Why would you want a wife who might not give you an heir?"

"There is no guarantee with any woman that children are possible."

He could see her body tighten as he spoke the words and knew he had made a mistake. "I do apologize. I only meant to say that you do not even know that there is a problem."

"That is an easy thing for you to say. But why would you even wish to take such a risk?"

There had to be a right thing to say—only there didn't seem to be. "All I can say is that it is a risk I am willing to take. My estates are not entailed. If we have no children, I am sure there is some worthy relative."

She turned from him, and he could see how tightly drawn her shoulders were, the blades almost meeting at her spine. She did not walk away, but stayed still, her face and body averted from him. "I do not see that it is so easy. It appears unlikely that

Violet will have a child, and who knows of Isabella. I have never heard mention of other relatives."

"It matters not." He tensed at the mention of Isabella. Was it the time to speak of her and all the possibilities of her departure? No, that would wait. He would win no favor with Clara by discussing the mistakes of his past.

She lifted a small piece of statuary from a side table and stared with apparent interest at the tiny shepherd. He did not believe that she could have told him a thing about it if he asked. Her whole focus was inward.

He waited for her to say something. The single lamp flickered, making shadows dance dimly about the room. He wanted so desperately to take that step closer to her, to feel the warmth of her body and to know that there was hope.

She placed the shepherd back on the table and lifted her head. He could see resolve in her posture.

"I have mentioned appearance, social perception, and the possibility of an heir as reasons we should not even consider marriage," she said. "These are all reasons that I don't understand why you would wish to marry me. I have not even broached the reasons that I would not wish to marry you."

It was his turn to feel discomfort. "Reasons not to marry me?"

"You are a bully." She said it as fact, without question.

"I beg your pardon."

"We have already discussed many times the ways

you pushed your sisters toward marriage. While I have come to understand your reasoning, I still do not agree with it. You see your own opinion as the only valid one. I do not see why I should wish to place myself in your power."

"I would disagree. I did the only possible thing in regard to my sisters—and regretting it now will make no difference. Yes, I trust my own opinion on most matters. And after watching my parents' failings, I knew that it was important to make strong decisions. If my father had done what he believed to be right, I would not have been forced to deal with their problems. I am no different than most others. Who does not think that he is right most often? But I do believe that I listen to reasonable argument."

"Violet did not find it so." She sounded so deadened of emotion as she spoke.

That was a question he was ready to handle. "Did Violet ever speak of arguing with me? It is so easy for her, and you, to claim that I do what I want without consult of others, but when has this been the case? Violet never spoke strongly against her marriages. If she had, there is the possibility that things might have been different. You have in the past expressed dissatisfaction that I never gave Violet a choice. Perhaps the truth is simply that she never asked for one—or at least not until long after it had ceased to matter."

"And Isabella? Do you deny that you knew she did not wish the marriage you planned? She fled rather than marry."

And so perhaps it was necessary to discuss Isabella. He had dreaded this moment. "Do you want me to say I am sorry about Isabella? I am. More so than you could possibly understand. If I had known how strongly she felt I would have tried to find another way." He was silent for a moment. He stared straight into her eyes and wished she could understand just how sorry. "I wish I had understood more at the time, but Isabella never spoke to me against the match—in fact, she agreed to it. If I had understood, things could have ended differently."

Her lips drew taut. "That may be true—although it seems unlikely to me. But I know Violet spoke to you against it."

"Yes, she did. I cannot deny that—but why should I have accepted her words when Isabella said nothing? And there were other considerations."

"Foxworthy's blackmail."

How much had Violet told her? How much did he need to tell her if he planned to make her his wife? "Yes, Foxworthy had proof that my father had been involved in treasonous activities."

Her eyes widened. So Violet had not shared that detail with her. There was a flash of compassion in her eyes, but then she drew herself back. "I did not know. I still do not see why that should excuse your behavior."

"And what would you have had me do?" Did she know how many nights he had debated this question?

"We have discussed this before. I do not disagree

with your main point, only your methods. Should not your sisters have had a choice?"

"If they had asked for one I would have considered it and in fact I did when—"

She cut him off. "You would have considered it. That sentence says it all. You believe it is your right to have the final say." She had fire in her eyes now as she stepped toward him.

"It is not me who believes in that right. It is society. The fact is I did have that right with my sisters." He took an answering step toward her.

Why did he not just tell her that in the end he had tried to stop Foxworthy, explain how far he had been willing to go to protect Isabella? He took a deep breath. He would do it. He would tell her everything—and then let her judge his actions—and their consequences.

She did not give him a chance.

"And why should I give you this power over me?"

That stopped him, but only for a moment—he would tell her the rest later after they had dealt with this issue. He placed a finger beneath her chin, drawing her gaze up to meet his. "It is a matter of trust in the end. When have I ever given you reason to doubt me? When have I not listened to you? You are not an easy woman, and still I take your words into consideration."

"Such praise." She tried to twist her chin from his hand. "I am not an easy woman and you grant me the privilege of listening when I talk. This is how you expect to win my hand?"

He held firm, keeping their eyes level. "I give you only the truth. Is not that what you want?"

Anger was filling her, he could feel her breath speed with emotion. She placed a hand on his chest to push him away.

"Yes, I want the truth. I just am not sure that you give it to me. I do not believe that you would leave me free to do as I wished if we married."

"I never said that I would." There, that was honest. "If I thought your actions were harmful I would try to stop them. I have seen what can happen when a woman is left unchecked." He dropped his hand from her face to catch her hand and hold it firm over his heart.

"Damn you." She spoke through gritted teeth and tried hard to pull away from him. "You have given me no reason to trust you."

"But have I given you reason not to?" He wrapped his other hand about her waist and pulled her tight to him.

She could only gasp as he pulled her toward him. Whether it was in response to the gesture or the question she didn't know.

"My mother was given free rein by my father and she ruined us all." He spoke so softly she almost did not hear his words. His heart was beating under her fingers, and she was intensely aware of each pulse. As the pace increased, she didn't know whether it was anger or her closeness that caused his reaction.

He continued, "My father gave her everything

she wanted, followed her wherever she went. She gambled, flirted, took other lovers, and still he followed her, did not stop her. She gambled until we had nothing left, and my father took the blame. If he had ever stopped her, my whole life would have been different."

"I am not your mother." Her heart felt pain for him, but she must think for herself, for the baby.

"I know, but still I must be on guard to be sure you never become her. I could never let a woman do to me what my mother did to my father—to all of us."

He was so damn stubborn. Why could he not see the problem with his logic, understand that she did not need to be so watched? Why could he not grant that she had a right to act as she chose?

She was every bit as much a person as he. "You could begin nasty habits as easily as I—and I would have no recourse."

He did not answer that. He did not disagree, but neither did he accept her words.

Why should she trust him?

When have I ever given you reason not to? His question echoed through her mind. It frightened her that she couldn't think of one. She was sure that at some point he had overruled her, but not a single one came to mind.

If she tried to think, all she could remember were the times he had espoused some unreasonable viewpoint, but when she argued, he did listen, and gave way.

Was it possible that if she stood up to him, he

would be willing to bend? She would never have thought so, but now she wondered.

He was holding her tighter now, grinding their hips together. Was he trying to tempt her to agree by such obvious moves?

"Marry me?" He whispered the words against her neck this time. "I will be a good husband to you."

She tried to push back against him; she needed space to breathe, to think. It was impossible to know what her mind wanted when her body was so insistent. "We still have too many points to cover."

"Like what?" He was laying small kisses just under the curve of her ear. How could he be so restrained? If she hadn't been so set on resisting, she'd have been tearing at his clothing.

"Like children," she gasped out, turning her head away from him as he laid assault to her cheek.

He groaned. "I thought we'd covered that one. I will be fine if we do not have them."

"Yes, but what if we do?"

"God, woman you drive me insane. How is that a problem? I thought it was what you wanted."

She took his momentary distraction and used it to ease back. Their torsos still touched, but at least she could turn her head with freedom. "I do. But I cannot see that we would agree on how to raise them."

He tried to press against her again. "How can you even think right now?"

This time she pushed hard, giving it everything

she had. "I can think because I—we need to. You cannot toss me such a ridiculous question and then try to brush it away."

He stepped back with a deep sigh. His chest was still rising and falling rapidly, and his eyes were so dark as to appear black. "Fine, we will discuss it then. Although I was only trying to demonstrate how we belong together."

Now that her freedom was granted, she was strangely loath to step away. She felt distinctly chilled without him pressed against her. "How do you plan to raise your children?" She was careful not to say "our."

He ran a hand through his hair, ruffling it almost to the point of humor. "I haven't really thought about it. I imagine the usual—a nurse, then a governess, then school if the child is a boy."

"There, we already have a profound disagreement. I would wish to send my daughter to school as well. I do not see education as the prerogative of the male sex."

"If that is your wish, we can send her to whatever school will take her." His gaze was on her breasts.

Clara almost felt the need to raise her hands to cover them. They would never have a meaningful discussion if he spent his time thinking about her bosom. Wrapping her arms about herself would show too much weakness. Instead, she turned and walked back to the desk, placing both hands upon it and staring at the shelf behind. He could not stare at what he could not see.

"Is there more?" he asked, moving to stand behind her.

"You mention a nurse and a governess. That does not tell me much about your own plans for involvement in your children's lives." She needed to know his answers. It was all she could do not to drop her hands to her own belly, to cradle the life within.

"I can only say again that I have not really considered the issue."

"Would you raise them as Violet and Isabella were raised? As you were raised?" Her voice trembled as she spoke.

"If you refer to the time before my parents' deaths, I will say that I would be proud to be the man that my father was during my childhood. He showed both care and discipline with both Violet and myself. As for after his death, Violet and I were both nearly grown. I did the best that I could with Isabella."

"And you would raise future children in the same manner?" She had heard from Violet how Isabella had been left in the care of the governess for months at a time. That was not a life that she would wish on any child of her own.

"Are two children ever raised the same?" He moved up close behind her, and she could feel the heat of his body again, the faint scent that was only he.

She should have chided him, made him move away, but in truth it was hard to push away the comfort his closeness offered. A woman could do the right thing only so many times.

She closed her eyes and tried to gather herself. Surely, she could manage his nearness as long as there was no actual touching involved. "You take the easy way out. Are you saying that you would do things differently?"

"I suppose I am. I am aware that I did not do things perfectly with Isabella. One always learns from experience, and I am sure I would do better a second time."

She wished she could turn now and see his face, catch the nuance of expression that must come with such words. Did he mean what he said, or was he only seeking to appease her, to win her agreement to his proposal? "So you admit you made mistakes?"

He was quiet for a moment, and then answered with more seriousness than she had yet heard. "I know you refer to things Violet has told you, that I ignored Isabella until I had need of her. I cannot deny there is some truth to that, and what truth there is can only be described as a mistake. But you must remember my circumstances. I was spending every waking moment attempting to put my parents' affairs in order and to keep my sisters fed and housed in the manner they were accustomed to. I do not, even now, see what I could have done differently. I might wish for a different ending, but I still do not see how I could have achieved it and still kept home and hearth together."

He placed his hands on her hips at the end of this statement and drew her behind firmly against him. Despite the seriousness of his tone, it was clear he was still occupied with other thoughts.

Should she give in? She was not satisfied with his answers. There was some reason to them, but they were not as full of reassurance as she would have desired.

Damn though, he felt good pressed tight against her. She could feel his firmness between her buttocks, and her inclination was to push against him, to wiggle in the manner that would drive him toward insanity.

This discussion was about power and control as much as anything, and she wished to show him just how much she had.

She knew that was not the answer, though. She might be able to win in this one area of their lives, but it did not mean he would grant her victory in others.

He leaned forward and nuzzled the back of her neck.

"Stop," she said, but without conviction.

"I can't," he groaned into her hair.

His hands slipped about her waist and then upward, cupping her breasts.

Now it was her turn to groan as his fingers flicked with expertise over her taut nipples. The silk of her chemise rubbed against the tips, the friction drawing another moan from her lips. "If we do this, it means nothing."

"It always means something." His fingers slipped over the edge of her dress, pushing it down as they sought her flesh.

"It does not mean I agree to anything but this, to sex."

"I could argue"—he was breathing hard, and it was difficult to hear the words—"but I won't—in truth, I do not much care at this exact moment."

"Just sex?" she whispered as she let her head fall back against him. Her arms were still firmly planted on the desk as he curved over her from behind, his fingers working magic on her breast, kneading, caressing, teasing, comforting. His lips worked their own magic over her neck and then moved to nibble an ear.

She swayed her hips against him, proving that she too could play, no matter how helpless her position.

His fingers squeezed tight, and she could feel the passion grow and flare. Skill and patience were relaxed as her skirts were pushed up. There was the whisper of fabric, and a single low curse from his lips, and then she felt him against her—hard, thick, and velvet.

He nestled in the cleft between her buttocks, and then his hands were on her hips again, raising her, lowering her until they were joined completely.

She pushed hard back against him, grinding, seeking her own pleasure. She shoved with her hands upon the desk, giving herself leverage. She would not be denied.

As if sensing her desires, one of his hands came around to cup and squeeze at her breasts again while the other slipped lower, raising the front of her skirts and slipping between her damp folds. She suppressed a squeal as he found that tender knot of nerves.

Then all was frantic.

Back. Forth. Squeeze. Release.

He thrust hard against her, his mouth closing on the back of her neck. Every muscle of his body was hard, tight. She pressed back, moving, seeking that final moment when nothing mattered.

Then it was almost there. She twisted slightly, heard his groan.

There. There it was.

His teeth bit into the back of her neck. His hand gripped her breast tight, almost too tight, and she felt him give that final surge.

The cry escaped her lips, louder than she meant as his thrust brought the world spinning about her, all thought lost in pleasure.

The door cracked open. She did not care.

The light from the hall shone in. She could not think.

"Oh dear. I did not mean to intrude." Even the deep masculine voice followed by feminine twitters did not seem worth noting as her body collapsed, its last spasm passed.

Chapter 17

Of course the feeling could not last. There were only seconds of enjoyment before reality closed in all too quickly.

She heard the door shut with a definitive slam, but not before a few more shocked giggles and squeals filled the room.

Masters released her from behind, pulling her skirts down as he went. Her fervent desire was to collapse forward onto the desk, hiding her head beneath her sheltering arms. If she could have simply vanished, she would have done so in an instant.

Life did not work that way. She pushed herself to standing and quickly pulled up her disheveled bodice, attempting to set everything to rights. She ran quick fingers through her hair and could find nothing out of place, it lay smooth against her head save for the desired curls, one small piece of order in her world. She stepped away from the desk and shook her skirts out. They fell smoothly from her waist to the floor; the few wrinkles in the many layers of silk would ease soon.

Her dress seemingly had survived amazingly undamaged. Her face was probably another matter, and she wouldn't be surprised if there was a bite mark on the back of her neck. Her shawl must be somewhere. Perhaps she could wrap it about herself and pretend that she was chilled. It was a cold evening.

But that was only the physical. Her emotions she carefully wrapped and put away for later. She must not let them matter now.

Then it was time to turn and face Masters. She had heard him making his own adjustments and was unsurprised to find him looking as crisp as ever. His hair was mussed, but he had done that before when he ran his fingers through it.

With some trepidation, she raised her eyes to his. "I did not see who it was. Did you?" She tried to hold her voice steady as she spoke.

"No. I believe it was Lord Wainscott who spoke, but I could not be sure. And I fear that some of the giggles may have been Miss Belinda Thwaite." His eyes were hard to read, but there was something there buried deep.

"That would not be good." That was a gross understatement.

"No, it would not be," he replied.

She leaned back on the edge of the desk, trying to find words to say. One of her first lovers after Michael's death had a fascination with illicit activities in public places, and she had caught some of his excitement. It was far different, however, to wonder at being caught than to actually be caught.

He stepped toward her, stopped, then turned and walked away. "What do we do now?"

"Why do you ask me?" she asked. "Do you really imagine that I have been in this situation before?"

"No, only—"

"You believe that, given my scandalous life, that I am used to facing public censure and should have profound advice."

"You deliberately misunderstand me, Clara. I meant only the literal words that I spoke. Do we walk out together? Separately? Do we announce our engagement tonight or should I put it in the papers?"

She closed her eyes against the pain she felt surrounding her. In all her imaginings, she had never pictured a situation as dreadful as this one. Or imagined him discussing their engagement in such a silky, determined voice. "I have not said that I will marry you. You presume much."

His voice turned cold. "Under the circumstances, I would not have thought it was a presumption."

Her head was beginning to ache, and for the second time that night, her stomach was roiling. "You are doing it."

"Doing what?"

"Assuming that you know best."

"I do not see that there is an alternative." His voice was gentler and he turned to face her. "I understand that you were not persuaded by my proposal, but surely now you understand that you will be ruined if we do not marry."

She rubbed her temple. "Yes, I do understand my fate if I do not become your wife. But it is my fate. It really does not concern you."

"How can you say that? I am here too. Surely our fates are intertwined." He was only a few inches from her. It did not bring the comfort it always had before.

"But you are a man. No matter what happens, the talk of you will only last a day or two at most—will, in fact, probably last longer if you do marry me than if you leave now and never speak to me again."

"I can't believe that is true."

"It is. I have moved in society far more than you. If we marry, there will always be sly comments, wondering if you are enough to keep me happy, and every time I even look at another man, it will be commented upon. Men will take great pleasure in pointing out who I am rumored to have shared my favors with. This would have been true even before tonight. After this, what reputation I had will be in shreds."

"Not if we marry." He spoke firmly and placed a hand on each shoulder. "Marry me, Clara, and let us face this together. I will leave here and go use all my contacts to get a special license. I will have you as my wife before the week is out."

There was temptation. Oh, there was temptation. Whatever emotion he had spoken with right after they were discovered had faded, and now he spoke with gentle persuasion. She wanted to lay her face against his chest and pretend that everything could be right.

She would say yes. She would tell him of the baby. He would take her in his arms and tell her he loved her. They would marry, and he would have the faith that she could make her own decisions and would not seek to control her. There would be long hot summers at his estates and the excitement of the season each spring. She would create the home she had always dreamed of—a homey, safe place to raise their child with love.

But that was a fairy story. He was already demonstrating that he did not trust her to decide on her own. He had spoken with persuasion, but also with command. He really did not see that she had any possible choice to make—and perhaps she did not. It was hard to see how she could go on from here.

There must be a way.

She stepped back from him and slipped around the desk. "We cannot stay here any longer. The talk will only grow by the second. Perhaps we were not recognized—the lighting is dismal—or perhaps those who found us will hold their tongues. I will not make any decision without knowing the truth." She turned and walked toward the door.

He tried to step ahead of her. "I will go first. I can report back what I learn."

He was doing it again, taking away her control. She stepped quickly, almost running, and placed her hand upon the cold metal of the handle. "No. I must do this."

She twisted the handle and stepped out into the hall.

She had left him. She had really left him. He had not bargained on it coming to this.

He pushed back the pain of her refusal and examined only the most manageable of emotions.

He had been shocked to be discovered. Somehow, the possibility had never entered his mind. It should have. Having sex in the library at a party was certainly not discreet or proper.

He caught a glimpse of his reflection in a darkened window and moved closer to straighten his hair, smoothing the slick waves back into place. He was amazed that no other mark of the evening's activities remained on him.

He still needed to face the crowds below.

She would marry him. There was no other choice. Surely she would see that.

He walked to the door with a confidence he did not feel. She had spoken correctly when she said that he did not know how to face scandal. Since his parents' deaths he had managed his life in order to avoid it.

There had been some talk soon after their deaths—a mysterious shooting did not go unnoticed—but his feelings had been numb at the time and he had been too busy trying to manage the debts they had left to be overly concerned with gossip.

He ran his fingers through his hair. Damn. He had to stop doing that or he'd be spending the evening staring at himself in the window trying to put it to rights. He yanked it flat again.

Had she been truthful in saying that she was capable of facing scandal after the life she had led? This was different from her other indiscretions.

This would ruin her.

She must see that.

Bloody hell. It was his duty to protect her. Grabbing the door handle, he stalked out into the hallway. He would do what was needed.

What was she going to do now? Walking out on him had been the right thing. She had no doubt about that. But what now?

She paused for a second outside the door, her innards turned to jelly. Always before when she had braved scandal and indiscretion, she had known before time what she courted. This time she was unprepared.

Still, she pulled back her shoulders and tilted her chin up. Let them talk. She was capable of handling this. She would not be bowed.

It was easier to face what was below than what was behind her in the library.

She took the first step and pretended that her legs were not shaking. She closed her eyes and imagined Masters's surety that she would marry him, his assumption that she had no other choice.

She would prove him wrong.

She let anger build within her. Anger could protect you from almost anything.

Two more steps.

Three more.

She reached the top of the steps and was about to descend when Anna Struthers came running up. "Don't go down there."

"What? Why?" She took a step backward.

"Rumors are flying. They think it was you, but

nobody is sure. The room was dark, and they could only see Masters clearly. If you come down these stairs, there will be no question."

Word could not have spread that quickly. "I don't know what you are talking about."

Anna gave her the exasperated look one would give a difficult child. "You know exactly what I mean. I've been told by three different people in the last two minutes that Mr. Masters was caught at a most intimate moment in the upstairs library—although not all of them put it quite so delicately. Miss Thwaite informed me it was you. Someone else informed me it was Miss Thompson—although how the two of you could be mistaken, I am unsure. The third did not know who Masters was with."

"Oh." It was not much of an answer.

"So if you sneak down the servants' stairs and enter through another door, it will seem less likely it was you," Anna suggested. "I would claim you were with me, but I was dancing with Lord Wilcox, and you know what a gossip he is."

"Yes, I do. Thank you for your help. I don't know—"

"Nobody should be forced to choose marriage or disgrace." With those few words, Mrs. Struthers turned and headed back down the stairs at a much more sedate pace than she ascended.

Clara headed back toward the far end of the hall. She was not exactly sure of the way to the servants' stair, but it should not be hard to find.

She was slipping through the door when she heard the library door creak open and Masters walked out. He walked firmly toward the stairs and did not look back.

She was tempted to chase after him and inform him of her plan, but the risk of being seen with him was too great. She slipped forward and was gone.

The world froze as he descended the stairs. Masters had never seen anything like it before. The whole room full of people stopped and stared as he came into sight. Only the orchestra played on.

It was all he could do to keep walking and not stop and stare back.

Then the whispers began. He could not hear a single distinct word, but instead, it was as if a swarm of bees had suddenly flown into the room. The buzz rose and filled the space, drowning out even the music from the orchestra.

Or perhaps it was only his head that was filled.

He forced his features to utter calm as he reached the main floor. He stepped forward and the crush parted before him. Nobody approached and nobody made eye contact.

He wondered if this was what Clara had lived with all these years. This knowledge that the whole room was speaking of you and not to you.

He paused and waited, seeing if anybody would approach.

No one did.

It was as if a magic circle had been drawn around him, one that nobody could cross and he could not leave.

He had heard of being alone in a crowd, but this was beyond the pale.

He walked toward Mr. Miles, a man he had known for years, and saw desperation flash in the man's eyes. He stopped. It would be unfair to force the situation.

"Oh, there you are. Peter was just wondering what had become of you. He thought you'd come down right behind him." Violet walked to him and smiled brightly.

At first he thought she did not know what had just happened, but then he caught her glance and saw full knowledge reflected there.

"I merely chose to linger over my brandy a few minutes. There is no crime in that."

"Of course there is not." Violet smiled and gave a gay little laugh for no reason that he could determine. "Come now, brother. Let me show you the portraits in the long gallery. They are really quite magnificent."

Before he even knew what she was about, he found his arm taken, and he was leading her from the room. Or at least anybody watching them would have assumed he was leading; in truth Violet had her nails dug in deep and there was no choice but to move in the direction she chose.

He tried to stop. "I must find Clara. She—"

"Don't even say her name, you fool," Violet hissed.

"But—"

"I am rescuing you for the second time this night. Please behave." She laughed again as if he had said something particularly witty, and then he found himself shoved through a door and dragged into an endless room filled with dour portraits.

Violet did not even pretend to look at them before beginning. "How could you? Have you no sense? No, of course you don't. You are a man. Why do men never think of the consequences of their actions?"

"I do not know what you speak of. Now if you'll excuse me, I must find Clara."

Violet rolled her eyes at him. He remembered Clara looking at him with exactly that expression. Where had she gotten to? He had not seen her when he came down. How had she managed to escape into the crowd? Given his own reception, he would have thought it an impossibility.

"Do not be an idiot," Violet said. "You know exactly what I am talking about. I am more shocked than I can ever explain that you would engage in such an activity. Mind you, I am not shocked by sex in the library, only that you would engage in it, my oh-so-proper brother."

"I never said—"

"Believe me, you don't need to, and at this point it would be impossible to deny. Lord Wainscott saw you, and was most clear in his identification. He is less sure of your companion, but gossip has already centered on the likely choices. Miss Thompson is leading at the moment—it is much more interesting to despoil the young and pure—but at some point soon it will be realized that she is most decidedly not a brunette, and then it will be too late. There are plenty who will be all too ready to believe this of Clara. I am probably the only one who cannot believe that she was foolish enough to become involved with you. Her other choices have been much more sensible. I've been afraid of this since I first saw you together, but I really did think she had much more sense."

"I beg your pardon."

"Don't glare at me like that. You know exactly what I mean. You are hardly the choice for either a woman who likes fun or one who wishes a peaceful home. And I believe Clara desires both."

He drew himself up stiffly, setting each vertebra of his spine in perfect alignment with the one below. He did not need this after the evening he'd had, but he could tell Violet was not about to desist. "I might be pressed to argue with the first, but the second? I can assure you that I intend to maintain a home of utmost tranquillity."

"As long as she does exactly what you say. And if she doesn't? How quiet will your home be then?"

"I can assure you that we will manage with great agreeability."

"Gads, you sound pompous. I take it from your reply that you have asked her."

"Yes." Not that this was any of her business.

"Ah." Violet suddenly lost her waspish tone. "She refused you. That is why you did not come down together. I thought at first that you would feel above marrying a woman of her reputation, despite the circumstances."

He turned and walked away from her to stare up

at one of the grim-faced paintings. Why did people never choose to look happy when posing for immortality? The man in question stared back out of the canvas with steely eyes and a decided downturn to his lips. Although perhaps it was only the weight of his jowls that kept his mouth at such an angle.

Masters grimaced; he was sure that his own expression was not far different at the moment. "I had actually asked her before events turned—difficult. Foolish man that I am, I let her turn me down twice—and I argued with her, trying to persuade her of my wisdom."

Violet came up and laid a soothing hand upon his shoulder. "That must have been unbearable for you. And you say you argued. I can't imagine that you didn't just tell her what was to be."

"I tried that, but the bloody woman refuses to see sense. She always wants to debate everything. I am constantly forced to defend my view."

Violet laughed then, a whisper-light but genuine laugh. "And I bet you don't always win. That is what really has your goat. This is not the first argument you have lost. I did wonder to see a woman—or a man, for that matter—who could stand up to your bluster."

"Oh, she more than stands up to it. She pushes back just as hard, and I cannot always persuade her. I fear this may be just such a case."

"Poor you." The comment was sincere. He could hear it in the melody of her voice.

"Why can't she understand that there is no choice? We must wed now."

"Give her time. This has been as much a shock to her as to you."

"I am not sure that eternity is enough time to make her see reason, and we certainly cannot wait that long. Every minute we delay only makes matters worse."

Violet answered, her voice turned serious. "I know that it feels that way to you, but society is more forgiving than I ever imagined, as long as one pretends to play by their rules. Once you are wed, it will only be months before invitations start to reappear. And then another scandal will replace this one. It becomes ever so boring to discuss the same matter again and again."

He wanted to grumble at her lightheartedness. This was his life. He needed control of it. His sister's smiling face stared back at him, and for a moment he was tempted to ask if this was what it had been like when she first wed Dratton. Had she felt so little power?

Was this what Clara felt, what she complained of?

He pulled away from Violet's touch, wanting to stand alone. He was a man who always knew the answers. Why now did they desert him?

He turned back to Violet, wishing he had the confidence in a happy outcome that her smile conveyed. "What do I do now? How do I persuade her?"

"Perhaps you don't." Her voice was calm.

"But I must—"

"I merely mean that perhaps you let her persuade

herself. Clara is not a fool. Give her time, perhaps only a few hours, and she will see the necessity of marriage. But let it be her decision."

"Her decision." He tried to understand the full import of those words.

"Yes, her decision—and not just because you think it is the best way to get her to come round, but because you truly think she deserves to—no, more than deserves, is entitled to—make her own decision. Do you think you can do that? If you cannot, I would advise that you run from this place and never think of her again."

"I can hardly run off, leaving her to face this alone." What sort of man did his sister think he was?

Violet strode back to him, her previous mirth forgotten. She caught his face between her hands and forced him to look at her. "I know you don't think you can, but I promise you would both be happier living in scandal than being forced together in unhappiness. Clara needs a man who can let her be herself. Can you be that man?"

Violet dropped her hands and did not wait for him to form an answer. "Just think on it. I don't think there is anything else you can do this night besides stand tall. Peter and I will stand with you, and I am sure Wimberley and Marguerite also." Violet stepped away then, and for a moment dropped her face from his view. Her voice became quiet, and it was almost as if someone else spoke. "And, brother, know that I do this as much for Clara as for you. I must admit there is some part of me that feels you deserve this and more." Then she raised her head again, and it was as if the words had never been said. Instead, she continued in her earlier tone, "Now the best defense is to pretend that it was nothing. I must go and find my fiancé. He will surely have more to tell me."

Violet swept out of the room, her skirts swirling majestically about her. He stared after her blankly. Her words had left him more confused than ever.

Combing his fingers through his hair, he caught himself and scowled. The blasted woman was driving him to all sorts of unseemly habits. His life had been far more manageable without her.

So why did being without her seem so impossible?

Clara paused at the edge of the ballroom. She had a choice to make. Oh, she had many choices to make, but this one was simple. Did she enter or did she flee?

It would be easy to leave now and put off until tomorrow the consequences of this night, to wait until she knew what her mind wanted—she was afraid that she already knew what both her heart and body wanted.

Him.

Why could he not have said simple words, told her that he cared, told her that he wanted to be with her forever? Why had it all sounded so cold, so final? Why could he not have pushed aside her arguments with declarations of affection?

Why could he not have spoken of love?

Love.

She wanted to scoff at the word. He did not love her, and she most assuredly did not love him.

Only—perhaps she did. She hated herself for it—she needed a man who realized that her opinion held—but she had long recognized that the mind did not control the heart.

She was delaying.

Did she enter the ballroom or not? Did she face public disgrace now or on the new day?

Would anything be better in the morning? Be easier?

No. If she was going to brave this out, she would do it now.

She closed her eyes for one moment, granted herself one brief second of relief, and then placed a mask upon her face as surely as if it had been a masquerade. She would be confident and seductive, act like nothing had happened. She would be the coquette they all imagined her, but one far more powerful than they could have dreamed.

She ran a finger over her lips, feeling their tenderness. Swollen and red—it drove men crazy and made women jealous. Pinching her cheeks hard, she tried to draw color into them. Their pallor would be a certain mark that she was worried, and worry would betray all.

Strong. Confident. Unashamed.

Those were the qualities that would make them stop, make them question. She could survive questions if they were unsure, but wondering if she could have done this. It was only if they were positive they knew the answer that disgrace would fall.

So let them wonder.

She swallowed, pushing away the lumps that formed in her throat—her voice must be husky, but clear.

She started to pull her shoulders back, but softened them instead. This was not the moment for the warrior. She must act as if there was no battle to fight, act as if she had already won.

A slow, easy grin spread across her face, and she sashayed into the room. All society turned and stared, and she kept her smile fixed, the mask truly in place.

Nobody looking at her would have guessed her internal devastation. She was a woman returning from a stroll, nothing more.

She flashed a grin first at a man, then at a woman, letting all understand she would not be conquered.

She stepped forward and felt them part around her.

There must be a friendly face here, one she could count on. Her glance passed over Mrs. Struthers. She would be a help, but not quite what Clara needed.

Ah, it was almost as if the heavens had sent an answer to her prayer—the Duke of Brisbane. He stood on the far side of the room staring at her along with the rest of the crowd. His look was kind rather than condemning, however.

If Clara had been asked how he would react, she would not have been sure. They'd had a brief liaison at the start of her wild years, but had parted on good terms. She had always considered him a friend, but had been aware what a stickler he was for propriety. He would never have dallied with her if she had been anything but a rich widow.

The possibility that he would condemn her for her actions was real, but as she met his dark eyes across the room, she felt no doubt.

She fixed him in her gaze and walked toward him, refusing to look to either side.

"Lady Westington." His voice was cool and deep.

"Brisbane." She could only hope she betrayed no tremor of uncertainty.

He continued to look at her, appraising, his mind still not made up. She could only stand and wait.

He held out his hand. "Would you care to accompany me in the country dance that is beginning?"

She grasped his hand in welcome.

Maybe she really could survive this.

Brisbane's arm was hard beneath her grasp as she let him lead her to the floor. The murmur of whispers followed her with every step.

He paused at the edge of the floor and leaned his head toward her, creating a moment of intimacy between them, an island of quiet in the storm. "Has he asked you to marry him? Do you need me to do some persuading?"

Did every single person think there was only one answer to her dilemma? "He did. I said no."

She could feel his shock. Those dark eyes widened and then grew tight, his lips tensed. "You will have to rethink that or not even I can help."

"Cannot or will not?" she asked before she could stop herself.

He drew in an angry breath. "Does it matter? I am here. I am your friend, but there are limits."

"Of course. I am sorry. I am amazed that you even risked this dance. I know how you value your reputation."

"Tonight the jury still deliberates. Few will risk a direct cut until they see in which direction the tide flows. I suggest that you make sure that it flows in your favor."

She could only nod as he led her onto the floor and they began the intricate moves of the dance, the pace and changing of partners allowing no further conversation.

Focusing solely on the music and the movement of feet and hands, she tried to block out everything else. Step, turn, step. Smile, nod, bow, smile. If she thought of nothing the world would keep moving and she could pretend for a few brief seconds that all was right.

Then the music slowed and stopped, and Brisbane was leading her to the edge of the floor. The murmur of gossip met her ears and she could hear her name whispered. Brisbane gave her hand one firm squeeze and then released her.

"Do the correct thing," he murmured.

She only wished that she knew what that was.

He did not walk away, but even with him standing next to her, she could feel that magic circle that surrounded her once again.

"You don't need to stay with me," she whispered to Brisbane while keeping a smile plastered on her face.

"I know," he said as he peered about the room, catching anyone who looked askance with a heavy glare. One unfortunate was even treated to the lifted monocle and narrowing of the eyes.

It was almost enough to cause a hysterical giggle to rise up in her throat. The whole world seemed askew.

"Oh Clara, how could you?" Violet's voice asked from behind. "I thought better of you."

Brisbane coughed. "I believe that is my cue to find another drink." He nodded politely at Violet and faded into the crowd.

"Why on earth would you have thought better of me? I would have thought we have been friends long enough for you to know there are few things I wouldn't do," Clara answered, trying to pretend she was lighthearted about the whole matter.

"Oh, not disappointed about that. You were merely unlucky to be caught—although perhaps you should have locked the door. No, I refer to being involved with my brother. I thought you had better taste."

"I thought a few weeks ago you were on the point of encouraging such a relationship. I seem to remember discussion of a dinner party invitation. And there is nothing wrong with your brother. Masters is a wonderful man. It is not his fault that things turned out as they did." She found herself rising to his defense as naturally as a mother protects her young—although she certainly had not the slightest maternal feeling about the man.

She turned more fully to Violet and caught the edge of a knowing look. "I do mean it," she continued. "Despite your own qualms about him, he is always trying to act in the best way he can. It is merely that he cares too much sometimes, I believe."

Even as she spoke she saw him. He had entered the room from the doors leading to the long gallery and stood surveying it like a hawk looking for prey. His eyes locked on her, and she knew she was his target. From across the room she could feel the pull of his glance. Her feet turned toward him of their own accord. Her toes curled under as she fought not to walk toward him, to resist the powerful draw.

"If you think so highly of him, then why do you refuse his offer to make you an honest woman?" Violet's question caught Clara off guard as she stared back at Masters.

It still felt as if he'd cast a rope across the room and caught her tight. It pulled ever harder, until she felt that she had no choice but to follow.

"I can see I'll talk no sense into you now." Violet's voice interrupted her thoughts. "I'll call in the morning and we can discuss this matter in great detail. I may be unsure of my own feelings for my brother, but there is little choice for you."

Clara lost the meaning of Violet's words as she saw Miss Thompson approach Masters and watched as the daring young miss pushed him backward through the doors from which he had just arrived.

"You'll have to marry me now," Miss Thompson demanded as he found himself bodily pushed back into the long gallery. He would not have thought such a slight thing could be so strong. Resisting would, of course, have been no difficulty, but he didn't want to risk more of a scene than was already being caused.

"There is already talk about us. We cannot be alone." He shoved a foot in the door before it could close. He was six inches of open space away from compromising a second woman for the night.

"That is why we must wed."

"But it was not you." He could only stare at her as if she had gone slightly insane.

"I know that and you know that, but nobody else seems to." Miss Thompson tried to reach around him to grab the door handle.

He didn't care how hard she tugged it. His foot was not moving. "I do believe that we are not the only ones who know."

She shook her head. "Of course I realize that. But it doesn't matter. You must marry me. My reputation has been ruined."

He did feel a gasp of responsibility. If he had not allowed their names to be publicly linked, then she would never have been suggested as his partner. "I do apologize for that, but I assure you that it will be quickly realized that you were not involved.

I understand the gossip all involves a brunette. I do not believe that anybody could mistake your golden locks."

His remark did not please her. Her brows drew together and she glared, her eyes colder than a January sea. "It was Lady Westington then. I should have guessed that she would never have been so helpful in arranging our match if she did not have her own motivations. She was clearly angling for this all along."

"I can only assure you that she did all in her power to ensure that you and I became better acquainted." It was the truth. Clara had worked hard to find him the bride he thought he wanted. If only he had realized sooner what it was, who it was that he truly did want.

"Does everything in her power include fucking you every chance she got?" There was true anger in Miss Thompson's voice.

He could only stare at her. He had never even heard a woman use such language before. Clara might be provocative, but she was never vulgar. "I have not said that it was Lady Westington."

"You don't need to, and even if it was not I don't care. You are supposed to marry me. You were going to ask me tonight."

The worst thing was that he couldn't deny it. He had been going to ask her. "I can only offer you my most humble apologies."

"No, that is not all you can do. You can ask me to wed you as you indicated you would." Miss Thompson kept her voice down, but it still felt as if she were screaming. He would have felt anger in return were it not for the clear sign of unshed tears in her eyes. "I will not be left behind for some brazen strumpet. The whole world knows of her and her lovers. I can't believe I ever thought she might be a decent woman, a lady."

"I can assure you that she is every bit a lady." It was easy to lose sympathy quickly when she spoke like that about Clara.

Miss Thompson drew herself to her full height, almost reaching his nose. "Well, if you want to keep her that way, I suggest we set a date soon. It will still any rumors that it was she in the library, and once we are wed my own reputation will be restored. I will let it be known how in love we are and that we could not wait. Of course, our engagement will have actually taken place earlier in the garden. I am sure your sister Lady Carrington will support our story. Should we not become engaged, however, I fear that the rumors about Lady Westington may be quite vicious. That would be such a pity, wouldn't it?"

Yes, it could be very hard to feel sympathy.

Chapter 18

⁓ ◌◌ ⁓

Clara lay in her bed, a pillow over her face. She could not remember having lived through a worse night. The night after Michael had died had been a nightmare, but there had been an emotional numbness that had blocked her from the worst of reality.

Last night had not been like that. If anything, the world had moved slower, every detail clear. There had been no pointed comment, no cut direct, but everyone had given her that second glance or moved to avoid contact with her. Judgment might not have been rendered, but it was clearly not far off.

She had lived on the edge of scandal for years, and had thought she could handle it with grace. There was, however, a great difference between almost a scandal and being caught in the thick of it.

And her pregnancy was not even known. There would be no way she could keep the child with her now. Her hand dropped to her stomach. She still could not feel the baby move within her, but she was ever more conscious of its presence.

She needed to act for both of them.

And then there was Robert. The date of his wedding to Jennie was finally set and Lord Darnell seemed pleased. How would he act when he heard what had happened?

If she didn't marry Masters, her world as she knew it was done. Last night she had spoken of choice, but in truth there was very little.

She could move to the far north or even to the Americas. She could use a different name and pretend the baby belonged to a deceased husband. Money, of which thankfully she had plenty, could solve many problems. But life as she knew it would be over.

Or she could marry Masters.

Her belly knotted at the thought.

In so many ways, it was everything that she wanted.

But in even more ways, it was not.

He would never see her as his equal if they came together in these circumstances. In all else she had held her own with him, given as good as she got.

Now she would be in his debt. He, the man, could survive this. It might even enhance his reputation.

She could not.

But did she have a choice?

In truth, no, she did not.

Throwing the pillow across the bed, she pushed up on her elbows and stared across her bedroom. The feminine, comforting appointments had always given her pleasure. Now they seemed to mock her, demonstrating all she had that was lost.

Masters's house was distinctly dour. It was hard to imagine how she could make it a home.

She was whining.

And of all the things she had been in her life, a whiner was not one of them.

She swung her feet off the edge of the bed and stood on the cold floor. A good splash of icy water and she'd put herself to rights.

Violet had said she would call this morning, and while a morning call normally did not actually mean before noon, Clara had a feeling that in this case it did.

She picked a cloth from the basin and began to scrub her face. Somehow, she would make this all work. She might have no choice, but that didn't mean she had no power.

She would make her own decisions in her own way. She didn't need Violet's help or anybody else's.

Masters strode across his study. His agent had sent the latest accounts down from his estates. He stared at the pages of figures, trying to make sense of them.

He needed distraction—distraction from the decisions he had to make.

Damn, the situation had been difficult enough before Miss Thompson had made her demands. Now it was impossible.

Why the bloody hell couldn't Clara have just agreed to marry him at the beginning? It had not been an elegant or thought-out proposal, but it had been sincere.

He had been slow in realizing what he wanted, but from the moment he had not asked Miss Thompson to marry him, he had been definite.

Clara was it. Clara or nobody.

Only now the world had tilted.

Clara did not wish to marry him, despite facing certain disgrace if she did not. Did she really find him so distasteful?

No, she was just being stubborn, refusing to see what should have been plain and simple.

Numerous curses ran through his mind as he considered just how wrongheaded she was being.

If only she were here to argue with him, to make him understand her reasoning. Then he could have tried to fight it, to make her see why his way was so sensible, so right for both of them.

"If you stare any harder at that portfolio, you're going to burn a hole right through it." Violet's voice sounded from the doorway.

He turned toward her with a scowl that softened immediately as he saw the concern deeply etched in her expression. "Good morning, sister."

"I don't see what's good about it." She took the thought from his mind, making no pretense at social niceties.

He raised a brow.

"Oh, don't even think of looking at me like that," she exclaimed. "You know as well as I why it is a horrid day. I've just been to see Clara and been told she is not receiving. She has never refused me before. She knew why I wanted to see her."

"Perhaps that's why she refused. She certainly

has a mind of her own." He felt his own mood darken at the thought. Clara was in need and he could not help, or she would not accept the help that he could offer. Only his failure to find Isabella had ever left him feeling so powerless. And even there he had his own shameful motivations and fears.

Now he did not. Even his personal feeling and desire for marriage to Clara were secondary to his desire to spare her.

He clenched his fists in frustration. "Why can't she let me help her?"

"By agreeing to marry you?" Violet asked it as a question, but it was not.

"Yes, what other way is there?"

"I don't know, but have you truly tried to find one? I have considered saying that Clara was with me the entire time, but there are too many who could gainsay it. Could you say that you were with somebody else? I would hate to smear another reputation, but surely there must be somebody."

"Miss Thompson is more than willing to fill the role."

"Miss Thompson? I did hear a rumor last night—it is possible. But that would mean—"

"Marriage—and not to Clara."

"Yes. You have clearly considered Miss Thompson as a potential bride over the last weeks. How do you feel about her now?"

He considered the cold, calculating girl who had confronted him last night. He had given her reason to believe his intentions serious, but nothing could have excused her behavior, her implied threat to Clara. "I cannot countenance spending my life with her. I had already decided that it was an impossibility before everything happened last night."

"But would you consider it for Clara?" Violet asked. "It will not remove all scandal from her name, but it will allow her a pretense of respectability."

The question was not unexpected. He had spent half the night debating the same question. He had forced it from his mind this morning—not wanting to face the truth—but there it was.

What was he really willing to do for Clara?

Clara had spoken of choices, and now here was his.

Would he willingly marry Miss Thompson to save Clara? Less than twenty-four hours previously he had been ready to propose to the girl. Why did it seem so unimaginable now?

"I see you waver, dear brother." Violet's tone was faintly mocking. She moved to the settee and sat. "Aren't you willing to marry without love for the greater good? Isn't that what you expected of Isabella and myself?"

"And so we are back to that." He came and sat beside his sister. "My whole life would be so much easier were it not for that."

"There is no way to avoid it, not with Isabella gone."

"And even if she is found, what will happen is not clear." He uttered the words with little emotion. His mind was so full of Clara and the decisions he must make.

"No, it is hard to know what will happen if she is found." Violet sounded bitter.

He turned to face her, full-on. "Most of the time I think you forgive me, that we are beyond what happened, what I did, and then—then I can almost feel you change as you sit next to me, and I fear we are back to where we started. Family, but not friends, never friends."

Violet was silent and then spoke with care. "Most of the time I do forgive you. I want to forgive you. I do understand why you did what you did. I can forgive you for myself, but when I think of Isabella, I find myself angry. When you forced me to wed my first husband, you were young, young and unknowing of the ways of the world, but with Isabella you knew—you knew what kind of man Foxworthy was."

"Yes, but I hoped he would not be a bad husband."

"You hoped." The flatness of Violet's voice spoke volumes.

"I could never have imagined how it would turn out, what would happen."

"No, I know you could not, no one could have, but still I cannot forgive you that she is gone, perhaps forever. I wish I could, but I cannot. We can be friends—I hope we have become friends—but the distrust and anger is still there."

"I do not forgive myself either. I may proceed as if I do, but I always wonder how I could have changed things, if there were other choices I could have made."

Violet laughed then, and it sounded almost genuine. "Choices. It always comes down to choice, both making them and letting others make them. And that brings us to the real question. Are you willing to wed Miss Thompson if it gives Clara freedom? Can you grant Clara the freedom of choice?"

"Yes," he said with fierce determination. "I am. Miss Thompson has given me until this afternoon to make a decision. I will tell her yes."

"You look like you've had a long night. I thought you had put such evenings behind you." Robert entered the room with a wide smile. Everything about him screamed of happiness. He must have just arrived back from Norfolk.

He clearly had not heard of the events of the previous night, events that could ruin his life too.

Clara lifted her head off the arm of the settee, removing the cool cloth she had across her forehead. "Yes, it was definitely a long evening—and not at all in the way that you imagine. And what are you doing here? Shouldn't you be in Norfolk with Jennie?"

"Jennie's here with me. We were married this past Sunday."

Clara bolted upright. "You're wed? And you didn't tell me?"

"Yes, we had the banns read the past three weeks. Everybody knew Lord Darnell had agreed and nobody questioned when the wedding was supposed to take place. We did not want to risk him changing his mind if that duke he had dreamed of suddenly entered the picture. I am sorry, Clara. There was not time to let you know."

"And you do not think he will have the marriage declared invalid? He could deny that he gave permission, and Jennie is not yet of age."

"We did consider that, but the whole county knows he has agreed. You know his concern for the family name. I cannot imagine him inviting the scandal of putting aside the marriage—particularly after we have spent the night together." The dear boy blushed redder than a freshly cooked lobster.

"I daresay you are correct. He will not put aside the marriage and risk that no one else would take Jennie, not even now."

Robert knew her well and did not miss the import of those last three words. "What has happened? What have you done now?"

She should have been angered by his tone, but she didn't have the energy. Even the relief she felt that he and Jennie were safely wed could not put aside her feelings of approaching doom. "I've truly made a mess of things this time, Robert," she replied, and then proceeded to recount the whole sordid story of the previous night.

He was silent for a moment at the end. His face had grown grim, and she was sorry to have ruined his happiness. "I will stand by you no matter what. And I know Jennie will also. But"—and he let the word hang—"you really must marry the man. I have never wanted to push you, but in this I must insist."

She wanted to argue that he had no right. He had no legal right, but her actions would affect him and Jennie. If she allowed the scandal to settle firmly about her, it would overflow to them.

Even if he cast her off and never spoke to her again, it would impact his acceptance in society. "I know," she said, rolling her shoulders in an attempt to ease the tightness in her neck. "It is not what I wanted, but I do see what must be done. There truly is no choice."

"Did my father leave you so turned from marriage?"

"How could you possibly say such a thing?" She frowned as she considered. "You know I had a wonderful marriage with him. We discussed it when I was in Norwich."

"And yet you are so opposed to marrying again. I do not understand."

Clara considered. "I loved your father and he loved me. And he certainly loved you."

"And you change the topic of conversation. I am delighted that my father cared so much for me, but it does not explain why you frown now when you think of him or of marriage."

"If you must know, I was just thinking that he was not perfect—but that perhaps was not fair. He died so young, and we all need time to grow into ourselves."

Robert came and sat beside her on the couch. He took her hands in his own. "Do you think I do not know that he was far from perfect? He would not have died if he was perfect."

"Surely you do not blame him for his death."
Clara felt a shiver of ice form within her heart.

"It is better than blaming myself as you do." He
spoke with absolute surety.

Clara turned to him, feeling as if her every fea-
ture had frozen. He spoke of her deepest fears.
This was what she had avoided discussing previously. "What do you mean?"

"Do you think I do not know? You explained
that you grew wild because you wished to have the
fun he always wanted you to. Do you truly believe
I think it is that simple?"

How could he possibly know what had happened on that last dreadful morning with Michael?
Nobody had been there but the two of them. She
did not say anything, but dropped her gaze to her
hands.

Robert continued, "I see the fear in your eyes
that you try to hide. Is this why we rarely speak of
it? You do not need to fear that I know the details,
but it has been clear in your every action since that
you blame yourself."

"Nonsense." She tried to sound convincing.

"I remember your pallor when they brought him
home. At first you only looked shocked, and then
I could see the guilt sneak in. I wanted to comfort you then, but you would never let me say the
words."

"I was a good wife to him—at least I tried to
be." She wasn't sure if she tried to convince herself
or Robert.

"Yes, you were. You were a wonderful wife to

him, and a good mother to me, for all that you seemed more like a sister. You reined us both in when needed."

"But he still—"

"He still died. Do you think there is anything that you could have done that would have prevented that? I refuse to believe that any action on your part could have changed what happened."

Clara lifted her gaze and met his eyes squarely. "I tell myself that often. Less often now than in the beginning. I do know it is silly to have held myself responsible for what was his action, but I cannot help myself.

"He wanted me to go with him that morning. He had a new hunter and wanted to go run free. I have never loved speed and danger the way he did, and I did not feel like indulging him that morning. I told him that if he wanted I would take my old mare and that we could ride along the river and have a picnic, but that I was not in the mood to go all out. He stomped out and left without me. If I had gone with him, he would not have tried that jump. He would have known that I could not follow. Everything would have been different if I had only gotten over my petty desire to have things my way."

"And given in to his petty desire to have them his way? Do you really think that would have changed things? I would bet he'd have gone over the jump at even greater speed trying to show off for you."

"But he might not have."

"And a branch might have fallen and knocked

him on the head or a dog might have run out of the bushes and spooked his horse. You can never know what would have happened."

She sighed, long and slow. "I do know that and I tried not to punish myself over it. But, sometimes, just sometimes, I could not help it."

Robert squeezed her fingers tight. "Is that what those wild years after his death were about? Punishing yourself?"

She laughed, with only a slightly bitter afternote. "Is that what you thought, that they were punishment? No, if anything it was the opposite. What I said when we spoke before was completely true. I was determined to take all the pleasure out of life I could. I was trying to live the way I thought your father would have wanted me to." She became still for a moment and then continued, "He had always said that I should marry again if anything happened to him."

"But you did not marry."

Clara worked hard to keep her inflection flat. "No, I did not marry. I have never even considered marrying again. Perhaps you are right and some of it was punishment, punishment for not living up to what he wanted me to be. Perhaps that is also why I have avoided marriage—fear that I cannot be myself and still measure up to someone else's needs. I will have to take the time to look at the problem with new eyes."

"I think that sounds like a fine idea." He turned to the door. "Now I must get Jennie. I wanted to tell you of our wedding on my own, but she is waiting."

"Yes, please bring her in so that I can wish her well. And Robert . . ."

"Yes."

"Do not tell her what has happened. Not today. Let us rejoice over your wedding. There will be time soon enough to deal with these matters."

"As you wish—but do not delay. It must be taken care of quickly. And Clara"—he turned back—"my father was right. You really should marry again."

Perhaps there was no other choice.

He left, and she wondered if there was any chance that she would be as happy after her own wedding as Robert had been when he entered the room.

She did not see how.

Masters stood beside the door to Clara's home. How did it manage to convey such a sense of home before he even entered the door? Even the knocker seemed to gleam more brightly than his own.

He should have sent a note announcing his intention to pay a call. She might have arranged not to be home if he had, however. Even now he risked being told that she would not see him.

He would not take no for an answer.

He would see her and tell her of his plans.

And then he would give her a choice.

He still wished to marry her, but if she would not have him, he would, in truth, marry Miss Thompson.

It was the only way to keep Clara safe.

Chapter 19

Clara smiled at Jennie until she thought the indents would be permanently left upon her cheeks. She picked up her wine and took another sip. She wished she could be happier for them.

No, that was not right. She was happy for them, as happy as anyone could be. It was only that she could not find honest joy within herself.

She heard the knocker clack on the front door and did not even turn. She took another sip.

Perhaps she would finish this bottle and then the next.

The mumble of voices rose from the hall—the porter's and—no, he would not come here. Her glass shook as she placed it back upon the table.

Robert had glanced at her as the voices rose in the hall. He did not change his expression at all, and still she could see his question.

Would she see Masters?

Was she ready to tell him yes?

Jennie chattered away, oblivious to the deep undercurrents in the room. Even with her own difficulties, Clara found herself wondering if Robert would tell Jennie everything later that night. She hoped he would. There should be few secrets within a marriage.

There was silence in the hall, then the sound of approaching footsteps, only one pair—Masters was waiting to see if she would welcome him.

"Excuse me a moment," she said as she rose. She did not want this encounter taking place here. "It seems as if I have another guest, and I fear it is some business I must attend to."

"Of course," said Jennie, as she inched closer to Robert on the settee. Clara imagined they would move in closer still as soon as she left the room.

Robert flashed her a brief smile of encouragement and then turned to his bride. At least they were happy. There was some satisfaction in that. She had not ruined their lives.

She walked to the door just as the porter raised his hand to knock. He stepped back, and she preceded him back down the hall.

Masters stood at the end. The light from the windows behind him cast him in deep silhouette, making it impossible to see his expression.

"Greetings, Lady Westington," he said.

She forced her face into a smile and answered, "It is good to see you—Jonathan."

"I was not sure if . . ." He paused as he registered her words.

"I thought we would talk in the library. We seem to have a great fondness for libraries."

"Yes, of course."

She turned and he followed her back down the

hall, past the parlor where Robert and Jennie sat.

"I've just had the most wonderful news," she said. "Robert arrived this morning with Jennie. They were wed this past Sunday."

"I am delighted to hear that. It must take a load of worry off your mind."

The weight upon her mind still felt so great, she could not have said if it had lessened. Still, she nodded.

Then they were alone. Masters had left the door open the proper number of inches, but with a decisive click she shut it fully.

"I am glad you have come." The words were softly spoken and were fully the truth. She was glad she had not had to send for him to tell him she had changed her mind. It already felt enough like begging.

She wondered if he had felt like this when she refused him.

He walked away from her, deeper into the room. "I was not sure you would be. I thought you might send me away. I was not even sure it was wise to come. Society has many eyes, and I was not sure you would wish anyone to know of our meeting."

"No, I am glad. It is simpler this way." She moved to her usual chair before the fire, waving him to the chair across from her.

Instead, he came and sat on the ottoman at her feet.

"I have something I must say," she began.

"No, let me speak first," he replied.

"If I do not say this now, I fear I will not have the words."

He hesitated, but then nodded for her to proceed.

Her gaze dropped to her hands, which were rapidly knotting and twisting the fabric of her skirt. It was impossible to remember ever being so nervous.

Her fingers felt as if they moved on their own, and it took extreme effort to move them to stillness. Then she raised her head and stared straight into his endless blue eyes. "It would be my great pleasure to accept your offer and become your wife."

There, the words were out.

He did not say anything, only stared at her.

What if he had changed his mind?

Masters did not know what to say. For a moment, his heart had filled with joy, but then he saw the misery in her face. This was not what she wanted. She agreed with desperation, not pleasure.

"You have decided you cannot face the shame?" he asked.

He watched as she pulled in a deep breath. "I cannot give up my whole life. I thought I could. Even standing there in that ballroom last night, I thought I could do it. But this morning I realized what the price would be. I want to be brave and insist that I can manage, but I cannot."

It was everything he wanted and yet nothing. "And so you will be my wife."

"Yes." She hesitated. "And there is something more."

Her hands were shaking, and he reached out and took them with his own.

"I am with child. The baby will be delivered in the late fall or early winter. It must have happened that one time in Aylsham."

And the baby is mine? He resisted putting the thought to words. He did not question her. He knew the child was his, but the shock of it kept the question echoing through his mind.

He was going to be a father.

And then another thought occurred. "How long have you known? Surely, you have not just realized."

Her gaze fell from his, and he could feel her hands clench to fists within his grasp.

She spoke very quietly. "I have known since the day before you told me you had decided to marry Miss Thompson."

"And you didn't tell me." It was not a question.

"No."

He rose to his feet suddenly, dropping her hands. He began to pace the room. "And what were you going to do? Take some potion and be rid of it? Or have you tried that already?"

"No." She rose to her own feet and walked toward him. "I could never have done that. I planned to go north until the baby was born. I had not decided quite how to proceed after that. I was either going to claim the child as my ward or pass it off as my maid's. I just don't know."

"You would rather have raised a bastard than tell me."

"I was coming to tell you, but instead, you told me that you were going to marry Miss Thompson."

"I would never have even thought of marrying her if I had known. You should have told me, regardless of all else."

"I wanted to, but I was afraid you would act like this. I didn't want you if you wished to be married to someone else. And all the reasons I did not think we would suit still stand."

"But you will marry me now—to save yourself?"

"Yes." Her voice was very small, even though she stood straight. "And the child. I could not bear to have the whole world know him a bastard. It would not be fair."

"And your other plan would have been?" He could not control the anger in his tone. "You have spoken to me so often of wanting your own choice, of how I should have given Violet and Isabella choices. Where is my choice? What choice did you give me?"

She did not answer, but chewed on her lower lip. He had never seen her look so young and vulnerable. She was normally so in control that he did not even think of her age; now it seemed unavoidable—still, it did not defuse his anger.

"I was wrong." The words seemed torn from her lips. "I do not say that often, but I will admit it now. I should have told you, consulted with you. You are correct, I was doing exactly what I have accused you of." She paused, and it seemed her nervousness increased. "But my question remains. Do you still wish to wed me?"

What should he say? He had come here with a plan so firmly embedded in his mind. He would tell her that he would marry Miss Thompson and then wait to see if she would talk him out of it. Now everything had changed.

He was going to be a father. How could he possibly not take her acceptance and let the rest drop?

"I do," he said.

Her lips twisted in a crooked smile. She looked relieved, but not happy. Her head dropped to her chest, and he could see her attempt to adjust to this new reality.

"However," he continued, "there is another option."

Her head jerked back up. "Another option?"

"You may have heard that there were rumors last night concerning myself and Miss Thompson. She approached me later in the evening and demanded that I marry her. If I do this, the rumors will all turn to her. Even those who are now sure that I was with a brunette, and that you were that brunette, will wonder and allow themselves to be persuaded. Why else would I wed her?"

"And the baby?"

He forced the words out between grinding teeth. "You can proceed with your plan. I cannot say that there will not be questions, but I am sure you can maintain some air of respectability for both you and the child." He could not say *my child*. That would make it too real, and he was not ready for that—not if he had to let them both go.

"You are really willing to do this?" She sank back in her chair, afraid her legs would give way.

"I would not have said so if I were not."

"You do not sound pleased with the idea. As of early last evening, Miss Thompson was still your choice for a bride."

"You know I changed my mind before all this happened."

"Yes, I do." She leaned her head back against the chair and stared up at the ceiling. "It is just all so much to take in."

He came and sat across from her. "Yes, it is."

"How do you feel about the baby? Do you want it, or is it just another responsibility? You clearly have a very large sense of responsibility and of your own duties in this world."

"I cannot deny that. I do, however, want the child rather desperately." His gaze locked with hers, and there could be no doubting the sincerity with which he spoke.

She lowered her head and met his gaze, her eyes searching. "But still you would let us go?"

"If it is what you want. I learned my lesson with Isabella. You cannot force others to be what you want them to be; it can lead only to disaster. I must accept that my sister would never have been driven to do what she did and then to flee, if I had not impelled her."

"I think I wanted not to have a choice. It is so much easier to let fate decide. I feel like such a fool. I demanded choice, and now I wish I did not have it."

He leaned toward her. "But you do have it. I cannot decide for you."

"Yes, then I will marry you." Her voice was the barest whisper.

She could not believe she had said the words—and not once, but twice that day. There was relief in having it done, however.

"There is one more thing," he added.

"What?" She could not imagine what else was left besides the details of planning. All things considered, the wedding must be soon—even then there would be talk, but society would soon move to the next scandal once the proprieties had been observed.

He rose again and paced to the window. He looked out for a moment before turning back to her and fixing her with an expression that was hard to read. "I have not told you the whole story about Isabella."

"I know you have not. There is much I have guessed from what you and Violet have told me and what gossip there has been. I know she disappeared and Foxworthy was killed. The world may not have fully put these two events together, but there must be some connection. And Violet told me of the blackmail. I know that your father made mistakes, mistakes which you have paid for. I do not need to know more."

"That is much more simple than it was and it leaves out several important pieces. Pieces not even Violet knows of."

That caught her attention. "What else could there be?"

"You know that Foxworthy was using blackmail to force me to let him wed Isabella."

"You know I do. We have had many arguments about it."

"What you don't know, what nobody knows, is that in the end—when I realized how opposed Isabella was to the match and what steps Violet would take to prevent it—I went to Foxworthy and I told him I could not do it. That I would face the consequences."

"It still would have been simpler to just give Isabella the choice." The words were out before she could stop them. Given her own recent behavior, she had no right to judge.

He flashed a look, but then continued, "Foxworthy was not willing to let it go. He demanded that if he could not have Isabella that I give him something else. He knew that his own power over me would diminish if things did not proceed as planned."

"But what could he do?"

"He had me sign more papers, papers that incriminated me in high crimes. He promised to keep my father's secrets if I would do this. I thought it would give Isabella a chance to find happiness before the world knew of our disgrace. I would already be ruined if the world knew my father had been engaged in traitorous activities. It did not seem like a large price to pay."

"But then Foxworthy was killed."

"And then Isabella murdered Foxworthy." He let the words hang.

She could only stare at him in confusion. Isabella killed Foxworthy. The very idea was preposterous. She had no words to say.

He saw the confusion on her face and gave more detail. "I told Isabella what Foxworthy had done, explained what he had demanded. I think I hoped that she would relent, would agree to the marriage and save us all."

"That is not what happened."

"No, it is possible that it is what she meant to happen. I did not know she had gone to see Foxworthy until later—until I found her standing over his body."

"But you cannot be sure—"

"I am sure in my heart. If you could have seen how she looked, you would have been sure too. I drove my sister to kill a man. There, I have said the words."

Clara could see how much it cost him. He had never truly admitted his own wrongdoing, and in those few sentences she could see it all. He was by no means as sure of himself as he pretended.

"If she killed him it was her own doing," she replied. "Just as I demand that you give her choice, so you must give her the responsibility that goes with it."

"I do not see it that way and neither does Violet.

She can forgive me for much, but not for that. Isabella will always stand between us."

"But if she is found—"

"If she is found—what? She will still have killed a man. There was some confusion after the event. Foxworthy was stabbed after he was dead, and we know that was not Isabella."

"Stabbed after he was dead? Perhaps he was not really dead before? Perhaps she did not kill him."

"He was dead." He said it with such finality that there was no doubt left in her mind.

"It makes no sense."

"No, it does not, but it does not change the fact. If Isabella returns, do we cover her crimes? The answer is, of course, yes, but it gives me little comfort. I do not know how I will face her after what I made her do."

"You did not make her do anything."

"It is not worth arguing—besides, that is not all I feel guilty about—it is those damn papers."

She looked at him with some confusion. "Papers?"

"The ones I signed admitting my own treason. Not all Foxworthy's papers were found with his body. The ones I signed were missing. I know Isabella took some articles from his desk. I can only assume the papers were among them."

"And so you have hunted Isabella."

"Yes. I would have searched for her anyway and just as hard, but—"

"—you feel guilty that your motives were not pure. You feel guilty that you believe she killed

Foxworthy because of you, and you feel guilty that you sought the papers as well as her."

"I do. It feels like I have lied to the world in not telling the truth."

"But who could you have told besides Violet? And I know she would understand—and forgive you. And why do you tell me now?"

"Because I have not found Isabella—or the papers. You know that I have given up—I cannot see how she will ever be found now, but you need to know that those papers are still out there. If they ever do turn up, I could be accused of treason—and as my wife, you have to live with the consequences as well. And if Isabella is found, it is always possible she would hang for murder. Do you really want to ally yourself with such potential scandal?"

She felt steadfast. Then she smiled, not a joyful smile, but one she knew was full of emotion and resolution. "I can manage that. I clearly have a talent for scandal."

He snorted.

And she laughed, a deep, full laugh that contained only the faintest edge of hysteria.

"We are quite the pair, aren't we?" she asked as the laugh trailed off. "You know of course that all the reasons we won't suit are still valid?"

"Of course I do, but they don't always seem to matter, do they?"

"No, they don't. I don't understand how you can be so irritating and still so inviting, but at least our lives won't be boring. I fear I am bound to you by temptation. I cannot imagine my life without you."

He came and sat on the ottoman again and took her hand, bringing it to his lips. "Yes, I think the one thing I can promise you is that we won't be bored."

He kissed her palm, softly—letting her rest it against his cheek. He leaned forward and let his face lie against hers. She could feel his stubble abrade slightly against her soft skin.

She turned her face to see him and watched as his pupils darkened, listened as his breathing sped.

There was so much in his eyes—all the words that they were not yet ready to say, but knew were true.

Her gaze dropped to his lips, and his breath caught.

Her other hand slipped lower. She felt him tense as her small, curious fingers began their exploration.

No, it would not be dull.

Epilogue

London, July 18, 1821

That blasted man. He had done it again. He had let her have her way.

He had told her the crowds for the king's coronation would be too great, too loud, too raucous. It would not be at all suitable to bring the children. They were too young to appreciate the spectacle and excitement of the event. They would not remember it. They should be left at home with their nurse.

And then he'd made the arrangements for them all to attend. He'd told her his plans, smiled sweetly, and acted as if it had been his idea all along.

He hadn't once indicated that she'd spent a full hour explaining why she thought it was important for the children to be there even if they didn't remember.

Damn that blasted man. If she didn't love him so much she'd kill him.

There was a small whimper from the crib beside her. Clara leaned over and pulled the thin blanket up over her sleeping daughter. The newborn was curled on her side, a finger lying softly against her mouth.

He'd told her it was too soon for another baby too. And then he'd promptly set about helping her have one—not that he'd seemed to object too much to that part.

What was a woman to do with a man who actually listened, even when he pretended he didn't—a man who had finally learned to tell her he loved her, who whispered his feelings in the dark recesses of their bed—a man who'd stood with her through scandal and disgrace—a man who complained only gently when the invitations started to arrive again, and she wanted to dance every night—although sometimes he persuaded her to stay home?

The baby kicked the blanket off and whimpered again.

Clara could only smile.

It was impossible to imagine life without baby Isabella. There had never been a doubt about what their daughter would be named. Bella would be Masters's second chance.

There was a loud cry from the next room, and Clara blew a kiss at the sleeping baby and walked to the door, easing it open.

Little Johnny was not happy. Her eighteen-month-old son sat upright in his bed, his face red from the scream. His eyes met hers in a clash of wills as she entered the room. "It is time to sleep, dearest."

"No." His expression said so much more than the single word.

She came and sat on the bed by his side, brushing his hair back from his face. The dark curls were tinged with red, just like his father's. "You've had your dinner and your bath and I've read you your story—more than one, in fact. You know it is time to sleep."

"No."

"Come now. Lie down and close your eyes." She ran her fingers through his curls again.

"Want Papa."

As if in answer to his words Clara heard the clatter of boots on the stairs up to the nursery. She sighed softly to herself. A proper mother would stop Masters before he entered the room and explain that their son could not have everything he wanted in life, explain that she had already told him his father was out and that he would have to make do with her.

Yes, that was what a proper mother would do.

She leaned over and kissed Johnny's forehead. "I think I hear Papa now. I'll tell him you want another story."

"Yes."

She heard the boots enter the first room, where their daughter slept. The footsteps paused by the crib, and she could imagine the glowing look on Masters's face as he stared down at their daughter.

She waited and heard the door ease open again.

"Still awake, are we?" Masters said as he entered. "Don't you know it's past your bedtime? Have you been giving your mother a hard time?"

"Papa!" Her son's voice rang with triumph.

Clara could only shrug as she stood and let Masters take her place on the bed. She handed him the book of stories that had become their son's favorite. "Only one, mind you. I've already read until my throat is hoarse."

"Of course," Masters answered. He looked up at her, and she could see that more than the joy of their family was in his eyes. "I'll be out in a few moments. And Clara, I have news—the very best news."

She raised a brow in question as she quietly left the room.

She heard the soft rumblings of the two male voices as she sat in the rocker next to her daughter's crib. The minutes sped by, and she was sure that at least one extra story had been told.

"He's asleep," Masters said as he slipped into the room, closing the door behind him.

"You know you shouldn't read until he's asleep. Nurse is always telling us that."

"I know, but it's a special night."

"Of course it is. The coronation is tomorrow. I am sure Johnny senses all the excitement in the air."

"No, not that. It's even better."

"Even better than the king being crowned?"

He crouched down before her until their eyes

were even. "Yes. Lady Connortan's recent letter was correct. There was a second redheaded governess in Norfolk. I sent one of the grooms who had known her since childhood to investigate, and he assures me it really is her. He says there can be no mistake. He would know her anywhere. He did not approach her because he did not wish to scare her off." His words tumbled out with excitement. "She was working for the Earl of Hunterdon, but she now has a position as a baby nurse with a Mr. Henry Wattington—I've actually done business with the man. Isabella has been traveling with Mrs. Wattington and their child. They were due to arrive in London for the coronation but there has been a strange delay, according to my man— something about the Duke of Strattonford. It made no sense to me. What is important is that if all goes well she should arrive in the next few days. I can't wait to tell Violet. Should I tell her now or wait? I still can't believe it. I have found Isabella."

Clara heard the excitement in his voice. Little Johnny would not be the only one who would have trouble sleeping. It was wonderful to hear him so joyful. He had worried incessantly in the beginning about what would happen when they found Isabella, but lately—now that they'd survived their own scandals—the thought of more did not scare him. In fact, he was positively shining with excitement. It would be hard to settle him to sleep. It would take quite a bit of . . . work.

Ah, the duties a wife was forced to perform. "Do you know, my love, I just received delivery

of a box of the very finest silk stockings? Do you
think they'll hold tight to the bedposts, or will they
slip loose?"

The gleam in her husband's eye as he pulled her
to her feet was enough of an answer.

At Avon Books, we know your passion for romance—once you finish one of our novels, you find yourself wanting more.

May we tempt you with . . .

- **Excerpts** from our upcoming releases.

- Entertaining **extras**, including authors' personal photo albums and book lists.

- Behind-the-scenes **scoop** on your favorite characters and series.

- **Sweepstakes** for the chance to win free books, romantic getaways, and other fun prizes.

- Writing **tips** from our authors and editors.

- **Blog** with our authors and find out why they love to write romance.

- **Exclusive content** that's not contained within the pages of our novels.

Join us at
www.avonbooks.com

AVON

An Imprint of HarperCollins*Publishers*
www.avonromance.com